FREAKS OF NATURE

ISBN: 979-8-9883406-4-5

FREAKS OF NATURE

Renate Rowland

RUNIK PRESS

Author's Note

Thank you for considering my book. For more details to determine whether this is a right fit for you, please check the list below.

Sensitive Content

This book contains explicit sexual situations and language intended for an adult audience (18+), as well as:

- MFM
- Rivals sharing (not why choose)
- Stalking/chasing
- Breaking and entering
- Dub/non-con
- Corruption kink
- Kidnapping
- Mask play
- Breath play
- Knife play
- Fear play
- Somnophilia
- Memory lapses
- Violence
- Murder/torture
- Arson
- Physical abuse and sexual assault of a character as a minor in flashbacks (age 15; non-graphic)

Emily

I fell into their trap,
and now I'm caught in the crossfire of their rivalry.
What I wanted was excitement, but what I got was twice as
much as I expected… and almost too much for me to take.
Almost.

It's wrong. I know it is. He's crazy, dangerous,
and he's been terrorizing me for his sheer entertainment…

The old me would've been appalled by the idea,
but I wanted to break out of that shell, didn't I?
That's why I left.

I should grab the bull by its horns and ride him,
or however that saying goes.

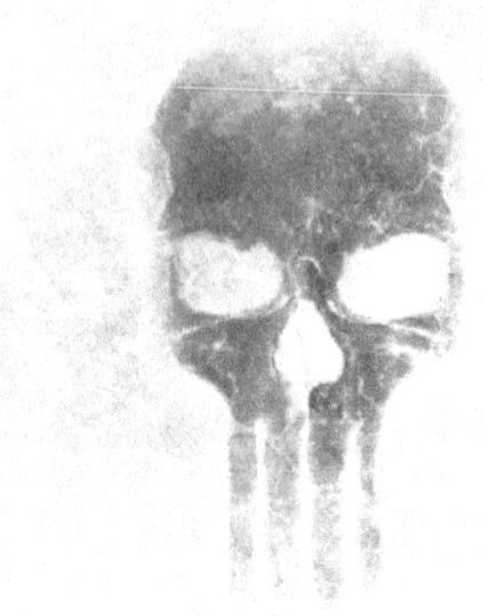

The night I caught her scent...

t's 2:36 am. Scrolling through my phone, I sit on my bike in the same spot across the diner where I park every night. I know it's late, but I don't want to go home. I'm itching for a fix.

Not drugs. I don't fuck with that shit, or drink for that matter. My itch is of a darker, more depraved sort, and it's one I can't satisfy alone.

I glance up from the screen right when she comes out of the alley. The sidewalk is busy, and she doesn't look my way, but my eyes rivet to her silhouette in those second-skin jeans and that black tank top.

My cock twitches.

Fuck, she's fine. Her tits bounce with her steps, and her shirt is low-cut, giving me a raging hard-on as I imagine sliding my shaft in between them.

A breeze plays in her dark hair. My breath stalls when she sweeps a strand behind her ear, and I get a clear view of her face.

The city noise disappears.

Her lips strike me stupid. They're full and lush, and I know I won't rest until I hear them moan my name.

My throat goes dry before I notice my mouth is hanging open. I run my tongue across my own lips on reflex and swallow.

I want her.

My free hand slides to my crotch, urging patience into the growing ache.

And I *will* have her, too.

Her eyes flick around, but they never cross the street to where I sit. She keeps walking, utterly oblivious to the sick desire she has woken in me. She's mine. My obsession. My poison. All fucking mine.

When she moves past my line of sight, my stare drops to her ass, and that's my cue. Fixated on her backside, I dismount to pick up pursuit.

I pull my hood down to hide my face; it's part of the game.

Weaving through the crowd, I stay on her tail. Every now and then she throws a glance over her shoulder like she can feel me following her, but I make sure not to attract her attention. I know how to blend in. She won't see me until I want her to.

She turns down another alley—one I know is dark and gets little foot traffic.

We have a lot of those. Castle City is a maze of turns and dead ends for someone who didn't grow up here.

Me? I know every block like the back of my hand. I have my bike, but I'm also no stranger to free running.

My skin prickles from anticipation. Hands stuffed into my pockets, I slip after her without my combat boots making a sound on the asphalt.

I give the alley a quick sweep to confirm we're alone, then reach into the front of my sweatshirt to pull out my mask.

Switching the light on, I slide it over my face and readjust my hood. I want it low for a more dramatic effect.

At last, I draw my knife.

It's the flick of the blade when I release it that brings her feet to a dead stop ahead of me.

She pivots, turning her head so slowly I swear I feel the air around us crackle from the fear rolling off her.

My excitement doubles.

A fresh wave of adrenaline rushes me, and I drink her in, my cock throbbing as it presses against my fly. Her skin has a touch of Mediterranean, mixed Hispanic maybe, but it's her eyes that nearly push me over the edge… because there's something else stirring under the fear.

And perhaps that scares her even more than I do. Her sneakers skip over the ground as she whips back around and starts sprinting down the alley toward the other end.

Sweet delight curls my lips. "Run, baby girl. You won't escape me."

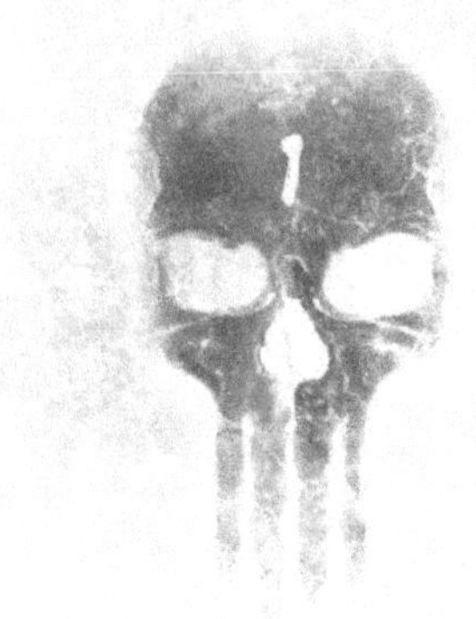

Em

I unfold the white sheet I picked off the table and gasp, my eyes going wide. "Did you see who left this?" I shout after Jake, who just finished busing the section.

"Left what?"

The cold sensation along my neck claws its way deeper under my skin. "Never mind." I fold the paper, feeling it crinkle against my fingers as I shove it into my back pocket. There's no way I'll show him the drawing.

I swallow my discomfort before moving on to the last table. It's been five days since my encounter with the man in the mask. He hasn't shown himself again, but I've felt his eyes on me every step. Whether I'm leaving my apartment for work or retracing my steps to go home after my shift, he's always there, a heavy presence hovering over me, a shadow.

Occasionally, I'll hear footsteps behind me only to swing around and find no one there. He'd have me thinking I was imagining it all, had he not made himself known in other ways.

It started with pencil sketches of me at work, serving tables; harmless scenes. But over the days, the drawings have become more unsettling. There was one of me walking home alone, arms hugged tightly around myself with an expression of fear as I glanced back over my shoulder.

How he captured the details in my features and eyes is remarkable, and at the same time, utterly terrifying. Like he stared directly into my soul.

And what's even more terrifying is that he's so familiar with my features that he started drawing me in poses he's never seen me in—couldn't have. Like the one that's burning a hole into my jeans now. In the drawing I'm asleep, my face relaxed, my eyes closed, the angle as if he's right on top of me.

A shudder runs over my spine as I wipe the table's sticky surface. I don't remember serving him. How did he come in and disappear without notice?

He's left other sketches for me to find beneath the wiper of my car on the street. He knows which one is mine. I assume he's been watching me get in and out of my apartment. This is the first time he's left one for me at the diner.

Yesterday, he left a sketch of me undressing in front of the window, which on its own is unsettling, but the view isn't from outside looking in. It's from the viewpoint of my closet.

It scared me so much, I checked the space for any signs of him having been there.

Of course there were none. He's fucking with my head. He wants me to think he was there.

But what's he waiting for?

"See you tomorrow," I tell my boss Laura after I finish my round and clock out in the kitchen.

Pulling the diner's back door shut behind me, I step into the dark alley.

An instant chill creeps over me.

I've only been working at the diner for a little over a week, but even before my encounter the other night, I've been getting the sense someone is watching me.

That's what I get for moving out here, I guess. I could've settled for a cozy life in a small town, full of dull friends and a husband who considered doing it with the lights on kinky.

But that wasn't for me anymore. Four years were enough. I needed more excitement in my life.

So that's what I got. A clean start in a new city, no friends, and no safety net.

It's a thrill to be on my own. My job at the diner is only temporary. I have a degree in communications, and I've applied for a few positions, but I need something to keep me afloat for now.

My shoes crunch on the ground. The hairs on my arms raise, and I instinctively perk my ears as my breathing shallows to take in my surroundings better.

I'm scared.

I admit I hate walking alone at this hour. It's the only time I miss my boring little home town.

A snapping sound at my back makes me jolt around. I expect a guy with a knife to jump out at me. In this city, you never know; crime is high. I remember the news report about the body of a woman being found in an alley a couple of weeks ago, strangled. I don't want to be next.

I stare down the pitch black tunnel, a cold hand of fear tightening around my throat. But there's no one there.

I expel a breath and spin back around to continue my walk home—

My feet freeze mid step.

Straight ahead of me at the other end of the alley looms a guy in a bright, neon blue purge mask; the one that has the glowing Xs for eyes and a wide stitched grin.

At least I think it's a guy.

He towers at over six feet, and despite his dark hoodie, I can tell he's athletic. He has wide shoulders and strong legs that end in black combat boots.

It's *him*.

Hands buried in the front pocket of his hoodie, he cocks his head to the side as I stare at him unblinkingly.

I'm utterly terrified. Is he the one who's been watching me all along?

I don't wait for him to make a move. I whip around and set off in a dead run down the dark alley.

I can hear sprinting sounds, but I don't know whether it's his or my own, and I'm too scared to look back. Steps echo off the brick walls as if he's closing in on me from all directions.

I don't slow until I reach the end of the alley. I veer left as fast as I can, and push more speed from my legs. I can't feel them over the adrenaline. Blood rushes in my ears and the drum of my heartbeat pounds behind my ribs—

I shriek.

My hands fly up, and I skid to an abrupt stop when a pair of boots land with a heavy *thud* not three feet in front of me to cut off my escape.

How the hell?

I'm face to face with him now, paralyzed by his sheer presence. There's something about him that dominates me without so much as a touch.

And I know I was right. There's a wall of muscle under that black hoodie.

He dips his head, hovering an inch from mine, and I swear I can feel him smile—a cruel, maniacal smile.

A prickle skips down my spine. I swallow, and my eyes rake over his mask before I'm able to recover my senses.

My feet are already back in motion. I make a 180, trying my luck in the opposite direction.

My lungs burn. Breaths burst out of me as I force more oxygen down and turn another corner—

My muscles freeze. My lips form a silent *No*, and I can't believe my eyes. He's right fucking there, ready to intercept me again.

I shoot for a narrow passage between two buildings, but I don't know where I am; nothing looks familiar anymore.

Panic blurs my vision. I catch sounds of metal somewhere behind me, the rattling of a chain link fence, him jumping onto a dumpster...

When I round the corner, he appears in front of me again, his chest heaving.

A sob hitches in my throat. I can't escape him. He knows all the shortcuts. How else is he able to beat me every time? It's not like he can be in two places at once.

He cocks his head to the side again in mocking. This time, he doesn't just stare, though. He draws his knife and flicks the blade out.

Raising his arm, he points the tip at the alley behind me and nods in the direction like he's telling me to run.

So I do.

I run like my life depends on it.

―――

I can hear his boots pounding the ground. It's all I hear as he chases me. I know he's right at my heels. He's faster. Any second he'll catch me and rip me back.

I get to the end of the alley. I cut the corner in a sharp turn, but I feel his hand closing around my upper arm.

I pinch my eyes shut. I don't want to see his mask. I'm so scared. I know that's it. He's got me in his clutches now.

A second hand grips my other arm, and I spin to crash into a chest. A scream ruptures from my throat as I squirm.

"Woah! Hey!" someone says.

They're not the words I expect. Nor the tone. The male voice is warm and laced with surprise.

"Where's the fire?"

I open my eyes and look up to take him in, the first human face since leaving the diner.

He's gorgeous. Tousled, dirty blond hair crowns his head, several inches on top blending into a buzz cut. A few long strands fall over his eyes as he peers down at me. I'm not sure about their color in the dark. I think they're green.

His chin is lined with light scruff and doesn't disguise the dimples in his cheeks when he crooks a grin at me. "You alright?"

"Yeah," I huff, still catching my breath. "There's a guy with a knife. He's right—" My voice cuts off as I look back over my shoulder.

He's gone.

"Someone was chasing me," I explain, returning my attention to the guy in front of me. I don't want him to think I'm crazy.

He straightens and throws a glance past me down the alley, but I know he can't see anyone there.

"Looks like he took off," he says with a shrug.

My gaze lingers on him. I bathe in the sense of comfort he prompts in me. I hesitate to move.

And so does he, like he's as reluctant as me to break the connection.

Warmth chases away the last cold tendril of fear. I become aware of my palms pressing against his hard chest. His T-shirt is soft and thin, and I can feel every twitch of his muscles under my touch.

"Um… sorry." Embarrassed, I curl my fingers and withdraw my hands from his chiseled pecs. I don't even know when they ended up there.

His eyes flit to my hands then back to my face, and I don't miss his grin stretching a little wider when he catches on. "No worries," he assures me with another easy shrug. I get the impression that's his usual quirky attitude.

I kinda like it.

"I'm Asher, by the way. You can call me Ash." He extends a hand. An array of dark tattoos winds up his arms like sleeves, then disappears into his shirt. Even his fingers are inked.

"Emily," I offer, sliding my palm against his.

"Nice to meet you, Emily."

Our connection is brief. Car noise rises around us, and I glimpse a bar across the street. I didn't realize I hit the main road.

Stuffing both hands into his pockets, Ash rocks on his heels. "So, where are you headed at three in the morning alone?"

"I was on my way home. I just got off work." I hike a thumb over my shoulder, then realize I have no idea which direction the diner is. "But I think I got lost. Do you mind pointing me toward 32nd street?"

He squints one eye with a cute twist to his lips, then says, "I can do you one better. How about I walk you?"

My breath hitches at his suggestion. Is he offering in hopes to get lucky?

My lips part, but before I can decline, he tips toward me. "You know, just in case he comes back," he tags on, brows arched.

Ash doesn't blink as he holds my stare, and I find myself swept up by his charm. Warm vanilla and a mix of amber and oak invade my airways. He smells divine. I feel my conviction dwindling.

I weigh my odds. I'm already running from a stalker. What are the chances of me stumbling into the arms of another, or someone worse?

"I'd like that."

19

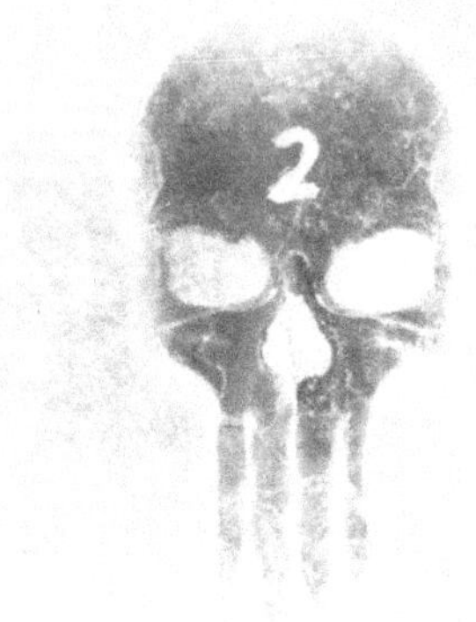

Em

bus the last two tables after the guests leave. We get a steady flow of customers right until closing, which is a lot later than some other places. In the week I've been here, I've never seen it empty.

Laura eyes me suspiciously from the counter. "Don't you look chipper for it being 2:30 in the morning. Wish I had your energy, girl."

Laura is a curvy woman somewhere in her fifties, but from what I can tell, she has plenty of energy to keep this place running on her own.

She wears an apron and street clothes underneath like me. The diner is a casual, privately owned restaurant, not one of those corporate chains.

I like working here.

But that isn't the reason behind the extra sway in my step or my grin as I gather the plates.

"If my sixth sense doesn't lie, and it never does, I'd guess you still have plans tonight. A date maybe?"

"Maybe," I echo with a teasing note.

Asher and I got to talking when he walked me home last night. My first impression of him wasn't wrong. He's laid back, funny, and a smooth talker.

He almost silver-tongued his way into my apartment.

Almost.

"So?" Laura prompts. "Who's the lucky guy? Where did you meet him?"

I wouldn't call him *lucky* just yet, but he did offer to walk me home tonight too, so let's see where things go from there.

"I bumped into him yesterday"—*literally*—"and we kinda hit it off," I tell her. "He's picking me up."

"Oooh, what a charmer," she drawls. "He handsome too?"

Hot is more like it. And that cologne of his… I feel my panties dampen just thinking of him and his big, strong hands on me again.

"Oh yes," I reply in a dreamy voice. "Yes, he is. *Very.*"

Laura clicks her tongue. "Sounds like my type."

"I heard that," Drew bellows from the kitchen at her back.

We both laugh, and I shake my head as I carry the dishes through the swinging doors. I love their heckling. When it comes to married couples, I consider them *#goals.*

In the back, I hand the dishes off to Jake, Laura and Drew's nephew. He's in his late teens and has been helping the couple out at the diner since he was tall enough to look over the counter.

Laura and Drew don't have any kids of their own. The two met when he was hired as the new cook way back in the day, then they took over the family business together after Laura's father passed away ten years ago.

"So… a date, huh?" Jake prompts with a nod, his chest puffed like he's trying to make himself appear bigger.

It doesn't work. He's a scrawny kid, despite matching my height.

"Yep." I avert his eyes, wiping my hands on my apron.

"That's cool." He shrugs and puts the dishes into the huge sink, trying to act casual, but I see the disappointment behind his demeanor.

I mean, he's cute, but a good ten years too young for me.

"Then you better not keep him waiting, girl," Laura urges me on. "A good guy is hard to find."

"True that. You might've snatched up the last one," I call back, winking at Drew.

His head does a little bob, and I catch a bashful smile stretching his lips as he turns to clean the grill.

I pull my apron over my head and hang it on the hook in the kitchen before I clock out.

When I slip through the back door, my heart gives a jolt. Asher is waiting for me across the alley, one foot braced against the wall, thumbs hooked into his pocket. Shadows tease over his dark tattoos where the ink is not covered by his T-shirt.

Hot indeed.

His hair is tousled again, and I have the urge to run my fingers through it.

His teeth tug on his bottom lip as his gaze drinks me in from top to bottom. I think the feeling is mutual. I notice the flexing of his bare forearms like he's itching to touch me too.

He told me he works at a custom auto body shop, so I already know he's good with his hands.

My skin flushes with the thought of them exploring me. "Hi," I say, my voice a little breathless.

He drops his foot to the ground and meets me as I descend the two steps toward him. "Hi."

The light above the door gives his green eyes a luster, and my knees go weak. He's so gorgeous I can't stop staring.

"How was your night?" he asks, breaking me from his spell.

I blink. My eyes flick to the graphic tee stretching across his well-defined chest. He's lean, not bulky, but I don't underestimate the strength and endurance weaved into every cell of his body.

"Good," I reply. "Busy. Makes the time go by faster." *Because I've been looking forward to seeing you,* I add in my head. "How was yours?"

His face has a few days' worth of a shadow now, giving the impression he only shaves every other. "Eh, work was alright."

He pivots down the alley, and I fall in beside him. I don't even look over my shoulder for my stalker. His presence calms me.

"Put a new engine into this sweet '54 Chevy Pickup," he says as we start walking. "It had a badass paint job, too."

That familiar quirky grin twists his features, and I can tell by his inflection how much he loves what he does.

What does that say about his own ride?

"Do you get to work on a lot of cool cars?"

"Usually, yeah. We're known for the crazy custom stuff you can't get anywhere else. Cars, trucks, bikes… you name it. Some clients drive all the way out here just for our work."

"Must come with a nice price tag," I prompt.

He expels a soft laugh. "Definitely!"

And apparently pays well too. As he walks on my right, I see the big watch on his wrist. It's flashy, and I'm guessing his clothes are not off the rack, either.

He's got money.

He has to have a fancy ride to go with his image, yet he walks the streets alone at night not worried about getting mugged?

"What about you?" he asks before I can dwell on his curious behavior. "What made you drop everything and move out here?"

I didn't offer him much about my circumstances last night. "I was looking for an adventure. A thrill."

"A thrill?" That draws another laugh, and I watch his head tip back. "Yeah, you'll find that here alright."

He isn't wrong. I've gotten myself a stalker within three and a half weeks of leaving my hometown. That must be a record of sorts.

His voice still carries a note of amusement when we come up to my place. "You want me to walk you again tomorrow?"

God yes! I'd love to make this a regular thing, but…

"Actually, tomorrow is my night off."

I expect a reaction of disappointment, but delight flickers in his eyes, and he smiles. "Even better. I pick you up from here when I get off. You said you've been in Castle for less than a month, so I assume you haven't seen much."

"No. Between my apartment and the diner, I haven't been anywhere."

"How about I show you around tomorrow? We can skip the touristy stuff, and I'll show you where the locals hang out instead."

I love the sound of that.

"Okay," I say, trying to sound casual as my insides do backflips. I give him an easy smile, but internally I'm beaming.

Ash holds my eyes like he knows.

Then his teeth tug on his bottom lip again, and I burst into flames. My thighs clench to answer him, leaving my pussy throbbing.

"I'll pick you up at seven," he says at last, releasing the undeniable hold his stare has on me.

When he turns to leave, I call after him. "Where are you going to take me?"

"It's a surprise."

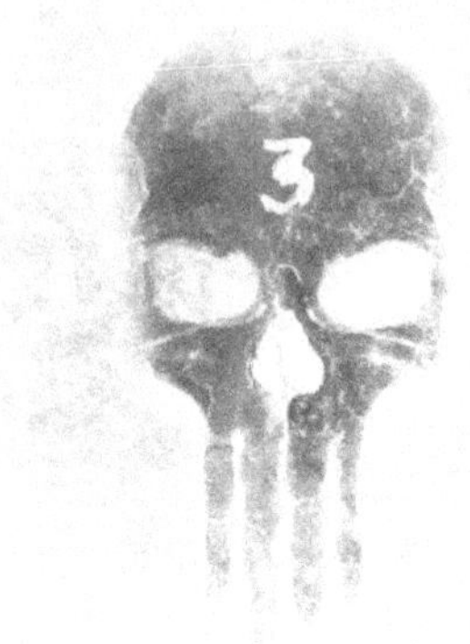

Em

At 7 p.m. sharp, Asher rings the doorbell of my apartment.

Mine is the only one on the ground floor, and of course he gave me an earful the first night he walked me home about how careless of a choice that is for a single woman.

"Be right out," I tell him through the intercom.

I put on my shoes, then grab my phone and keys to meet him at the door. I notice how clammy my hands are as I shove both into my back pockets. My heart patters in an unnatural rhythm. I haven't felt this excited since getting into my car to make the long drive here.

Excited in a good way, of course. Being chased by a psycho doesn't count.

Ash's smile is a match, igniting a flame in my core. His eyes sparkle wickedly, and a tingling reaches all the way to my toes.

He shaved for our date. His chiseled dimples greet me. "Hey!"

"Hey!" I echo in a clipped breath.

Despite the West Coast's mild climate, he's wearing a hoodie, and when I glance over his shoulder toward the curb, I see why.

"Ever been on a bike?"

My jaw goes lax, and I simply stare at him, too stunned to form words. I've never even seen one up close.

"You wanted a thrill, didn't you?"

I let out a laugh, shaking my head. "I sure did."

I'm terrified, but I'm not going to chicken out now. His proposition is enticing, and I know I can handle it. I'm ready to push my limits to new heights with him.

Ash gives me a nod. "You should probably grab an extra layer, though."

"Right! Gimme one minute," I say already on the move.

I'm in and out of my apartment in less than that, clutching a hoodie that I pull on as I walk up to him already seated.

His motorcycle is all black except for a white Japanese kanji painted onto the front fender. I gesture toward the symbol. "What does that mean?"

"Falcon." He chuckles, handing me a helmet.

"Interesting choice. Does that mean it goes fast?"

His chuckle turns a shade darker. "Oh yeah."

I slide the helmet on and mount the bike behind him. There's a whole lot of touching going on, from my arms around his chest to my boobs pressing against his back.

And don't get me started on my thighs.

If the draft from the ride won't give me goosebumps, my contours molded to his sure will.

"Hold tight," is the last thing I hear before he cranks the ignition.

My body vibrates as the engine roars. I feel the power between my thighs. The ripples chase up my spread legs through my core, and I hug Ash tighter on reflex.

This is going to be so much fun.

Fast is an understatement. We haul through the city at lightning speed. How he weaves around traffic, keeping control of this beast of a machine, is beyond incredible.

I'm utterly aroused.

We stop to grab a bite to eat from a taco truck he swears by. His voice is muffled, but I catch every word. "You'll love it," he shouts through the helmet as he slows.

I'm not even surprised when we roll up. The choice is on point with what I've seen of his personality so far. Quirky. Casual. Easy.

And he's not wrong. I do love it.

I'm almost a little disappointed when he puts his helmet back on, hiding his face. He even looks hot when he eats, and the whole time, my eyes were glued to his hands and mouth.

Street food really was a genius move. I could've watched him lick his fingers clean all night long.

After that, Ash takes us out of town. We leave the bright city lights behind as we gain elevation and make our way into the mountains.

The highway has a steep drop down one side. I know I'll have to face it on our way back, but the view is breathtaking.

We climb higher, chasing one sharp turn after another while he feeds the throttle.

The friction between us is maddening.

Leaning the bike into the winding road, my body matches his. Each fast turn we take brings us closer.

I want him.

I want his weight on top of me. I want him to bend me until I break. I've never felt so alive. I feel invincible.

We reach the mountain top. Ash pulls into the parking lot that has signs for hiking trails. I also see several picnic tables. It must be a popular spot during the day.

Or maybe...

"Is this the local lovers lane?" I joke, removing my helmet.

Ash's laugh bellows through his own before he pulls it off.

"Maybe." He offers me a sly grin, his hair falling over his eyes in all his roguish splendor.

He holds my stare, doing that thing with his lip again, and I can see him playing with his tongue as his teeth bite into the flesh.

God, I want to bite that lip for him.

I dismount first while he tugs the leather gloves off his hands.

I put my helmet down on the seat I vacated and shrug out of my hoodie to leave it with the bike. The light breeze up here doesn't warrant an extra layer.

Turning my back on him, I amble toward the mountain drop. It's quite the romantic lookout over the city lights below.

It's quiet, too. Crickets chirp and wind rustles through the trees, but there's not a soul here besides us.

Ash comes up on me from behind, his hands encircling my waist.

He's no longer wearing his hoodie either. His arms are bare as they wrap around me, and the friction of his skin sears me through my tank top.

"I thought it's only fair since you got to do all the touching," he murmurs, his husky voice right by my ear.

The hum of his timber ripples down my spine where my back presses against his chest, and I suddenly feel too hot, even in this. His hands remain on top of my shirt, but the hem rides up my stomach, exposing more skin to the elements.

It's exhilarating.

The thought of being out in the open where someone might see us is awakening dark desires in me I didn't know I had.

The tip of his nose brushes down my neck, and I moan, dropping my head back onto his shoulder.

I melt into his touch. My hand comes up to rove through his hair as my body arches, encouraging him to explore me further. I want his mouth to devour me.

His warm breath lingers at the base of my throat, riding the growing anticipation in me. I throb all over.

I feel his lips part, and when his tongue licks up the side of my neck, something hard registers in the slick drag against my skin.

My breath hitches. "Holy shit! Your tongue is pierced?"

How did I not notice?

His chuckle returns to the shell of my ear, the edge to his voice darker than before. "Among other things."

OH. MY. GOD! *Does he mean—*

I don't get to finish the thought. Ash whirls me around, and the look in his eyes is my answer.

His mouth crushes against mine, his firm hand at the back of my neck guiding me, and my lips part for him. I let his tongue in—let him tease me in the most exquisite way.

Our moans mix while Ash explores me, sliding further with each skilled flick. I feel him everywhere from the roots of my hair to my fingertips and toes. The primal need in his kiss is inescapable. It consumes me. It's a taste of what sex with him will be like. Fierce. Deep. Unrelenting.

My fingers clutch the front of his shirt, and he eases up enough to grant me a breath.

We both pant as his lips linger over mine. His hands drift, caressing my curves and mapping a path to the hem of my shirt.

He slides underneath it.

I don't stop him. My arms wind around his neck to give him free reign. My skin buzzes under his touch. It's addictive.

Ash inches higher. The breeze dances around my waist as he raises my shirt in the process, exposing me, and I know he won't stop at my bra.

My teeth nip at his bottom lip to give a little tug. I want to feel his hands on me, and I don't want him to be gentle.

"Fuck, Emily," he groans when I release him. "You're going to make me come playing rough like that."

I'm so wet for him already, but his ragged voice sends a fresh wave of lust through me. The hard length of his cock prodding me through his jeans is a promise that he can destroy me in a single thrust.

Ash lets out another curse, then breaches the constraints of my bra, pushing it up over my breasts along with my top.

My nipples are hard and sensitive when the pads of his thumbs roll over them.

He strokes me roughly.

His hands squeeze me without apology.

He feels so good I'm ready to mount him right here. A car could drive up, hikers could return from the trail, someone could be watching us from the shadows… but I don't care.

Ash answers my body's need. His hands drop, palms rounding my ass to pick me up by the back of my thighs.

Hanging on, I lock my legs at his back. He moves us a few paces, and then there's a picnic table under me.

I know I'm about to do something very, very stupid. I'm about to have unprotected sex with this man I only met days ago.

I'm still on birth control, but I'm fully aware of the other risk I'm taking. No doubt, Ash has plenty of participants eager to jump him.

His mouth breaks from mine, dipping to the crook below my jaw with a ravenous desire that chases a fresh surge of heat up my spine. It's a kiss full of sin. A kiss that burns my very soul. Like he's the devil himself, and he's come to collect.

There's no other explanation for the hold he has on me. With my thighs spread around him, I yield as he nudges me backward onto the table.

Bent over me, Ash's lips trace the front of my throat before skipping lower.

I grip his shoulders and suck in a sharp breath when he latches onto my right breast. His tongue is hot, swirling in wet circles around my nipple while his diligent fingers work the front of my jeans.

Looking up at me, he flicks his piercing over the pebbled tip of my breast in a taunt.

My pussy throbs with need. His green eyes are striking at night. Like something unnatural that wants to devour me.

Pinning me with his stare, he eases his hand past the zipper into my fly.

His eyelashes flutter. His knuckles stroke my clit over my panties, and I know they're soaking wet to his touch.

With a muffled moan around my breast, he pulls the material aside and slides across my bare flesh.

I whimper. I'm so close my muscles tremble.

Ash flicks my nipple with his piercing again. "Fuck me, baby girl," his voice implores me. "I want to feel you come around my fingers." And then he pushes two into me in a slick glide.

The tingling races toward my core, adding to the pressure my body struggles to contain. It's too much too fast.

Ash moves his fingers in and out of me, his thumb pressing down on my clit, and my orgasm explodes.

I convulse. My hips buck under him as I grind against his hand, his fingers still pumping in and out of me in a quick rhythm.

My walls clench around him in a steady beat with my pulse when I hear a cracking of branches. My eyes flick to the side and what I see makes the rushing blood in my veins run cold.

The glowing blue stitches rendering a face.

A scream ruptures in my throat. I push at Ash's shoulders to make him move, but he doesn't catch on.

"It's him. He's here!" I shove him harder, as my bare tits retain his attention.

"Who?"

"The guy with the mask," I reply, struggling to adjust my bra and shirt with him still on top of me. "The one who's been chasing me downtown."

Ash straightens, his eyes scanning the shadows by the trees.

After a long moment, he turns back to me, shaking his head with a skeptical expression. "I don't see anyone."

I feel a drop in my stomach. I'm starting to believe I'm imagining him too. How would he have tracked us all the way out here on that rocket of a bike?

35

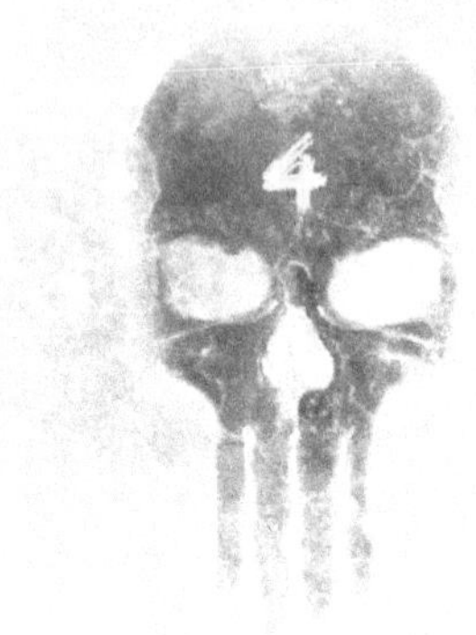

Ash

*P*erfect. *Fucking. Timing.*

I curse inward.

Emily's scream pierces my ears. I feel her feeble attempts to push me off, but I'm reluctant to comply.

"It's him. He's here!" Her legs kick at my sides as she tries to sit up.

"Who?"

"The guy with the mask. The one who's been chasing me downtown."

I take my time to straighten, then drag my eyes over the tree line.

"I don't see anyone."

But my words don't reassure her. When I turn my head back to her, I recognize how scared she is.

My shoulders drop, and I run a hand through my hair. I know the moment is ruined.

"C'mon." I nudge my head toward the bike. "I'll take you home."

Emily looks up at me with a hint of surprise, like she expected me to keep going despite the abrupt shift in her.

I can't lie. I want to. I want to fuck her so badly riding home with the bike thrumming between my legs is going to be torture. I'm so hard it hurts.

But I don't push her. I need her to trust me for this to work out.

I zip and button her jeans before dragging her ass off the picnic table to lead her back to my bike.

Her hands are still trembling when she pulls on the helmet.

I get on and wait for her arms to wrap around my chest. I'm not used to the feeling, but I fucking love it.

Her thighs slide against mine. Her breasts press to my back. Once she's settled, her fists clutch my sweatshirt, and I start the bike.

Emily's body molds to mine without fear. Whether we make a sharp turn or go straight, her shape remains soft. The speed doesn't scare her.

She's so fucking perfect, I think, checking my mirror as I zip through traffic.

When I pull up to her apartment, I shift into neutral and leave the engine idling.

Emily dismounts.

The instant her hands slip from me, I want to pull her back. I don't want her to sleep in this shitty place alone, in this shitty neighborhood.

I flip open my visor and watch her remove the spare helmet I grabbed for her from the shop.

When she holds it out, I take it.

I don't say anything. I know what happens now depends entirely on her next words.

She sweeps a dark lock of her hair behind her ear, stalling.

I'm tempted to follow the motion down her body. I recall the smooth feel of her naturally tanned skin. The taste of her nipple on my tongue. The slick, hot glide of her cunt against my fingers—

Fuuucck! My cock jerks as it swells another painful degree.

Grinding my teeth to will it down, I hold her gaze, a swirl of mesmerizing hazel and blue.

Her chest rises with her inhale, then her lips part. "Will you walk with me again tomorrow?"

A grin stretches behind my helmet. "I'll be there," I promise.

She's going to be worth the blue balls I'm currently nursing.

We have her right where we want her.

———

My cock is still throbbing when I decelerate, and I have a feeling the persistent hard-on is not going anywhere until I take care of it the old-fashioned way.

The garage opens on my approach. I pull in, taking off the helmet and gloves before I dismount.

I leave my stuff on the bike, then punch the button to close the garage behind me.

Stomping into the house, I lift a middle finger in passing to flip off the motherfucker sprawled out on the couch; I have a pressing matter to attend to before dealing with him.

I keep my eyes on the hallway in front of me. I don't need to look at him to know he's grinning.

"Asshole!" I shout without turning.

His laughter carries back to me as I slam the door.

I'm going to jack off right now, but I might jizz in his cereal later on principle.

39

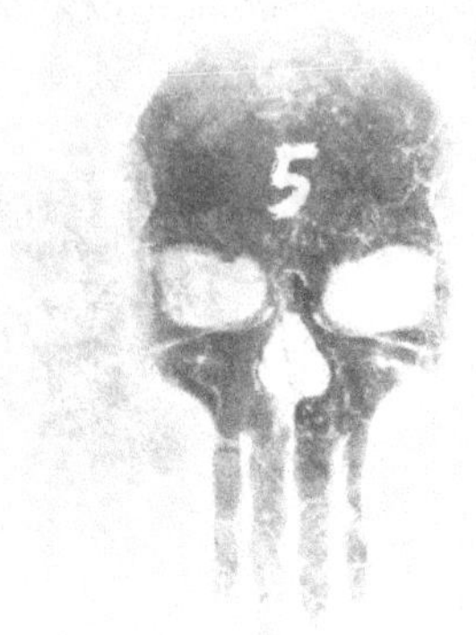

Em

"Can you turn that up," I ask Drew, pointing at the small TV he keeps in the kitchen.

I recognize the footage of the news report about the young woman who was found dead right before I moved here. The same anchorwoman now speaks about the discovery of a second victim as new images flash on the screen. "Marisol Fuentes appears to have been killed days ago," she relays.

"That's correct, Susan," the reporter at the scene picks up when the feed switches to an apartment building which is clearly marked with yellow tape, stretching behind her. "According to the authorities, both victims show signs of having had consensual intercourse prior to their deaths. But is that merely coincidence or a pattern?

"After the body of 22-year old Shelly Baker was found a month ago, police have been looking into ex-boyfriends as possible suspects; someone who is jealous or feels betrayed by her moving on. However, with this second victim, more questions about the motive and connections between the two arise.

"Did her killer know about her personal life? Had he been stalking her and lying in wait for her lover to leave? He might even be a scorned lover himself out for revenge.

"The bruising on their necks suggests the assailant might have been wearing gloves, and the DNA found under the victims' fingernails remains inconclusive, so no arrests have been made, but the police says it's only a matter of time."

"What a shame." Laura shakes her head beside me, a hand splayed on her chest. "I'm so glad you're no longer walking home alone at night thanks to your gentleman caller."

I stifle a laugh at the term. I have my car, of course, but parking is a bitch downtown, and the walk to my apartment is only a few minutes. Still, I'm glad, too, that I ran into Ash.

"I don't know," Jake says over his shoulder while rinsing the dishes in the sink. "Sex and asphyxiation? If you ask me, sounds like a fetish gone too far."

"Seriously?" I stare at his back, my brows raised. "You think he got himself off by choking her?"

He huffs as though amused by my ignorance. "No." He turns his head toward me. "I think *she* might've been the one who got off."

"Boy!" Laura's tone warns.

I cringe. "That's sick."

"What?" He shrugs, refocusing on the dishes. "Breath play is a thing, you know? Supposedly, it makes you come harder."

I can't believe my ears. "Who tells you this shit?" He's too young to have that kind of experience.

"The Internet."

Now I'm the one to let out a huff. "Don't believe everything you read online," I advise him, removing my apron.

True, after four years with a boyfriend like Nate and his lack for adventure, I'm looking for more excitement when it comes to sex, but I'd have to really trust a person to give breath play a try. I mean, my life would literally be in their hands.

I step outside and don't see Asher.

Pulling my phone from my back pocket, I check the time, even though I know I'm not early.

Dread prickles across my nape as I stuff it back into my pocket. *Did he forget?*

No. He promised. But maybe he fell asleep.

I shift the weight on my feet. I don't know whether I should wait for him or walk home alone.

A screech like nails on a chalkboard rakes up my spine, making me cringe. I swing my head left to check what made the noise when my eyes land on *him.*

My heart punches up my throat. He's ambling toward me, mask hiding his face and his pace almost leisurely as he drags the tip of his knife along the brick wall in a taunt.

It's a terrifying sound. I can almost feel it, like claws ripping through my flesh.

For a moment I'm so scared I can't move.

I swallow my fear, and my feet regain their mobility. Eyes on him, I shuffle backward a few steps before my mind catches up, and I turn to run.

My pulse continues to accelerate even after I round a corner, and he can no longer see me. The last time I tried to outrun him, I got lost. Am I better off hiding?

I duck in between two dumpsters and catch my breath. But I don't feel safe. Tipping my sight upward, I check the roof tops for movement.

The alley is quiet.

I listen for footsteps and don't hear anything but my booming heartbeat and the cacophony of traffic on a nearby street.

I stay there for I don't know how long. I resist the urge to pull out my phone afraid the light of the screen will give me away.

My hands tremble. I'm left in darkness with nothing but my broken breaths.

At last, I dare to step back out into the alley.

I exhale in relief and pivot my stance when a strong arm snares me, pinning my own down to trap me in his hold.

I know it's him. I don't have to turn my head to see the mask as he cages me against his chest. I recognize the black hoodie.

Something sharp presses to the dip below my jaw, forcing a whimper from me.

"Shhh," he whispers.

Despite all my instincts, his low voice is soothing at my ear. The swell of his chest is rock-solid but warm, and with his front pressed to my ass, I know he's aroused by this.

A dark and depraved desire stirs in my core. I can't explain it. And a part of me is ashamed to admit it.

Before I'm forced to confront my dilemma, his arm releases me. The tip of his knife stays in place for another second, and his gravely timbre reverberates in my ear. He growls one word:

"Run!"

———

I don't hear him chasing after me, but I can still feel his breath down my neck.

He could've killed me.

His knife was right there at my throat, our bodies flush, and an unspeakable charge crackling between us.

The tingling sensation his hard contours stirred in me remains. *Fuck!* I liked the way his body pressed against mine from behind. I wanted him to take me like that. Wanted his rough hands on my hips, his cock driving into my pussy without mercy.

It's wrong. I know it is. He's crazy. Dangerous. And he's been terrorizing me for his sheer entertainment. I can't let him catch me.

I keep running.

I'm panting, cold sweat trailing down my back when the roar of an engine rushes up on me, and a motorcycle comes flying out of the crossing alley to my right.

A cry rips from my throat. I expect a collision, but he manages to brake in time.

Heart leaping out of my chest, I stare at him, wide-eyed, and it takes my brain another second to catch on. It's Ash. I recognize his heather gray hoodie; it's the same one he wore on our date. It has a skull logo on his left pec with what I assume is the name of the auto shop written underneath.

He flips his visor up. "Shit!" he shouts over the sound of the bike. "My bad. I didn't mean to run you over. I was looking for you when I didn't catch you at the diner. Sorry for running late."

I'm so glad to see his face. I'm not even mad. "It's fine," I wheeze, grabbing my side to nurse an oncoming stitch. "But we should probably exchange numbers." If I had known he was on his way, I would've stayed put.

"Good call."

I draw another deep breath into my lungs, and his eyes narrow on me. "Are you okay?"

"Yeah! Yeah, I'm fine," I huff, waving him off.

His scrutinizing gaze does a rake over my body, then he nods toward the helmet strapped to the back of his bike. "Hop on. I'll give you a ride home."

My head swivels to throw a glance over my shoulder down the alley. The rush of fear mixed with adrenaline is an utterly new high to me. It's addicting.

I refocus on Ash. The thrill of running into my stalker makes me want to take a risk, and the words tumble from me before common sense can put a damper on my high.

"Let's go to your place."

I catch the glimmer of surprise and delight in his eyes before I unhook my helmet to climb on behind him.

"Ready?"

The engine rumbles between my thighs. He angles his head toward me, and I reply with a *yep* as I wrap my arm around him.

We haul ass through the streets.

I swear Ash is racing his own shadow the way he rides. Timing each stoplight perfectly, he swerves around cars that appear to stand still.

My heart batters my ribcage with the ongoing rush of adrenaline. I don't know where he's taking us, but we're quickly leaving the busy downtown scene behind.

The drive is not far, though. After a few minutes, he decelerates on a long stretch of road flanked with single family homes.

No wonder he considers my living arrangements low standard.

Only I could never afford to live here. Not on my own. With a roommate maybe; once I got a better job than waitressing.

A garage door rises a short distance ahead. Making a stealthy approach, he slows to a crawl; at least compared to the speed we were going earlier. It's the middle of the night, and he probably doesn't want to piss off the neighbors.

He cuts the engine as we pull in.

"Don't tell me you still live with your parents," I probe with trepidation, removing my helmet.

Ash throws back a laugh, then shakes his head. "No."

Living in a house instead of an apartment makes him appear so grown up. He's too good to be true.

I notice that the garage is big enough to fit two cars, but has been converted to a workshop for his bike. There's tools and painting equipment too.

Ash closes the garage behind us and takes my hand to lead me into the house. There's a living room to our left, an open concept kitchen to our right, and a hallway straight ahead, which is what he tows me toward, peering back at me over his shoulder.

The hooded look in his eyes makes my stomach quiver. I know we're both eager to pick up where we left off after getting interrupted on our date.

His free hand twists the knob of the door at the end. I assume it's the master. We passed by a second bedroom that's shut, and if Ash does indeed have a roommate, he must be out since there was no other vehicle in the garage.

Lucky me.

Ash's room is tidy. Other than a very inviting king-sized bed, a dresser with a TV on it, and a lounge chair in the corner, there's not much to it I can see in the ambient lighting coming in through the curtains.

He tugs me over the threshold and lets go of my hand before shutting the door.

I sit down on the long side of the bed, leaning back on my hands to watch him take off his hoodie and shirt in one go. He chucks the bulk toward the chair, then gets to unlacing his boots.

I kick my sneakers off in response too.

When he straightens, I finally get a good, long look at him. He's marvelous. Lean muscle flexes under my attention, drawing my curiosity to his tattoos. The designs spread up his shoulders and over his chest.

Both sides are covered with ink of images and words. I make out some skulls, tendrils of smoke and snakes, all in a very dark theme. I associate them with violence and death. A dark past perhaps?

My eyes skip over his smooth chest and latch onto the trail of hair disappearing in the waistband of his jeans.

I bite my lip as my thighs twitch. I remember him mentioning being pierced in more places than just his tongue, and since I can now see it's not his nipples…

We'll, *I'm thrilled* is an understatement.

Ash pulls out his phone and queues some music before setting it down on the nightstand.

I open my legs for him to step in between, and when he does, the bulge of his fly is at my eye level, daring me.

I push off and reach for his button.

"Nu-uh." His grip cuffs my wrists. "Not so fast."

My pussy pulses with him holding on to me, and I swallow as anticipation ripples through my core at his commanding tone.

Ash releases my wrists. "Tit for tat." He gestures with his head toward me, his sly grin matching the quirk of his eyebrow. "Take off your top. All of it," he demands.

I meet his smile and do as I'm told, tossing it somewhere behind me.

Ash's grin widens. "Such a good girl."

Heat floods my pussy at his praise. I never understood the allure behind the term until I heard it from him. I want to be good, but how can I be good if I want to do bad things?

Like *really* bad things. Things that normal couples didn't do. Things that were considered dirty. Depraved.

Ash lifts his right hand to my breast, teasing my tender nipple between his fingers. His teeth rake over his bottom lip with the motion, and I wonder whether he's remembering sucking it.

"Now you can touch me," he finally says.

My fingers flick the button. Eyes riveting to his face, I drink in his reaction as I tug the zipper down slowly.

I notice the jerk of his Adam's apple from anticipation. I feel it too. It rages through my veins like an inferno.

Sliding my hands in from the top, I push his jeans and boxer briefs down.

His cock bobs free.

My eyes catch on the silver captive ball ring nestled right below the head then drop to the horizontal barbell at the base of his shaft.

Not one but two?

My throat goes dry. The piercings are not the only thing suddenly intimidating me.

He's big.

Bigger than any guy I've ever been with. Ash's shaft is long and so thick I'm not entirely sure I can fit all of him.

"We'll make it fit," he says, reading my wide eyes and gaping mouth.

I pick my jaw off the ground when he takes my hand and slides my palm over his stiff length, curling my fingers around him.

Fuck, he feels good. His pulse beats against my palm as I stroke him root to head, his hand guiding mine. His skin is smooth, shifting over the rigid shape like silk.

Ash surrenders a moan when I tighten my grip, and my thumb teases the ring.

My needy pussy thrums at the sound of his pleasure. I need to hear more. Need to feel more.

"How does that work with condoms?"

"You'll still feel it," he replies, his breath jagged. "Just not as much."

"And you always use condoms?"

His green eyes scrutinize me briefly. Then he removes my hands, taking them by the wrists again. "I make rare exceptions," he drawls, nudging me backwards onto the bed.

Pinning my arms on either side of my head, he feathers his lips over my mouth. "But I get tested regularly because sometimes they do rip." A velvet kiss makes my eyes flutter. "I'm clean, if that's what you're wondering. And I can pull out before I finish."

The weight of his hips settles in between my thighs, and his pecs brush my pebbled nipples. I tingle all over, from my fingertip to my toes, to the roots of my hair.

The friction between our bodies increases. I ache to feel him inside me.

"I'm on the pill," I blurt. "Knocking me up is not an issue. I just got out of a four-year relationship, and I never stopped taking it even though I haven't been with anyone else."

"Same guy for four years, huh?" His soft kisses dip below my jaw. "Sounds serious."

I tip my head back as his lips map the front of my throat. "We were engaged, but I couldn't go through with it. So I bailed."

Ash chuckles darkly. "To look for a thrill?"

I look down and catch the wicked glimmer in his eyes when his pierced tongue swirls my nipple in a lazy circle.

"Can't blame a girl for wanting some excitement in her life," I reason. "He definitely wasn't it."

A slight tilt to his head, Ash stares at me in challenge. "Still looking?"

How much of a thrill could I handle? My experience level is basic at best, and he's probably into some kinky stuff. Why else get your dick pierced? "What do you have in mind?"

"Let me blindfold you?"

I cringe. "Um… after being with a guy who was reluctant to have sex with the light on, I was really looking forward to the visual experience."

Ash jerks up, blinking. "What?"

I release a sigh, and he must've read my expression that I wasn't kidding about my disappointing sex life.

"Girl!" He rolls his eyes before they refocus on me. "Next, you're going to tell me he didn't eat your pussy either."

My teeth clamp down on my lips to stifle a laugh.

Ash shakes his head, then settles back down, his face hovering inches from mine.

Eyes locked, his mouth lowers to mine. "Do you want to get properly fucked, baby girl?" he asks, amusement in his tone.

I reply with a chuckle. "Yes please."

"Let me blindfold you, and I'll make it worth your while." He parts my lips with his, teasing the answer out of me.

"Fine," I moan into him. "Just this once."

He gives air to a hoarse laugh, then straightens on top of me, primed to push off.

Adjusting his briefs, but leaving his fly undone, Ash rushes out of the room.

I prop myself up on my elbows.

I hear a door down the hall, and he returns five seconds later, a black bandana in his hand.

"Where did you just pull that from?" I ask as he bends over me again to cover my eyes. Swift fingers work a knot at the back of my head. "It smells nice."

"The dryer."

I wonder what laundry detergent and sheets he uses. The notes spreading through the cloth's fibers are dark and musky like men's cologne, but not his. The difference is unmistakable.

His own cologne must've overpowered the fragrance.

"How's that?" His fingers release the tie, hands shifting around to cradle my head. "Too tight?"

I give him a light shake. "No. It's perfect."

I can't see anything. The room was already dimly lit, but with the cloth forcing my eyes shut, only darkness greets me.

I like how it feels. My anticipation rises with the loss of sight and not knowing what he's going to do next.

And that's not all.

I'm immediately more aware of his touch. His weight on top of me. The friction of him between my thighs.

Everything becomes heightened.

Ash hovers over me, his thumbs tracing the edges of my jaw, and I don't need to see. I can sense the heat of his smile on my face.

"You're perfect," he stresses in a husky voice, his lips caressing mine.

One of his hands lets go to brace his weight as he deepens his kiss and nudges me flat onto my back.

I open my mouth to him on a moan.

Ash counters with equal sounds of pleasure. His teeth tug on my bottom lip, then nip my chin when he moves lower, his hips grinding against mine.

My eyes roll back into my skull. This is so hot.

His tongue curls into the dip of my throat, then slicks a trail down my sternum.

He drifts to one side, and I arch up when he sucks my right breast into his mouth while his hand engulfs the other, working me simultaneously.

I ride the high. He feels so good. I want him to devour me.

A desperate whimper escapes my lips, and he chuckles with satisfaction. "So needy, baby girl?"

But Ash answers my call. He straightens, and his hands come together at the front of my jeans.

I lift my hips. Patiently, he undresses me until I'm completely naked before him.

My breathing judders. He takes my knees, sliding his palms along the inside of my thighs to open me to him.

I feel the chill air of the room on me, and I shudder knowing that I'm on full display. I can't hide anything from him. He sees me now. All of me.

"So beautiful," he murmurs, his heavy hands spreading me until I can't go any further.

His thumb traces my wet seam, back and forth, teasing me before stalling right at my clit.

The mattress shifts under his movements, and then his tongue lashes out. He thrusts it into me, spreading my seam to grant himself entrance.

My muscles tremble. Stroking my clit with his thumb while his left arm wraps around my leg to keep me from squirming, he has me close to climaxing already.

I feel it peaking.

I cry out as I thrash in his hold, my arms flailing to grab a hold of anything. I buck against his mouth.

But Ash is not done. Thrusting two fingers up into me, he does the curling motion to stroke my G-spot and sucks me harder.

He's relentless.

He doesn't just do this for my sake; he revels in giving me pleasure. His tongue curls inward to meet the smooth glide of his fingers. He devours me like it's his calling. Like he's never tasted anything so good.

And that piercing?

Each time his tongue retreats, he flicks across my clit, then slides back in. I can't take it. It's too much.

Ash makes me come again, and adds a third finger to his thrusting motion.

"Is my baby girl ready to get properly fucked now?" he asks, his voice drawing nearer as his fingers stretch me.

"Yes! Please," I beg him.

He frees his hand, and I hear the rustling of his clothes.

The mattress under me tilts to the side as he sets one knee down for leverage and settles between my thighs.

Left hand on my knee, he slides the little metal ring adorning his cock across my pussy.

We both moan.

"You feel so good, baby."

Ash aligns the blunt head at my entrance and crowns me, giving me only the tip before sliding my leg over his shoulder. I tense. Even after all *that*, I feel myself stretching to fit him.

He lowers himself down to kiss me while sinking his cock gradually deeper, bit by bit. He doesn't retreat. He drags the piercing along my tight walls, pushing on with firm intent.

It's overwhelming.

I wrap myself around him. Matching the soothing motion of his lips, I suck in clipped breaths. There's pain, but I relish the burn that comes with the pleasure.

I open my mouth to him, submitting to the slick demand of his tongue and letting all of him in.

Ash gives it one last push.

I flinch from the sharp sensation. A whimper makes my lips tremble against his as my pussy is forced to adjust around the thick base of his shaft. But I take the final inch he has to give.

"Good girl," he groans into my throat, his mouth slanted over mine. "That's it."

Our tongues tangle as he rocks into me with increasing fervor.

His thrusts gain momentum. Ash retreats further, coming at me with more force on each drive.

He winds me up.

One hand gripping my thigh, the other one bracing himself, he straightens without slowing his pace. His breathing turns ragged. Hoarse grunts reach my ears, and my stomach tightens.

The pressure in me builds and builds until there's no stopping it. He rails me with every inch of his pulsing length.

And I feel it. *Oh, do I feel it.* He reaches places inside me he shouldn't be able to reach.

Faster. Harder. The words ricochet in my head like bullets.

My toes curl. My womb contracts. With my hips angled up, I come.

I cry as my walls grip him to hold on, but the suction on his retreat counters me. He keeps pumping in and out with short quick thrusts, a low growl chasing his momentum.

His grip flexes on my thigh. Ash jerks into me, twice, then pulls out abruptly.

His weight lifts off the mattress as he flips me onto my stomach, and before I can get my bearings in the dark, he's back. He hauls my hips up and thrusts into me from behind in one slick glide.

I thought he came already, but when he fills me again, he's just as big and hard as before.

He fucks me harsher now, his fingertips at my hips digging into my skin. He pulls out so far, the piercing at his tip catches my clit each time before he follows up by slamming the second piece of jewelry into the sensitive bundle of nerves.

Ash plunges into me so raw and deep I clench the sheets in my fists. My whole body trembles. I'm so close to coming again, but this time it's more. Maybe it's this position. Maybe it's his piercing pounding my G-spot combined with the external stimulation. This time it feels like I'm going to explode.

My mouth opens, and I cry out when I go off. My walls squeeze him, clenching and unclenching to pull him into me.

Spasms rake me while his hips come at me again and again until he too finally climaxes. He locks into me in one final brutal thrust.

Ash stills, his cock jerking inside me to release every last drop.

I grind back.

I can't help it. He feels so good inside me. I want to feel him come again.

At last, he pulls himself free. He rolls me over and rips the bandana off my head.

My eyes settle on his face, but there's no wryly dimple at the corner of his mouth. His smirk is cold; almost cruel.

A chill races up my spine.

He holds my stare as he thrusts two fingers into me, pumping them in and out.

I can feel his cum dripping free. There's so much of it.

"Lick them clean," he says, bringing them up to my mouth.

My lips part on his command, and I suck them in.

"That's it. Good girl," he groans, his hooded gaze pinning me. "You like the taste of us, don't you?"

I nod, swirling my tongue around his fingers, swallowing greedily.

Even though he removed the bandana, it's all I smell. Like the scent burned itself into my mind.

Satisfied, he withdraws, but remains hovering.

"We're gonna have *so* much fun together," he promises, an unusually rough edge in his voice.

My pussy acknowledges him with a pulse. It's a betrayal. Something in me answers the call of this dark side.

I follow the brief drop of his eyes to my lips before he kisses me. Then his groan fills me, deep and sensual like he's kissing me for the first time.

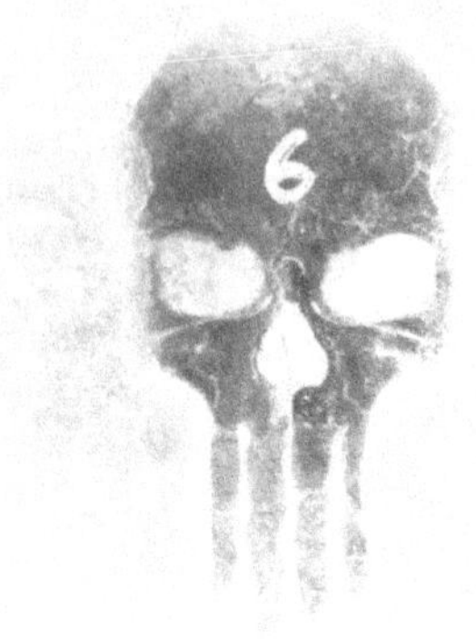

Ash

I park my bike in the rear of the shop and stroll in through the staff door that leads directly to where we work on cars.

An old-school radio is playing on a workbench.

"Is that you, Ash?" Isaac asks when I let the steel door slam shut behind me.

I look over to where a sturdy man's jean-clad legs poke out from underneath a '67 Hemi Road Runner that's getting overhauled.

I offered to give him a hand, but he declined. Supposedly, he used to have one just like it, and he wants to do that one himself—won't let anyone else even touch it.

And nobody argues with him. The shop is his baby.

"Yeah," I grunt. "Where's Mace?"

We're a team of five working in the garage, but the three of us are always first to come in and last to leave, not counting Isaac's daughter Tatum, who runs sales in the front of the shop. Rob and Jason will roll up within the hour.

"Painting!"

Figures. He's been talking about nothing else since sketching the design.

Pushing the plastic curtain that divides the workspace aside to step through, I find him squatting by the Nova's right front fender in paint scrubs and mask, the detailing spray brush in hand.

I know he's got earbuds in, listening to a different kind of music than Isaac, but his sixth sense goes off the second I enter, and he turns my way.

"I owe you donuts." I toss him the bag, and he catches it one handed, crushing it to his chest.

"I'm glad you remembered." His voice comes out muffled through the facemask.

"Got your favorite too."

"The pink ones?" Setting the brush down, he removes the face masks and grins. "Nice. Thanks."

"Oh no," I disagree with a laugh. "Thank *you.*"

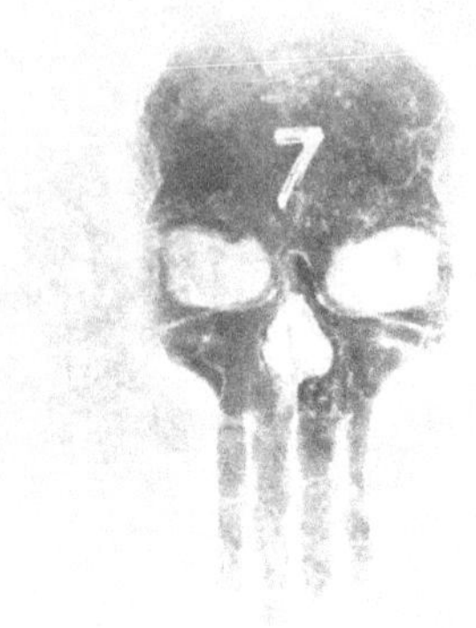

Em

I get to the diner at 6 p.m. to relieve Cathy, my counterpart, of the day staff. While Jake comes in with me, Laura and Drew are already here.

As he's busy behind the grill, he greets me with a smile and a wave that I return when I clock in before slipping my apron over my head to meet Laura out front.

We hustle through eight hours, chatting about everything and nothing while customers keep a steady flow going.

Of course, she needles me with questions about Ash.

He woke me this morning with fresh coffee after he'd already showered, which I hadn't heard at all. Nor had I felt him slipping out of bed once I fell asleep with him spooning me, still in his jeans. I was out like a light.

Letting me borrow his hoodie, he dropped me off at my place on his way to work, but he said he'll pick me up again after my shift.

And I hope the night after that as well. I know we're moving fast, but I want us to become a regular thing.

At the end of the night, I switch my apron for his sweatshirt, which I left on the hook in the kitchen, and say goodbye to Drew and Jake.

Ash awaits me in the alley out back. He's scrolling on his phone but looks up when I step out.

He grins. His helmet sits on his lap; mine is strapped to the backseat.

"Miss me?" I drawl, taking the short flight of stairs down to him.

His dimple deepens. "*Hell* yeah."

He puts his phone away, and I slide in for a kiss, my fingers clasping his jaw.

His groan hums through me. "Damn, baby girl. If I start kissing you now, I'm not gonna stop."

I like the sound of that.

"Promise?" I purr against his mouth. My teeth nip at his lip, and I swear I can feel the heat radiating off his body.

He gives me a soft grunt, then motions at my helmet. "Get on."

I let out a laugh, but comply.

I slip the helmet on and tug the long sleeves of his hoodie over my fingers before wrapping my arms around him. I get why he's wearing gloves. It's not just the wind; bugs sting like a bitch at high speed.

We're back at his place in what seems like minutes. He pulls into the garage and lowers the door, this time from the bike instead of the switch by the wall. Like he can't wait to be away from prying eyes fast enough.

It makes me giddy.

We dismount, then the helmets come off, along with his gloves. Arms snaked around one another, we're already kissing as we push into the house.

We make it down the hallway to his bedroom, lips locked, my hands tangled in his hair, his finding their way under my shirt.

Ash's heated touch roams my bare skin with growing passion—my waist, my ribs, my back.

When we stumble through the door frame, I kick off my shoes before breaking from his kiss to rip the hoodie over my head. Then my hands dive under his.

He doesn't need another cue. He helps me get it off and lets it drop behind him.

I watch the flare in his eyes ignite as my palms slide over his smooth chest. His tattooed pecs are too big for my small hands. I splay my fingers to grasp more of him.

My curious fingers drift lower to explore the ridges of his abs. The muscles flex under my caress. He's rock solid everywhere.

Ash wears his jeans low; no belt. I bring my hands together over his stomach, hovering where a darker trail of hair leads to his fly.

I can feel his anticipating stare on my face as I release the button and drag the zipper down.

My eyes flick to his. "You know," I say, pushing his briefs and pants down over his hips, "I've been thinking about this all day."

He squints through one eye. "Is that so?"

"Mm-hmm." I give the waistband a tug, then motion for him to sit on the bed.

Ash plops down, leaning back onto his elbows.

Eyes on him, I lower myself between his legs. I run my hands over his thighs from his knees toward his crotch, sliding inward.

The slow, teasing motion earns me a groan. Ash bites his lower lip the way that makes my inhibitions crumble.

My pussy clenches at the sight of him. I lean forward, stroking his thighs like that again and watching his cock twitch in response.

I take his stiff length in my hand to stand him up and squeeze him a little while stroking him with my thumb.

His pulse beats against my palm. I think he's swelling more at my touch, and I'm considering the possibility I might very well choke on him. With or without the piercing.

A bead of pre-cum awaits my tongue at his tip. I flick across to lap it up, then direct my attention to his jewelry.

Capturing his hooded gaze, I tease the ring. My thumb skims the length of his shaft down to the metal barbell in a slow pump.

My worry of whether I'm any good at this is cut off by the hiss through Ash's clenched teeth.

I close my lips around the head, my tongue swirling the ring again before I slide lower.

The smooth head of his cock glides across the roof of my mouth toward the back and panic tickles up my nape. I pause, using my hand around the base of his shaft, because I don't think I can fit it all.

I keep the pumping motion going, sucking him deeper down my throat, bit by bit to push my limits. I love the way he fills me. I can't get enough. He feels so good.

My hand falls away as my lips stretch around the thick base, and then, oh God, take it all.

My hips rock. My clit throbs. The sensation of him at the back of my throat almost makes me come. It's tight and slick and hard to breathe, but I don't stop. I slide his length over my tongue again and again, taking every last inch.

Saliva pools around the seal of my lips. I swallow, and my throat squeezes him on his next thrust.

I moan around him as he fills me all the way to the back again. My pussy aches. I need him there, too.

The hum that carries from my lips up his shaft earns me another groan, and his hips buck to thrust himself deeper. I don't think I can take it.

My extended tongue swirls the barbell seated at his base and somehow I *do* manage to overcome the crude intrusion.

A wave of pride chases through me at that.

"Fuck yes! Play with it," Ash's strained voice urges. I know he's close. His motion grows fervorous as his breaths come in shorter, quicker grunts.

And then he arches off the bed.

Ash spills into me with a gush down my throat. I swallow, greedily, my hands squeezing his thighs to take in all the strength he has to offer.

"Fuck, baby girl." Ash fans his fingers through my hair. "*I'll* be the one thinking about this all day tomorrow. *And* the next day," he tags on with a little snort.

I withdraw my lips from around his cock.

"Strip," he says in words as much as with his eyes. "I want you naked against me."

I push to my feet, and start with my jeans, taking everything off slowly like I'm putting on a show for him.

Ash drinks in every move. He unlaces his half boots without looking down, and toes them off before scooting further back onto the mattress.

"Turn around," he tells me when I crawl up to him. "I want your ass grinding on me."

I stretch out over his chest, my head beside his, resting on his shoulder.

"Spread your legs for me, baby girl."

I lift my feet, and set them down on either side of him, baring myself toward the door which is still open to the hallway.

"Raise your arms."

I comply, giving him better access to rove my front.

Ash's palms stroke my breasts, rolling my nipples into even harder pebbles. My right hand in his hair, I tip my head back and arch off him, my ass grinding on top of him.

"That's it, baby girl. Just like that," he coaches me.

Goosebumps prickle my skin. Eyes toward the window behind us, I focus on his touch.

His dominant hand skates lower. His fingertips brush the crest of my pubic bone, then curve over.

Ash cradles me in his palm, fingers sliding through my slick folds.

I'm so fucking wet.

He acknowledges the same with a groan that sends shivers down my spine. I can feel him getting hard again.

The grind turns rough. His left hand shifts to my right breast, his arm of steel wrapping around my ribs and pinning me to his chest.

"Come for me, baby girl," he huffs, his breaths as ragged as mine.

His stroking grows even harsher. I ride his hand without shame, giving myself over to the impending climax.

The tremors take over. They're coming at me in waves, faster and faster when I hear the creak from the door.

My head snaps up and my eyes land on the tall, dark figure stepping into the room… his combat boots… his black hoodie…

Blood drains from my face with a cool tingle across my scalp. A gloved hand lowers his hood, and I get a full view of the mask.

No! No, this can't be happening.

"ASH!" I push at the arm that's trapping me.

Ash ignores my plea, and for a split second I think I might be hallucinating.

My heart pounds up my throat. I choke on a scream, squirming in his hold, trying to get free despite the vise he has me in.

But his fingers work me relentlessly. I can't fight the climax. The man by the door reaches for his mask and raises it slowly.

I shatter the instant he reveals his face to me. I can't contain my cry as I buck against Ash. The same green eyes… same dirty blond hair…

He's a twin!

A *fucking* TWIN!

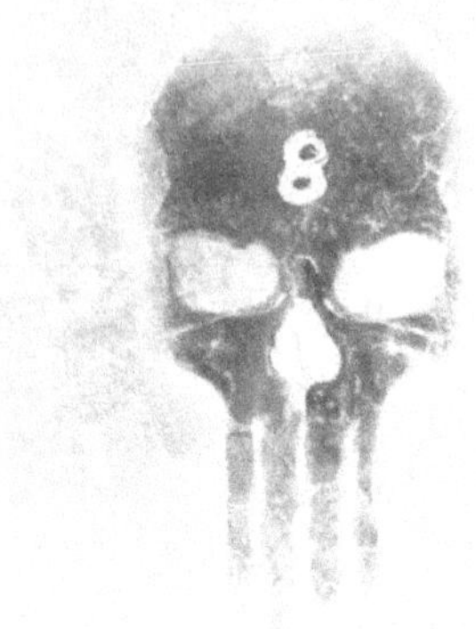

Em

"Meet my brother Mason."

Ash's words are like ice down my back as he sits us up, and I'm face to face with the man who's been stalking me.

I close my legs, but his hand is still there.

"C'mon now, don't be shy, baby girl. Technically, you already met him."

If I weren't so terrified, I'd scoff. I wouldn't exactly call our encounter in the alley a meet-cute.

Ash's fingers grip me, his voice kissing the shell of my ear. "You even let him fuck you."

Oh no.

His twin's lips curl into that same cruel grin from last night as he takes a step, plucking the black gloves from his hands.

Approaching the bed, he stuffs them into the front pocket, then reaches up behind his head, pulling his hoodie and the T-shirt underneath off in one go.

I flinch.

"Uh-uh." Ash's hold on me tightens. "Relax! We're not going to hurt you. We just wanted to scare you a little bit," he justifies with a note of amusement.

Then his voice turns raspy again. "Now be a good girl and spread your legs for my brother," he tells me, removing his hand from between my thighs. "Give him a taste."

My legs go numb. And I do it. I open myself up to him.

Why do I do it? Why do I want this?

Mason closes in on me, all slow like he's stalking his prey.

A wave of need crashes over me with the way his intense eyes devour every inch of my bare flesh.

I ache.

He gives my hips a tug, pulling me off his brother's lap.

Ash resumes kneading my breasts from behind. I watch with rising anticipation when Mason lowers himself. He slides my legs over his broad shoulders, splayed hands gripping my thighs, then his tongue darts out.

Eyes locked to mine, he lashes at my clit with the hard metal of his piercing.

My body unfurls in ecstasy.

Ash takes notice. "Do you like watching him?"

"Yes." I groan, bucking against his brother's mouth. His chin is rough, long past a five o'clock shadow, and I don't care if I'll be sore later.

My release crests. I tense.

I'm teetering right at the edge when his tongue thrusts into me, his lips forming a hot seal as he sucks.

The orgasm rakes through me full force. Mason moans into me, the vibration adding to my high while I thrash with panting breaths.

He lets me ride out the wave against the sweep of his tongue before he straightens between my thighs.

His knees settle on the edge of the bed, the mattress dipping under his weight. My legs still slung over his shoulders, he takes my hands and guides them between us.

His teeth rake over his bottom lip in a deliberately slow drag, watching. "Hold yourself open for me," he says, his voice a shade darker than Ash's as he leads my trembling finger to my pussy.

Ash's palms slide down my sides to cradle my ass. He gives my pelvis a tilt so I can see EVERYTHING.

Mason frees his cock.

His left hand at the back of my knee, he flicks his piercing over the tender nub at my clit.

I twitch from the jolts that shoot through my core on each pass.

His lips curl. He drags the pierced tip of his cock along my seam, relishing the trembles it draws from me as I glare up at him.

He lingers at my entrance, and I swear I catch him winking at me right before his grip on my knee tenses, and I feel the pressure.

My mouth opens to a silent gasp, but no air reaches my lungs. Mason spears me in one thrust. He used only his tongue to get me off, and my walls are not prepared for his size. I cry out, but he cuts my voice by crashing down on me. He steals my breath as he fills me so fucking deep.

With my legs up, he folds me in half. His thumb strokes my clit in rough circles, and his tongue fucks me as roughly as his thrusts. He pounds into me.

Hard bumps of more piercings along the top of Mason's shaft register, adding to the stimulation of my already sensitive parts on each drive while Ash's cock grinds against my backside. His hands rock my hips into his brother. There's no escaping them. My walls clench and I come again.

Mason speeds up like he's about to come too.

"Mace!" Ash's voice carries a note of warning.

Mason ceases his assault, chuckling against my lips. "I think my brother wants to cut back in." Then he pulls out.

My lips hang open. I brace myself against his chest as Mason takes me around the waist and picks me up like I weigh nothing.

Ash adjusts his position underneath me, lying flat on his back before his brother sets me down on his lap in reverse, my legs bent on either side, his cock probing my slit.

I sink down, taking the hard length he offers me.

Mason's left hand cradles the base of my skull. Urging me onto my elbows, he grants me a closer view of his piercings. They're not the same as Ash's. Where the captive ball ring adorned his brother's cock below the head, Mason has it at the base, a vertical barbell running through his skin at the tip instead.

And I was right about additional ones. I catch sight of four little beads at the halfway point of his shaft on top as he retreats to stand at the side of the bed.

My stomach forms a knot. I know where this is going.

Mason's pupils are so large, his hooded eyes appear black. His right hand strokes his cock at my eye level, giving me time to take in its intimidating size.

"Stick out your tongue." He guides the tip to my waiting mouth. "Let me see how far back I can reach."

I comply, and he eases himself past my lips, sliding along the roof of my mouth all the way back.

"Watch those teeth," he cautions.

I gag and force more air through my nose, keeping my jaw lax like before when my mouth closes around his thick base, meeting up with the ring piercing his skin there.

His right hand joins the other at the back of my head. "Atta girl." Fanning his fingers through the hair at my nape, he grants me a few lazy thrusts. "Look at you, taking both of us so well."

I taste myself on him as I hollow my cheeks and suck.

Ash's hips thrust up to match his brother's rhythm as they fill me to the brim.

"Fuck, I love this view." His palms squeeze my ass, his thumbs spreading me open and prowling my crack.

His touch stalls over my clenched hole, drawing circles. "Do you like me playing with your ass, baby girl?"

I can only moan in response.

With that as validation, one of his hands leaves me briefly, then a slick thumb pushes into me.

I curse inward, because *yes*, I do like this. It's dirty, it's depraved, and I want to come like this so fucking bad.

His thumb thrusting into me, Ash bounces me on his cock while Mason rails my throat at an accelerating pace. His head tips back. He's going to come.

A soft growl pushes past his lips, and his fingers curl in my hair. The pressure in my stomach builds. My muscles quiver.

Mason gives a shove to the back of my throat, emptying himself into me, and I come so hard I think I might die. Sparks fleck my black vision.

I swallow as fast as I can before choking. He sits so far back I can't breathe. The narrowing motion squeezes his shaft, milking every last drop from him.

Bucking under me, and pushing me into Mason, Ash fills me too.

But as the high of my orgasm wanes, a hot flash of anger flares through me. I want to kill them for this dirty trick.

Ash collapses onto the bed behind me, his arms landing with a *plop*, legs sprawled out.

Mason lets out a laugh. "I think you killed him."

He catches my glare and withdraws his dick to tuck it away before I can take a bite out of it.

I scramble off Ash's limp body, shoving Mason out of the way to get my clothes. My shame emboldens me momentarily. I know he's still the same psycho who held a knife to my throat, but I've switched into flight mode. If they think I'll spend the night so they can have another go at me, they're delusional.

My hair whips around my face as I yank my damp panties on. My tits bounce. My bra is next, then I lunge for my jeans.

I can already feel more wetness gathering between my thighs. Ramming in one leg after the other, I sense his amused gaze on me, but I don't look at him. I finish with the fly and reach for my top.

I've never gotten dressed so fast in my life. My face is flushed. I slide it on, ripping the hem down over my stomach. I don't want him gawking at my nakedness for another second.

I stuff my feet into my loosely-tied sneakers, glad I don't have to waste time lacing them, then pick up my phone, which has tumbled out of the back pocket of my jeans. My house keys are still tucked into the front when I double-check on a panicked reflex.

I don't spare Ash another glance. He's out cold on the bed. Shoving my cell into my pocket, I storm out of the room, my hair whirling with my fierce movement.

Mason's grip on my elbow stops me before I reach the front door. He spins me around. "Where do you think you're going?"

"Home!" I tear myself free in a motion as sharp as my tongue.

"On foot?" he mocks. "You're not gonna get a ride at four in the morning. Let me take you."

Be alone with him?

I scoff at his audacity. "I'm not going anywhere with you," I declare, my hand gripping the handle of the front door as he turns back down the hallway.

I rip it open and see another black motorcycle parked at the bottom of the steps—a twin for Ash's except the falcon kanji on that one is gray instead of white.

So that's where he'd hidden it so I wouldn't see it in the garage.

I swing the door shut behind me and follow the walkway at the side of the house to get to the street where I take a right, marching down the road we entered the neighborhood on.

My breath hitches. I don't know what I'm doing. He's right. I won't get an Uber. I can't walk all the way home. I'm fucked.

Muttering to myself, I hear his bike behind me. He gains on me in seconds.

Mason pulls up on my left. I don't acknowledge him, but in my periphery, I can see he's back in his black hoodie, a helmet for me nestled in his lap. Matching my pace, he swerves lazily side to side like he's mocking me again.

I hug my arms around myself and keep my eyes straight, but I don't miss the derisive swivel of his head before he accelerates to come to a stop a few feet ahead.

My legs halt. We both know I have no leverage for a stand-off, and as I reflect on my lack of options, I have to admit he's persistent.

And not to mention patient for an asshole. Lifting the helmet from his lap, he extends it toward me, and waits.

I won't go so far as calling the gesture chivalrous—there is no honor in what he did—but he could've said fuck it after I declined his offer and stormed out. Yet here he is, making sure I get home safely.

I drop my arms with a sigh and march up to him, hands balled into fists. Before he can catch the tears welling in my eyes, I snatch the helmet from him and strap it on, then mount the bike behind him.

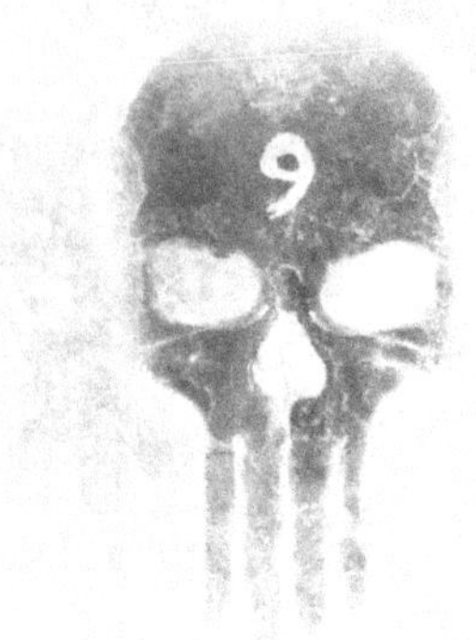

Mace

My gloved hand reaches back to rub the outside of her thigh any chance I get.

I know it's no consolation, and won't make her despise me any less, but I don't want her to think we're done with her now that we had our fun. This is far from over. I'm only getting started, and I need to placate her somehow to get her to trust me.

Her body remains tense against mine; nothing like the way it molded to me earlier. She's pissed. Understandably. But she didn't exactly put up any resistance; she opened her legs… rocked herself against me. I would've stopped had she told me to.

Instead, I listened to her body's cues, to the exhilarated beat of her pulse matching mine, to the desperation in her kiss.

Fuck, I want to draw her like that, with her features tense, lips parted in a moan, and eyes pinched shut in ecstasy as she took the full thrusts of my cock to the very root. I could sketch her from memory alone. Even the image of her deep-throating me has burned itself into my mind.

My fingers squeeze her thigh. I can't stop touching her. I need to taste her again. Feel her legs tighten around me.

Her muscles flex against my palm.

I've seen her ride with Ash when I followed them, the way she leaned into him with full confidence and a sense of intimacy. There's none of that ease between us. Her fists clutch the front of my hoodie to the point where her knuckles turn white, but I know if it wasn't for her fear of falling off, she wouldn't hold onto me at all. Like I'm all sharp corners and edges, and she's afraid to get bruised.

I revel in the fact that she can't escape my touch on the bike. For this brief moment, she's all mine. I don't have to share her.

I pull up to the curb at her shitty apartment. Emily is off the seat, undoing the clasp beneath her chin before I get my visor up.

The light of the street lamp blinds me, but I catch the shimmer in her eyes as she removes her helmet.

My right hand locks around her wrist when she lowers it.

I tug.

"Let go!" she snaps at me.

I don't. "Not until you tell me why you're crying."

"What, you can't guess?"

"I want to hear you say it." I can't let her go like this. I know what I saw. I know the truth.

Her hands clutch the helmet tighter. I feel her tremble. "You… you…"

"*I?*" my voice coaxes her.

"You took advantage of me. I didn't agree to that."

"You didn't *disagree*," I counter. "Tell me why you're really crying." She's holding back. She's afraid to admit what I already know.

"I…I…"

"You?"

"I…"

Come on.

"I liked it."

There it is.

I watch her shoulders sag when she forces out a hard breath. "And I hate that I'm not even mad," she adds in surrender. "Because that was the best sex of my life."

My helmet hides my grin.

I loosen the cuff around her wrist but don't let go of her yet. Holding her gaze, I brush my thumb over her smooth skin. "I saw it in your eyes that first night in the alley," I tell her. "I recognized the hunger in them."

Her mouth twists in contempt. "So you decided to share me with your brother?"

My jaw tightens with her shot at my motives. I need Ash. He never strikes out. He has a way with words where I shine in action.

That's not to say I'm not skilled with my tongue; I just prefer a more brazen approach, but I admit it takes a specific type to match my freak.

I don't go for the obvious, though. I like a challenge. Sometimes they need a little nudge, a little encouragement to dare venture into my depraved depths.

Like Emily.

I couldn't risk losing her before I even had her. Ash was my only option. I had to use him to reel her in, but she's mine.

Even if she doesn't know it.

I drop my hand and swallow my chagrin before I respond. "Ash and I like to share a sweet treat from time to time," I say in a blithe tone.

She scoffs. "And what am I? Your Twinkie?"

"No." I let out a laugh, shaking my head, then clarify, "It takes three loads in three holes to fill a Twinkie."

Emily doesn't appreciate my joke. She expels an appalled breath, then rams her helmet into my chest.

I catch it in one hand before it drops as she whips around, marching toward the building's front door.

I hate this run-down neighborhood. She isn't safe here.

I call after her, "Does that mean you don't want me to pick you up after work tomorrow?"

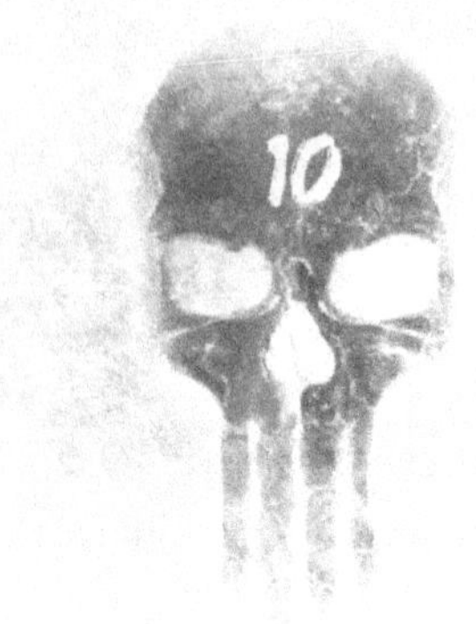

Ash

"I need someone to take that custom V-rod for a spin to see how she handles," Isaac's voice hollers a short distance from me.

"I got it." I push out from under the truck I've been working on this morning, the wheels of the dolly squeaking with the motion.

I kick to my feet, snatching the key from the old man's open palm before Mason even gets a word out.

He throws up his hands and scoffs. "You always do that."

"Because I'm the older one," I remark, a self-righteous curl to my lips.

"27 minutes don't give you the right to call dibs every time."

I give air to a soft laugh. "Sure they do."

I turn to mount the Harley but still catch Mason flipping me off in my periphery. Twisting the key in the ignition, I start the bike and rev the engine.

"You better not scratch that paint job, asshole," he calls after me when I peel out of the garage bay.

I only take her a couple of blocks. With the wind tangling through my hair, my mind drifts back to Emily. I can still feel her nails teasing across my scalp.

A chill races up my neck that has nothing to do with the adrenaline rush from my speed. And yet it's twice as exhilarating.

My fingers flex around the throttle. I don't want to give her up. I know Mace and I had a deal, but after coaxing her out of her shell and seeing how she took both of us like she was fucking made for it, I want more of that.

And I think she does too. As a matter of fact, I have a feeling we unlocked something she didn't even know she craved.

But can I convince Mason to share her?

When I return to the garage, I find him in the break room, having lunch.

"Hey." I pull out the chair across from him and spin it around to take a seat. "We should talk about Emily," I say, crossing my arms over the backrest.

Mason's eyes narrow, his sandwich raised to his mouth.

"I have a suggestion for you," I continue, leveling my gaze on him.

Jaw tense, he grinds his bite slowly as he lowers the sub onto the wrapper in front of him.

I watch him swallow. His chest inflates on a long inhale that I know is practiced restraint. I've seen it enough.

I take my queue when he shoves his food to the side and laces his fingers, giving me his full attention. "I'm not bowing out," I declare. "The way I see it, I'm the one who won her over. I should get a fair chance."

I know Mason had no intention to share her with me other than that first time, which cost me a bag of donuts, but I demand a shot at Emily. He never would've gotten her without my help.

I raise my hand in a placating gesture. "I know you wanted her to yourself, and I'm not expecting you to step back either, what I'm suggesting is we share her… take turns… whatever she's comfortable with, but we both play equal parts."

"No." Mace shakes his head, his muscles in his face taut.

"You really think you can charm her all by yourself?"

My twin's eyes harden at my insinuation.

"We wouldn't be in this situation if you believed that," I add, taunting him further.

I see his mind doing the math behind his stare.

Blinking slowly, he lets out a resigned sigh. "What if she doesn't want to?"

Tipping my head, I arch my brow suggestively. "She didn't seem to mind last night."

Mason's lips twist into an affirmative grin. The little amused huff that chases his smirk suggests he's on board. Relief and excitement shoot through me.

That went better than I expected.

Refocusing on his lunch, he tugs on the corner of the wrapper to slide the sandwich back toward him. "It might still take some convincing, though," he says, lifting it to his mouth.

"Don't worry." I rise, flipping the chair back underneath the table. "I can smooth things over with her."

"Nu-uh," he mumbles around a mouthful of the whole grain. "You don't get to call dibs on that one. *I* got this."

I throw my head back on a laugh. "You think *you* can convince her to an arranged threesome?"

"Yeah!" Mason's eyes are level and dead serious, gone is the amusement from a second ago.

I take the challenge. "Wanna make that a bet?"

"It's gonna cost you more than a bag of donuts this time," he stresses. "I'll ask her tonight when I pick her up at the diner," he tacks on before taking another bite.

Dammit! He will fuck this up. *I* have to be the one to ask her. I need this. "I'll race you for it," I counter.

"Bitch, you still *owe* me a rematch. You only beat me because I got stuck behind that damn Prius going thirtyf—"

"Will you two ass-clowns cut it out already and maybe act your fucking age?" Isaac yells from the open door of the break room, cutting through our squabbling. "I swear I'll rethink my decision to leave my shop to you idiots."

I swing my gaze back to Mace, nailing him with a hard stare. "Good luck!"

Then I walk out.

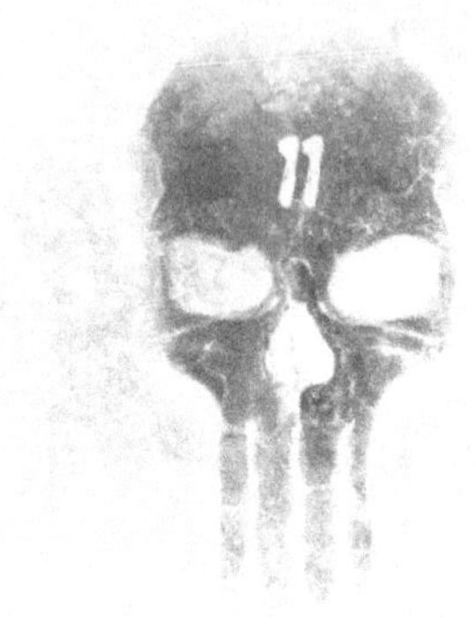

Em

"Do you mind if I take off half an hour early?" I ask Laura, sagging against the counter, a hand pressed to my belly. "Cramps are killing me," I supply with an eye roll.

It's the best excuse I can come up with. I need to make my escape before Ash's psychotic twin shows up.

I have no doubt that he will.

"Sure, honey." She gives me a nod and gestures to the back. "Go ahead. I'll finish up."

My heartbeat punches up my throat so hard I can barely breathe. I rush past Drew and Jake to exit out into the alley not a minute later.

I exhale in relief. The flood of adrenaline in my veins ebbs when I find it deserted.

I don't linger. My pace is faster than a brisk walk, but not quite a jog. Dread chases me until I lock the deadbolt of my front door behind me.

Only now can I relax.

In my bedroom, I strip out off my jeans. I grab my pajamas and underwear before making my way to the bathroom. The smell of diner grease clings to me. Especially my hair. I scrub until the last bits are replaced by the fresh scent of cucumber and mint.

My long tresses are still damp when I brush my teeth and get ready for bed. I don't bother with blow-drying them. I'd rather deal with them in the morning.

I wipe a hand across the foggy mirror, and my eyes catch on my tired reflection when I hear a thud from my bedroom.

My head snaps around toward the disturbance. The drop in my stomach hits like a ton of bricks.

What the fuck?

Holding my breath, I perk my ears for sounds of motion, but I'm only met with silence. Not even a squeak from the old building's floorboards.

I force a swallow down my dry throat and push quietly out of the bathroom.

On bare feet, I sneak along the stretch of hallway separating me from my bedroom until I get a full view of the scene. What I encounter makes the blood rush from my face.

It's Mason, the window open, a crowbar in his hand.

I know it's him behind that mask. There's something about his presence that reeks of danger.

He cocks his head. "Think you can hide from me, baby girl?"

The tool lands on my bed with a light bounce, and I whip around to make a run down the hall to get to the kitchen. I need a weapon.

My hand finds the door frame as I make the sharp turn. With Mason right on my heels, my fingers skip along the counter, ignoring the drawer of cutlery. I need something bigger.

I draw the chef's knife from the block, and when I spin back he's already there.

"Now what do you think you're gonna do with that?" he mocks, taking a step towards the outstretched blade in my hand.

Letting the tip bite into the skin below his jaw, he dares me to strike.

My fingers tremble. I can't do it, and he knows it.

Eyes wide, I swallow, and he doesn't miss his opening. Mason is on me in the next beat, his fist closing around my fingers on the knife's handle as he whirls me around.

Wet hair smacks my face. He brings the blade's cool tip to my throat. His other hand cuffs my left wrist, wrapping around my waist and caging me to his chest.

"Gotcha!" He presses his masked face to my cheek, his voice a low hum. "If you want to play with knives," he taunts, dragging the blade carefully down the side of my throat, "all you had to do was ask."

He keeps going lower, brushing the tip down my chest, flicking my nipple over the camisole I'm wearing. The thin cotton can't hide the hard shape. Heat flares across my skin with his breath at my ear.

"Maybe next time." He rips the knife from my hand and it clatters against the counter as he slams it down.

Pulling my arms back, he shifts my wrists into one of his hands and tucks something from his pocket to tie me up. I can't see what it is, but it's soft, like cloth, where he winds it around my elbows, locking them in a bent position.

When he's done, my chest juts out with the forced arch of my spine. The strain on my shoulders is almost painful.

My vision blurs from another spin, and he dips before I can refocus on his mask. Restrained as I am, he throws me over his shoulder and returns to the bedroom.

The heavy thudding of his boots comes to a stop at the foot of my bed. My back hits the mattress, and an ache shoots through me at the contortion of my arms underneath my weight. I wince.

His amused huff carries to my ears. Panic lances through me, watching his hands go to his belt. Digging my heels and shoulder blades into the mattress, I scoot up the bed to get away from him.

I don't make it far before he rips the strap through the loops, and his knees settle on either side of mine. Leaning over me, he slides it under, then fastens the belt around the meaty parts of my thighs so tight, the leather bites into my skin.

Fuuucck.

My spine arches on a whimper. It turns me on. My traitorous pussy salutes him with a pulse.

Another dark chuckle worms its way through my ear canal. *He knows.*

Mason slides his fingers into the gap between my thighs, feeling the damp spot that's growing where my boy shorts meet my wet slit.

"Is that for me, baby girl?" His fingers curl over my needy flesh as he rubs me.

I squeeze my eyes shut and clench my teeth, denying him my reply, but my body betrays me again. My hips grind into his motion.

His left hand grips the front of my throat, palm forcing my jaw up as his fingers dig in at the sides.

My eyes fly open.

"I asked if that's for me," he repeats in a growl, his other hand dipping into my shorts to meet me skin on skin.

"Y-yes. It's for you, Mason," I whimper already close to coming.

"Say it again. I want my name on your lips when you come." And then he spreads my slick seam, thrusting his fingers into me at a quickening pace.

Every muscle in my body tenses as the rush overtakes me. His thumb strokes my clit and my walls clench around him while his left hand continues to squeeze my throat.

My vision flickers. I'm at his mercy. My lips part with a plaintive moan, forming his name as my climax peaks.

"That's it, baby girl." Mason's grip on my throat loosens, his voice hovering over me. "So eager to please, aren't you? But we're not done," he adds, withdrawing his hands from me completely. "I like to keep score, and by my count, my brother is ahead. I don't like it when he beats me."

He pushes off the bed, and my eyes follow him around my room in a haze from the aftermath.

He walks up to my dresser. Pulling the top drawer open, he rummages around the contents like he's looking for something particular. I'm not sure why he's so interested in my underwear until—

"What do we have here?"

Fuck me! I throw my head back into the pillow with a groan. He found my toy stash.

"Cute." He pivots toward me, holding up a slim, purple vibrator. "We both know you can fit bigger than that," he acknowledges with a little laugh behind his mask, then dives back in. "Let's see what other toys you got in here."

Please no. I sink into the mattress in shame.

"Ha! Now we're talking."

I know what he found before my eyes catch the silver glint of the butt plug.

He tips his head to one side, suspicion in his tone. "Have you used this before?"

"No," I groan. I have plenty of practice with the vibrator, but I'm still working up the nerve to make use of the plug. It was an impulse buy a little while back, and it's been taunting me ever since.

"It's a bit ambitious in size for a beginner. Guess you like a challenge. I knew I liked you." His hand makes another dip into the drawer before he shoves it home.

I don't miss the sadistic glee in his gait. Loot in hand, he returns to me, dropping his stash on the mattress beside me to nudge me over onto my stomach.

My body complies without reason. Mason has reached into my mind and is now pulling the strings of my deepest, darkest desires like I'm his puppet.

I turn my head to draw a breath through the tangled strands of my hair and the pillow when his weight settles on top of me.

"You ready to have some fun, baby girl?" he prompts, hauling my hips off the bed to meet the ardent bulge behind his fly.

I manage no more than a grunt before his fingers dip into the waistband of my shorts and push the cotton down my thighs where it stops at the belt still firmly in place.

"You have no idea what this view does to me," Mason growls, his palms rubbing up and down my arms, tugging on my restraints. "Imagine all the unspeakable things I can do to you like this… all the sinful ways I can corrupt you." He does another rough pass down my forearms, grip lingering on my wrists. "Moan for me."

The queued response leaks from my lips, and I grind back on reflex, searching for the friction of him.

"Mmm. So compliant," he muses.

He releases my wrists. His big hands skip to my ass, spreading me open, thumbs tracing the edges of my pussy.

Another deep, pleased growl carries to my ears. His praise ignites a fire in my core. I ache to feel him inside me. To have his throbbing cock stretching my inner walls.

Mason's weight shifts behind me. When his touch leaves my needy flesh, and there's a rustle from him removing his mask, my anticipation crests.

The mattress dips under his movements. My skin flushes as he takes his time. The wait for him to touch me again is agonizing.

He gives me no warning. He eases the vibrator into me, sliding it against my tender folds. The glide is cool and smooth, and I know he lubed it. His hands are slick too.

His thumb circles the tight rim of my rear, applying pressure before pushing in.

My lips part to a silent moan. My eyes squeeze shut. Mason's groan chases me…

Then he turns the vibration on.

I cry out as he fucks me slowly. My body trembles. It's different when *he's* using the toy on me—when he's the one in control of my pleasure instead of me taking care of myself. The sensation is so much more intense.

He moves in and out of me with a matching rhythm while my knees press together from the restraint around my thighs. Face buried in the fluffy down pillow, the muscles in my neck pinch as my spine arches. My weight is braced on my chest, my breasts riding the friction of his thrusts.

I love the pain he spurs. I chase the feeling, letting it push me higher until I climax.

"Oh God…" Shivers rake through me. I'm drooling as the ongoing vibration draws a symphony of whimpers from my throat.

More waves crash over me when he pulls the toy out and rubs it across my clit.

I groan.

My body convulses.

I don't know if I'm still coming or about to come again.

"That's my girl. So needy. So hungry."

Mason's voice rings clearer without the obstruction of his mask, but my brain has trouble grasping his words with the way he stimulates every nerve in my body.

"Think you're ready for that challenge now?"

Oh fuck! He means the plug.

My muscles tense.

Mason removes the vibrator. Then his thumb. "Relax for me."

And then I feel it, the cool, slick steel probing me, stretching me beyond the size of his finger.

"Just. A little. More," he coaxes, pushing it deeper with persistence despite my distress.

It's too big. The pressure is too much. I don't think I can…

A groan ruptures from my throat in relief of having claimed the widest part of the conical shape.

"Yes, baby. Fucking swallow it."

The sensation is something else. I'm full, but not full enough.

"You want my cock?"

"Yes," I groan into the pillow, my hips squirming in a restless motion.

"Then come for me, baby girl." Mason slides his long fingers into my pussy. I think it's three, but I'm not sure. "I need one more before I give you what you want."

Rough knuckles stroke my clit. I'm being stretched too far. I can't possibly take any more, and yet I know he will fit his cock regardless.

Nudging the plug, he pumps his finger in and out of me in a slow rhythm at first, gaining speed. Sloshing sounds fill my ears. I bottom out. I feel myself unfurl for him.

My body convulses in its restricted position, and a cry of raw, unrestrained pleasure shatters my skull as white lights pop in my vision.

Mason rewards me with a deep, gratified sound before both his hands disappear. I can hear him undo his pants. Then he's back, the tip of his cock prodding my pussy.

He pushes into me with a single thrust. "Feel how hard you make me?" he taunts, retreating and slamming back into me. "That's all for you, baby girl."

While toying with the plug, his free hand cuffs my wrists for leverage, and he picks up momentum. His lower piercing teases my clit. My stomach clenches. His thrusts rail me deep and hard at a quickening pace, sending ripples through me.

His short breaths come fast. "Fuck, you look beautiful like that," he pants. "The only thing missing is you choking around my brother's cock."

His words send me over the edge as his hips pound into me again and again. My body grips him. My climax crashes over me so violently my vision goes black. I can't even draw air into my lungs.

My body's spastic clenching milks him, and Mason's hoarse growl explodes like thunder. He rears into me in one last punishing drive to claim his own release.

Flush with my backside, his hips jerk as he spills. I feel him pulsing against my walls.

A shudder passes from him to me before he pulls out. He zips himself, then removes his belt and at last the tie around my elbows.

I collapse. My useless limbs can't hold me up.

When he leans over me, his massive upper body braced on his hands at either side of me, his hips grind into my ass with intention, his weight pushing the butt plug.

Mason's breath feathers across my cheek, but his content hum reaches something beneath my skin. "I'm going to leave this in," he rasps low at my ear. "I want you to get used to that feeling of having your asshole stretched, because next time you run from me, it's going to be my cock filling you."

His lips give my temple a peck, and then he's gone, out the window and back into the night.

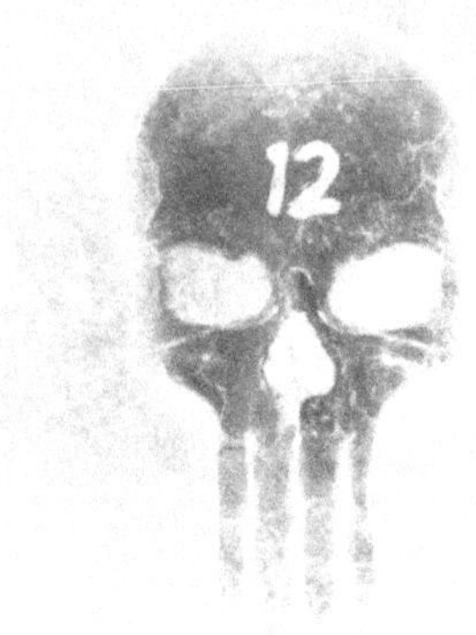

Mace

I clutch the mask in my grip and stare up at the brick building that's so very familiar to me. I'm far from the worst thing to climb through her window.

The fingers of my right hand curl toward my palms. *She isn't safe here.*

A distinct memory tries to claw its way toward the surface, but I squash it.

No one's safe here.

Rough hands seize the front of my shirt and drag me to my feet. I sway in his grip. Matted strands of my hair stick to my forehead.

The guy, Thomas, I've heard his friends call him, is one of five men in the dingy living room. Broken beer bottles scatter on the floor while a bigger one with a dark liquid sits on the table crowded by the rest of the spectators.

We're tonight's entertainment. Dad handed us off to Ely for 24 hours.

"Hit him again," a deep voice prompts, thick, white smoke seeping through his stained teeth as he removes the cigar long enough.

My wrists are tied behind my back, so are Ash's, but even if they weren't, we couldn't put up much of a fight. We're scrawny for 15-year-olds. Due to being malnourished, not because we lack the genetics.

Thomas draws back his fist, and in the next moment I feel my skull explode. White-hot pain flares across my cheek. My vision flickers.

He punches me so hard I stumble and collapse to the floor again, unable to catch my fall because of the cuffs cutting into the skin around my wrist. I'm pretty sure I'm bleeding.

He yanks me back to my feet. My shoulder screams with pain, and my ribs are bruised, but I hold my chin high. I glare up at him two feet above my eye level.

Black, merciless pits stare back, daring me to cry. But I won't. I don't make a sound. Not even when his fist retracts to deliver another blow to my gut.

I lurch forward at the impact. The only reason I don't drop to my knees is his grip at the back of my shirt collar. He buries his knuckles in my stomach, making my teeth punch down on my tongue.

The taste of metal fills my mouth. When I swallow the bitterness, I feel the burn all the way down my throat, and it no longer stirs a repulsion.

I welcome it. I let the taste of my own blood fuel me.

"Stop it!" I hear Ash shout. "Don't fucking touch him."

But there's a quiver in his voice. From the corner of my throbbing eye, I see his flailing shape, struggling against the hold at his shoulders. He's on his knees, a guy named Jonathan restraining him as he's forced to watch my turn to get beaten.

They all like to watch.

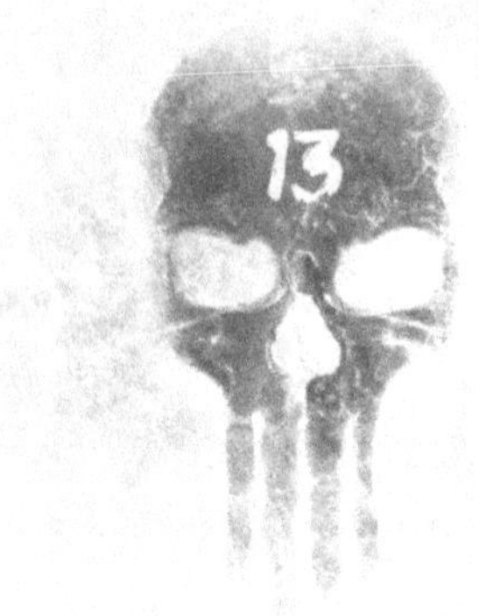

Ash

"So, what did she say?" I ask Mason when I finally find him in the shop's locker room.

We share the same DNA, but we're not attached at the hips. Other than living together, we don't crowd each other. We keep our own schedules, and he left the house before I got out of the shower this morning. I never found out what happened when he took Emily home after her shift at the diner.

Flicking the latch on the metal door next to his, I pull it open to drop my backpack inside. "Is she interested or not?"

"I think she's considering it," his smug voice reports from the other side out of my view.

My hackles raise, and my fingers slowly unclench from the backpack's strap as I straighten. "What do you mean with 'you think'?"

I don't like the sound of that. "You didn't ask, did you?" I deduce.

He pokes his head around the slim metal door and grimaces. "Kinda."

"Kinda?" My eyebrows shoot up with my volume. "How do you 'kinda' suggest a threesome to someone?"

"I told her she'd look better with your dick in her mouth as I was railing her, and she didn't disagree."

My expression falls. "You didn't," I mutter.

Mason's face lights up, and I don't miss the proud edge in his tone on his nod. "I did."

A bold grin stretching his lips, he has the nerve to wink at me before he slams his locker shut and rounds me to walk away.

I don't know what comes over me. I'm still wearing my leather jacket when I wrench him around by the front of his shirt and slam his back into the locker wall.

"You son of a bitch!" I growl, my breaths heaving as my chest swells with rage.

My fingers clench his shirt in my fist, but he just smiles back coldly, unruffled. His voice is dead calm. "Relax, man. I didn't do anything she didn't want me to. She was *very* willing."

The smug edge in his tone and sadistic glimmer in his eyes remain. I'm not the slightest bit relieved by his words. I'm familiar with his manner of persuasion.

My fists twist at his front, and a soft snicker ripples from him. "Is that what you're pissed about?" he probes. "That I had her all to myself... and she liked it."

I shake my head in disbelief at his tactics... his brazenness. I knew I'd regret letting him do the talking. I should've handled it myself.

Mason isn't like me. He had it worse and never got over what we've been through as kids. He's a hidden time bomb in my basement. "You're really fucked up, you know that?"

A flare ignites in his eyes. "I know what I am," he sneers. "I'm not hiding it."

Grinding my anger between my teeth, I give him another shove against the lockers, making the metal groan, then release my grip to let him walk.

———

I avoid my brother for the rest of the day. I have a drop to make after work for Mr. DeMarco, one of the bosses who control Castle's underground businesses.

Mason and I ran away from home at 16. We had already been through hell, and living on the street, surviving on scraps wasn't new to us. But we were older now, and new opportunities presented themselves through connections we made.

Before we had bikes, we made deliveries for Mr. DeMarco on foot. We quickly developed our free running skills and memorized shortcuts; no one could match us. We gained a reputation. Respect. Trust. We made a name for ourselves. For the first time in our lives, we felt invincible.

It became addictive.

We would chase each other, betting on who'd be the one to make the drop. More often than not, we'd show up with a busted lip or a black eye. We were always competing.

After putting the code into the keypad, I enter the gentlemen's club through the back.

The bouncer there gives me a nod, already expecting me, I assume. He doesn't bother with patting me down, either, and lets me go about my way.

I don't see much of the club itself as I take the narrow and dimly lit hallway to the back where the boss has his office.

Two burly guys stand guard, one on either side of the door, their hands clasped in front. Mr. DeMarco's men all wear pressed suits and com pieces visible in their ears; unlike the guns they hide under their jackets.

I stop, facing them, and wait, but neither of them moves, their expressions stoic.

My eyes flick from one to the other. Pulling my hands from my pockets, I gesture lazily between them. "So, which one of you ordered the lap dance?"

Neither of them cracks a laugh, but the one on the left finally gives the door a sharp knock—probably afraid I might actually hump him.

Christopher's voice answers from inside. "Let him in."

The same guy unlatches the door and opens it wide, jerking his head in a motion for me to enter.

"Thanks fellas," I chirp on a light note as I brush past.

Christopher, Mr. DeMarco's personal assistant, sits at the massive mahogany desk, flipping through paperwork. His slim frame is dressed in a perfectly tailored suit, reminding me of a department store mannequin. He's a few years younger than me, and from what I've heard, eager to handle all of the boss's needs.

I watch his manicured hands make annotations next to the printed text in front of him before flipping another page.

He's efficient, alright.

My eyes shift to the large padded envelope on the desk. A smaller, fat one with my name on it lies on top.

"214 Arlington Drive." He barely looks up as he pushes the stack toward me.

The address is one of the more frequent ones, which makes the drop-off easy. They know my brother and me.

Pocketing my payment, I swipe the package off the desk. I don't know what it contains; it's not my business. All I know is where to take it, and I don't ask questions.

I swerve the Hayabusa through the late rush hour traffic and make the drop all the way across town before checking the time.

It's 8:30.

I know Emily is at the diner by now. I need to talk to her and do some damage control. We exchanged numbers that morning after Mace and I pulled the switch, but this is something I need to do in person.

I park my bike in the alley. Helmet in hand, I swing the backpack over my shoulder and walk around to the entrance of the diner.

A chime above me goes off as I push through, causing several glances to drift my way. It's busy.

I scan the dining room for one familiar face and freeze when I see her. She's gorgeous. Her cheeks have a rosy flush that sings of excitement and exertion in equal measure. A look I've seen on her before.

A heatwave hits me. Blood rushes to my groin at the vision, and I feel my dick throb behind my fly.

I watch her address an elderly woman at the table she's clearing. Her mouth curls into a smile.

Those full lips...

As if suddenly sensing my stare, her view lifts and slides my way. Her expression changes.

Oh no.

The moment her sight locks on to me over the crowd, she flinches back a step, probably thinking I'm Mason.

The plates balanced on her forearms slide off, and a shatter of dishes explodes in my ears.

Fuck.

I close my eyes and groan before rushing to her side to help her pick up the shards. It's my fault she dropped them, after all. Well, technically my twin's fault.

She's kneeling in front of the mess, and I squat down, dropping my helmet to free my hands.

"I'm sorry," I mutter low when she doesn't look up at me. "I didn't mean to cause a scene. I just wanted to apologize for Mason's behavior."

I don't know the specific details, but judging by her reaction and her trembling hands lifting the ceramic pieces, I figure they're pretty bad.

Her lashes flick up, her eyes finding mine at last. "Ash!" my name leaves her lips like a revelation.

I only manage half a nod of affirmation before a boy comes up behind me with a broom and a small tub, practically shooing me away.

She gives him a soft smile. "Thanks, Jake."

We drop the broken dishes into the tub as the kid cleans up the rest.

Emily pushes to her feet. I reach for my helmet, doing the same, and follow her toward the kitchen.

"Can we talk," I prompt. "Just for a minute."

"What makes you think I even want to talk to you after how you tricked me?" she fires back with a hiss.

God, how did I ever let Mason talk me into that?

"You're right. I'm really sorry. That was wrong on so many levels, but you and I, we had something. Just hear me out, please."

"Ash…" The sound of my name is laced with a sigh I recognize as rejection, and I can see the drop of her shoulders confirming the notion. She keeps walking without looking back at me. "I don't know. I—"

"Please." I cut her off by taking her hand and whirling her around to face me before she can disappear through the set of double doors.

I can be bold too when I'm desperate.

My breath stalls for a second while simply taking her in. My eyes flit over her features and catch on her mouth again. I want to kiss her, feel her soft lips press to mine, and my arms holding her against me.

I back her into the wall. "What we did was fucked up, I know," I start, lowering my voice to a whisper only for us to hear. "I'm sorry for tricking you. We thought you'd be into it—the scaring, the adrenaline rush, the thrill of being with both of us. But we were never going to hurt you."

My lips hover mere inches from hers, and the warmth of her breath sends a need through my body.

"And Mason isn't bad," I explain, holding her stare. "He's just… *Mason*." I give her a shrug, not knowing how to put it into words. But I can't bad-mouth my brother. "I don't know what he said, or did last night… all I know is that I still want this."

My thumb circles the soft skin of her hand I'm still clasping, and she doesn't flinch away from the gesture. Her gaze flicks to our tangled fingers, then back up to me. I don't dare move.

We stare at each other for several long seconds, locked in our bubble. I see her chest rising and falling heavily, her lips slightly parted, and I physically ache to be inside her. To sink into her soft, tight heat.

I want her. I can't give her up.

"Can I pick you up later?" I ask, a pleading edge to my voice.

Her eyebrows twitch, and I can see the uneasiness forming there, so I tag on, "I don't expect anything, I swear. I just want to talk."

Emily's features relax, and I know I have her.

"Okay."

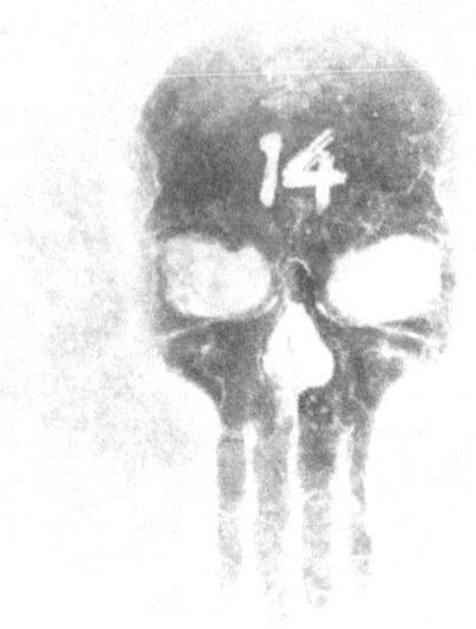

Em

Have I completely lost my damn mind? Why did I agree to him taking me home?

I wipe down another table, replaying my moment of weakness. I'm so fucked. His green eyes and the dimples when he smiled made my knees soft. I couldn't say no to Ash.

And to Mason?

Yeah. I'm fucked, alright.

My shift is nearing its end. As we're clearing the final tables, Laura nudges my side with her elbow, one eyebrow arched. "Did you see the hands on that boy?"

Before taking off, Ash grabbed dinner to go. Something I suggested from the menu.

Her voice carries a dreamy lilt. "Mmm-mmm. I would've loved to watch him polish that burger off right here in front of me."

I'm about to say *'You should see the way he devours tacos'* but then decide to keep that to myself.

"It's good to be young, girl. Go for it, and enjoy the ride," she says, stacking two dirty plates and turning toward the kitchen. "Every inch of it," she adds with a wink over her shoulder.

I jostle my head and laugh as she disappears. If she only knew he comes as a package deal.

Scratch that.

She'd probably encourage that even more. Double the fun and all.

I'm not so sure, though. Can I really commit to both of them? They're brothers, and the last thing I want to do is drive a wedge between them. I couldn't live with myself if I broke their bond.

But maybe if we're all on the same page…

God, this is insane. The old me would've been appalled by the idea, but I wanted to break out of that shell, didn't I? That's why I left.

I drop my shoulders on a sharp exhale. Laura is right. I should grab the bull by its horns and ride him, or however that saying goes.

I'm surprised when I find Ash in the alley on foot and not with his bike. But he said he wanted to talk, and that would be hard with helmets on, I guess. Plus, walking gives him more time to spend with me.

"You know, I can always pick you up out front. We don't have to make it look like we're sneaking around." He's wearing a white graphic tee and blue jeans, standing at the bottom of the stairs that lead down to the alley. Leaning back into the rail, hands in his pockets, he's looking up through the rogue, dark blonde strands of his hair.

He gives me a crooked smile.

"Nah, it's alright. I'd be leaving out the back anyway." I take the two steps down, and he straightens from his lean, immediately towering over me again.

"Hi," I say hoarsely, staring up at him.

His grin stretches, and I can't fucking help the heat creeping into my cheeks under his attention.

"Hi," he echoes, mimicking my tone.

The brief silence that wraps around us is charged with longing. The skin at the back of my neck prickles, and I can almost feel his hand there, threading through my hair as I imagine him kissing me.

Ash shifts first. "Thank you for hearing me out," he says, kicking off into a leisurely stroll which I match beside him. "I didn't want you thinking Mason and I do this on the regular. The tricking women, I mean."

Well, doesn't that make me feel special.

"But you've shared before?"

"Yeah," he admits, running a hand through his hair. "But usually they are fully aware of the situation."

"And give their consent, I presume," I throw in as a side note.

"Yeah, *that!*" he huffs embarrassed. "Definitely that!"

I turn my eyes forward pensively while keeping pace. I believe Ash's sincerity. Even Mason doesn't strike me as a serial rapist. He's good at persuasion, though. His method is *all hands* no talk.

Although there *is* tongue involved.

"Believe me, I know my brother's ways are questionable," Ash goes on. "He gets off on pushing boundaries; including his own. And I'm not saying I don't like a good challenge, but I prefer things a little more... *subtle*," he adds in a suggestive note.

Ash's approach of wooing me is a lot less aggressive. He's sweet in his own way. But Mason is right. I can't pretend that his manner of pursuit is not affecting me. He knows more than he should about me. More than I admit to myself.

"It's hard for people to get past his armor," Ash explains. "He doesn't date."

"And you do?" I arch a brow, side eyeing him.

He shrugs. "Off and on. Nothing that lasted more than two months. The excitement fades after the conquest."

"And that's what I am? A new conquest?"

I watch him smirk, those infamous dimples forming again. "I haven't quite figured that out yet. But I meant what I said earlier inside. I'm not ready to give this up." He motions between us. "It's uncharted territory for me too."

Meaning his continued interest in me despite having already gotten in my pants. Twice.

"And you like it?" I prompt, turning onto the walkway leading to my building.

"It intrigues me." We walk up to the door and stop. "*You* intrigue me," Ash stresses, his hand reaching for mine, making me face him.

Then he takes another step to back me into the door and bring his body flush with mine.

I suck in a quick breath. My nipples are hard as his chest presses into me. It's just like inside the diner. Heat shoots south through my belly like a lightning bolt. I feel it pooling between my thighs, and they give a little twitch at the need of wanting him there.

His left arm snakes around my waist to hold me closer still. His eyes are heavy. They drop to my mouth, then he dips his head, closing in slowly. "So yeah," he whispers, lips feathering across mine. "I like it. I like it a lot."

Ash kisses me, gentle at first, but growing gradually in demand, and I let out a moan, sinking into the warmth of his body.

As my lips part, the tip of his tongue flicks out to tease me. He makes my toes curl, exploring and nipping before nudging past my teeth.

I open for him. Sliding his tongue deeper, Ash reminds me of his skills with the piercing.

I feel my hips undulate in response. More wetness pools between my legs, aching for friction, and I want to wrap myself around him with an unapologetic desperation.

Releasing my hand, Ash runs his palms over my body more eagerly. I steady myself on his shoulders, and he squeezes my ass as he grinds the hard ridge at his fly into me, mouth still fused to mine. The electric current spreads from his kiss to every part of my body. He sets me on fire. I don't want him to stop.

But I know we have to.

"Ash." My voice comes out strangled, and I give his shoulders a squeeze.

He surrenders a sigh. "I know. I'm sorry. I got carried away."

His words retain a heated rasp as he forces himself to pull away.

"Fuck," he groans. "What are you doing to me, baby girl?" Ash shakes his head, and I bite my bottom lip to stifle a grin. It feels so good to be desired.

He lowers his forehead to mine, his eyes suddenly serious. "I want you as much as my brother does, but it's up to you, Em, not him. I'm not backing down. You choose."

With that, he straightens, and I know he's about to take off, but he swings back one more time. He takes my right hand, lacing his fingers with mine and sliding them between my thighs.

He gives me a squeeze. "Think of me when you finish."

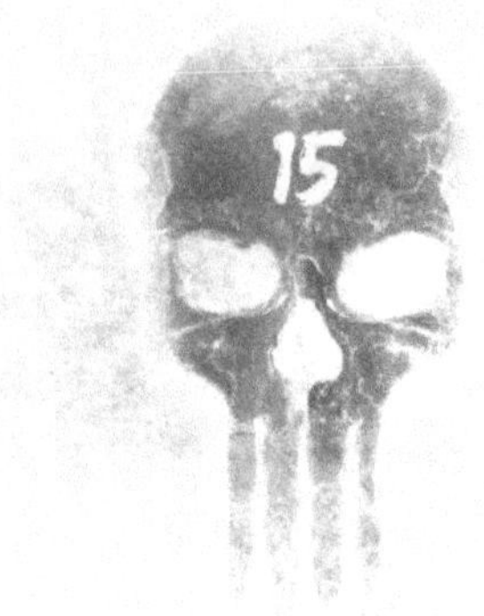

Mace

Standing on the edge of the rooftop, I remove my gloves and work my fingers, clenching and unclenching my fists to test the stiffness.

They're fine now. Whatever caused the sensation a couple of weeks back has passed, but I still recall the ache in my hands after waking up from another episode.

I look down at my hands with a strange unease. While the tenderness is gone, the recurring blackouts remain.

I stuff my gloves into the front pocket of my sweatshirt and pull out the mask. I don't switch on the LEDs, but I slide it over my face and raise the black hood to cover the rest of my head.

My breath immediately strains through the small air holes.

The lack of oxygen doesn't make me panic anymore; I've gotten used to the sensation. But it's more than that. When I put on the mask, something flips in me. The reduced flow of air gets me high…

…makes me hard.

I feel the swelling behind the restriction of my jeans already, and I know the throbbing ache is going to increase shortly.

I have something fun planned.

The thrill of the anticipation is the sweetest part. The inevitable release is only the finish line, and I want to withhold that for as long as I can. I want the chase.

Or, in this case, *the hunt.*

The back door of the diner opens, and I watch Emily step out, descending the stairs with a worriless bounce to her step.

She hasn't reached out to Ash again yet. We decided to give her space, and she seems to believe she's safe walking home on her own.

I scoff at her false sense of security. She has no clue what's lurking in the shadows.

Without my boots making a sound, I ghost along the rooftop's edge to stay on her tail as she starts down the dark alley. Her arms are crossed at her front like she might be regretting her decision now; she doesn't look so confident anymore.

Perhaps she senses me after all.

Her silky black hair billows in her haste. Still in my silent pursuit, I watch her shoulders creep up her neck, her posture tense, eyes shifting nervously. She looks ready to jump out of her skin at the sound of a scurrying rat.

I want to stall and savor the moment. She's so vulnerable right now. She has no idea how easily I can overpower her. Turn her from my prey into my victim.

She's almost at the first corner, and my breath comes a little faster now. I clench my fists before pushing off into a sprint. I need a running start to clear the gap.

Right before the drop, I kick off the ledge and jump across the alley onto the next building, a rooftop a couple of feet below.

My landing isn't silent. Gravel crunches beneath my boots as they go into a slide, and I know she heard it three stories down, but I don't look over the edge to confirm. I don't want her to see me yet.

She's aware of me now, because I want her to be, but she doesn't know about all the other times I followed her, stalked her home, watched her sleep. I'm sick like that. I get off on this little game and the fact that I know things she doesn't.

I want her to be ignorant, so every time she hears a noise in her apartment or feels a breath on her neck in the dark, she'll wonder whether it's really me or if it's her mind playing tricks on her.

Yes, I know things she doesn't. I know that she doesn't want to admit that she wishes it *was* me.

My hands grip the rail of the fire escape as I fling my body over the edge, dropping quickly from level to level. Every step is second nature.

I see her head shoot up, scanning the alley ahead, but the ricocheting echo of my movements makes it hard for her to pinpoint their source. She doesn't know where I am.

I jump the last five feet and land in a crouch on the closed dumpster behind her.

The heavy drop of my boots against the metal sounds like an explosion, and Emily whips around.

My adrenaline spikes at the sight of her. Her eyes lock onto me in shock and her face pales.

A jolt rakes through me. It settles in my thighs as more blood rushes toward my groin.

I have her now. She's mine.

I straighten my legs, rising slowly to full height, my eyes riveted to her through the slits of the mask. Heat shoots up my neck when taking her in, and I draw a long breath as my heart starts beating faster.

I have her right where I want her. Just her and I. No one will come to her aid. No one will even hear her scream.

Her chest moves up and down rapidly as she realizes the same and begins backing up. A smile curls my lips behind the mask. I cock my head to the side in a taunt.

I reach into my back pocket, drawing my knife and flicking the switch. Pointing it at her, I say, "You better run, baby girl. You don't want me catching you."

Emily doesn't disappoint. I knew she wouldn't. She twists around and breaks out into a full sprint.

That's my girl.

More delight rushes me. With my skin on fire, I jump down and race after her, knowing she can't match my stride.

Before she can clear the sharp right turn onto the main road, my fist seizes the back of her shirt. I yank her around to face me, caging her against the building.

Emily lets out a shriek. Her arms flail, trying to fight me off. We're right at the corner, just out of view.

I put the tip of the blade to her left cheek, leaning in. "No one's going to save you. No one cares."

A trickle of sweat glides down my back. I won't hurt her, but she doesn't know that for sure. She doesn't believe even *I* have my limits. Doesn't know where I draw the line.

And it's the not-knowing that scares her.

Emily freezes, all fight suddenly drained from her, though the fear etched across her face remains.

My heart pounds heavily beneath my ribs, but I keep my breathing calm, relishing the electric charge between our bodies.

Neither of us blinks.

"You see that bike across the street?" Using the blunt edge of the knife, I nudge her head in the direction around the corner. "That's where I park every night, watching you through the windows of the diner."

A small gasp slips across her parted lips at my confession, and my eyes charter the front of her throat as it hitches.

Then they roam lower.

My stare trails over her breasts, catching on the distinct peaks of her nipples through the fabric.

I tilt the knife in my right hand at her cheek, then drag the tip down, tracing her jawline slowly. "I promised you we'd play with knives, didn't I?"

I map the soft shape of one breast, flicking the tip with my knife.

Fuck yes!

Her body arches against the blade, earning my play a little whimper. I knew she'd be into this.

I thread my free hand through the hair at the back of her neck, and give a light pull. Without taking my eyes off her face, I drag the flat side of the knife down her front, letting her feel the pressure of the tip along her stomach.

The blade skips over the waistband of her jeans. I clear the length of the zipper and slide the knife home in between her thighs.

Emily inhales sharply. Her hands squeeze my shoulders as my thumb strokes her clit through her jeans. Her eyelids flutter…

…and then she *fucking* moans.

Something in me snaps. I move back and forth in a slow slicing motion, letting her grind on me while melting into the blaze of her core. It flares through the material.

She's so fucking bold.

She rides my hand over her clothes, and I almost drop the knife. I want to feel more of her. Want to feel her soft flesh against my fingers when she comes.

I retract the blade, folding it one-handedly and returning it to my back pocket while my left hand still fists her hair, forcing her chin up.

I slide the mask to the top of my head, letting her see my face, and lower my lips to hers. But I stop before they touch. "And you remember what else I promised you, don't you, baby girl?"

My bottom lip feathers over her mouth as I inhale her juddering breath. "What I said I'd do next time I caught you?"

My voice is rough. Possessive.

"You knew, but you played my game anyway," I remark. "You must want me pretty damn bad, I take it."

I pull back, and whirl her around, my right arm wrapping around her, locking her body against mine as I pin her to the wall.

Palms up by her chest, she braces herself, every muscle flexed with apprehension.

"What do you say, baby girl? Do you want me to fuck you right here in the alley? Pull your pants down and give it to you hard and deep?"

My hips find their mark. She's a perfect fit as I grind my throbbing cock into her ass.

Fist tangled in her wild tresses, I dive into her neck and groan. My eyelids grow heavy. The scent of her floral perfume sends a ripple down to my thighs, making me harder and urging me on.

Her body shivers in my hold. I skim my nose up to the sensitive skin beneath her ear, breathing out in a whisper, "I bet this is the hottest thing you've ever experienced." I tighten my arm around her small waist, relishing the little gasp it draws from her. "And I'm not even inside you yet."

My mouth scorches a path down her neck as I kiss and nip at her taut skin. Each bite declares my claim on her, willing her to submit.

"Let me be your nightmare," I rasp, my lips never leaving her skin. "I'll make you wake up drenched in sweat, my name a scream on your lips."

Her muscles relax in my hold. With her shape melting into mine, I slide my right hand under her shirt. I brush along her flat stomach, skating slowly higher up her ribcage toward her breast.

My palm runs over her hard nipple, and my cock threatens to tear through my fly. The pebbled tip is sharp and distinct beneath the thin fabric of her bra.

Emily arches against my front with a plaintive moan when my hand strokes her up and down. Letting go of the wall, she reaches back for my neck. She bends for me, molding herself to my body like water.

"That's it, baby girl." I give her breast a firm squeeze, then dip my fingers inside the cup, pulling it down. "Let me ruin you."

I tease her nipple, rolling it between my middle and forefinger while cradling the full weight of her in my palm. "Better me than some random thug jumping you on the street."

She scoffs at that. "You're no different from any other guy cornering me to take whatever he wants."

Her body doesn't stop undulating against mine, and I pick up on the goading lilt in her tone. *Baby girl wants to play.*

I laugh darkly. "I'm different because I'll never hurt you." Drawing my hips back, I thrust forward. "Fuck you, good and deep, but never harm you. You'll always be safe with me."

I roll my hips into her again. My grip in her hair as unrelenting as the one on her body, I have us both panting.

"The devil I know versus the devil I don't?" she muses with shallow breaths.

"Exactly. And don't deny that you like me hunting you down. That it turns you on; I know it does. You love being scared: the adrenaline rush... senses cranked to the max... hyper-aware of every touch...

"Your nipples are so hard right now, I bet your skin is buzzing."

My hand releases her breast, and I inch south to get my proof. I pop the button then lower the zipper, taking my time and savoring her anticipation.

I ease my hand into her open fly and hold my breath, pushing her underwear aside. My fingers glide along her slick seam…

I moan.

"I knew it. You're so turned on and fucking wet right now."

The bare feel of her puts me in a chokehold. I trace the length of her, giving extra attention to her clit as I edge her. I want her as close to coming as I am.

"Not yet, baby girl," I tell her when her body trembles in my embrace. "Get these pants down for me."

She lets go of my neck, and I withdraw my fingers, working my own jeans over my hips with one hand to free my stiff length from its confines.

I keep a possessive hold on her hair.

When she's ready for me, I slide my hand over her wet opening again from behind. This time, three fingers sink into the inferno to meet her soft flesh.

Emily moans again. Her little muscles flex around my knuckles lightly. She feels so fucking good.

"Put your hands back on the wall." My cock standing fully erect between our bodies, I pump my fingers in and out of her in a rough motion. I want her dripping down my wrist.

Her sounds turn whimpering. "Don't you dare come yet," I warn.

Pulling my fingers from her heat, I flatten her chest against the brick at her front and guide the head of my cock to her wet cunt. I tease her with the vertical frenum barbell, letting her swallow just the tip before I retreat and ease back in.

Emily clenched around me, so fucking eager to take it all, and I give her another inch. And then another before pulling out.

"Just like that," I praise her, drawing my hips back and sinking into her again but no deeper than before. "Soak my cock, baby girl. Get it nice and slick. You're going to need it when you take it up your ass." She's getting every inch of me eventually, just not like this.

I keep a grip on my shaft. Feeling her wet and ready heat bare against my skin, I shudder on each stroke. It's not something I commonly allow myself. Like Ash, I always use protection, but with Emily, I want this.

Although I would've pulled out too, if she weren't on the pill. She doesn't need to know that I'm shooting blanks.

Ash and I both had vasectomies. We made a pact that our DNA will end with us, but we like to keep that to ourselves. It would only raise questions as to why we took such drastic measures, and neither of us feels particularly inclined to disclose details about our upbringing.

My grip becomes slippery. "Are you ready for me," I hear myself ask.

Anticipation has me strung like a wire as I prowl the path to her tight hole with the slick tip of my cock.

I feel Emily tense. Her breaths judder.

I push.

I enter her gradually, letting her crown the head for a few seconds to adjust—I'm bigger than the plug; I knew she'd struggle. Then I proceed with my intent.

Another whimper carries to my ears, this one tinged with distress. "Mason… Mason, please. You're too big. I can't…"

"Yes, you can, baby girl." I press my lips to her neck, and my hand settles on her right hip, squeezing her gently while drawing circles with my thumb in an effort to chase away some of her tension. "Your body was made to take me," I affirm, sinking deeper. I can't stop now that I have her pinned between the wall and my chest. That I've gotten a taste of her that way.

"You've been starved, little flower," I say, releasing my fist in her hair. "Let me feed your dark needs. Let me be your devil."

I slide my left hand up her throat to the base of her jaw. My thumb traces the edge, depressing the soft tissue below while my voice stays by her ear. "Let me show you how good it feels to be bad." And then I give her one final thrust, burying the last few inches of my cock inside her tight passage.

Emily lets out a moan that's all pleasure, and I twist her head, planting my mouth over hers to devour it.

More sweet moans pour into me as I start fucking her slowly, swallowing each one like they're the best meal I've ever had. And other than her divine pussy, they are.

"You take it so well, baby," I rasp. Grip firm on her jaw, I seal my lips to her, and make her bend for me.

My right hand leaves her hip. Finding my way to the cleft at her front, I impart some more attention there and slide the tip of my finger under the hood.

Emily jerks at my touch, but I only hold her tighter.

Adding pressure, I tease little circles while exploring further. Wedged in between her toned thighs, I flick over the sensitive bundle of nerves in my path.

I'm rough. I stroke the length of her seam unapologetically, curving my finger up into her as far as I can reach. I need to feel her shatter.

Emily's body grows tense, then she convulses violently in my arms.

I ease up on her mouth to suck in a breath. "Don't stop coming," my voice chokes out. She feels so good clenching around me.

I work her without mercy, thrusting my hips into her. Harder. Faster. I'm so close.

I run the tip of my middle finger over her seam again and again until I feel my own climax peaking. The force lances through me like a bolt of lightning.

Locking my hips into her, I release every drop I got while my fingers continue their assault.

As my shivers subside still buried inside her, I feel her little muscles flexing around my cock again. She's building up to another climax.

My fingers stroke her clit. "You like the feel of me inside you, don't you?"

"Yes!" she cries out as the spasms of her climax lash at her again. "God yes!"

Fuck, I love the sound of her voice like that. So raw. So uninhibited. No guilt or shame from taking pleasure in the act. *That's* how I want her.

After letting her ride out the second orgasm, I step back and zip up.

Emily wrestles with her jeans. I watch her perfectly-shaped ass disappear and miss the view already.

I give her a spin, pulling her towards me to fasten the button at the front myself.

She looks up curiously. My thumbs trace the bare skin of her belly as my hands linger at the waistband. Her lips are parted and her face is still flushed.

I suppress a grin.

Hooking her by the waist, I pivot us around the corner to let her see how close we are to the road.

"Oh shit!" Her eyes widen. People are literally walking right by us.

Now *that's* a thrill.

Tipping her chin up with the same hand that wound through her hair so possessively earlier, I lean us back against the wall, this time at the side of the building for everyone to see us.

My thumb skims her jawline. I caress her gently, memorizing every detail of her face from the furrow between her hazel blue eyes to the freckles across the narrow bridge of her button nose and the full, defined shape of lips.

I can read the question on her face before she speaks.

"Why would you choose to share me with your brother?" she asks, her brow scrunched in confusion.

I narrow my eyes on her, my comeback ready. "Maybe I like watching him fuck you while your eyes are on me, anticipating my next move, wondering whether I'll join in or just get my fill watching," I insinuate with a smirk.

Tracing the bottom edge of her mouth, I lean in, my voice low. "And I'll see your fear," I stress. "The nervousness in your stare as it pins mine. I'll see what you're trying to hide. That you're scared of me. Scared, because you don't know the sick and depraved things I want to do to you. All the dirty fantasies I have. It's the thrill of not knowing what to expect that will get you off. So… while he's the one pounding into you, it will be *me* who gets you off. *My* eyes… *my* presence pushing you over the edge. The chill creeping over your skin pulling your muscles and making your nipples hard, that's *me*. And that gives me power. I want you afraid of me."

I withdraw my hand and tug the mask back down over my face. "My brother may have you, but he will never own every part of you like I do. *I'm* the one in your head. The one under your skin. You belong to *me*."

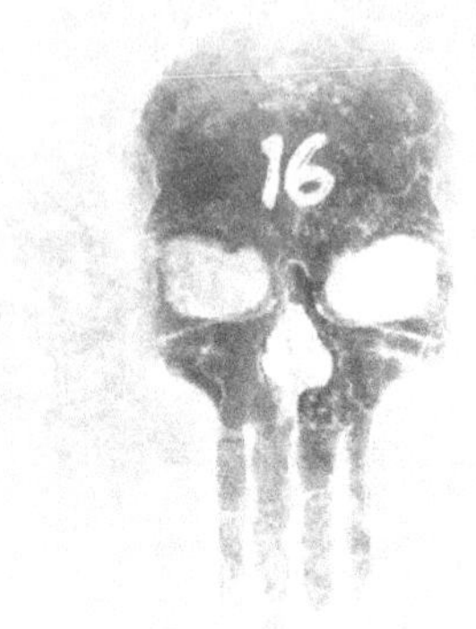

Mace

I roll onto my side, hugging my knees into my chest and curling inward.

"They're going to pay," Ash growls in a whisper. "For every punch… for every kick… for every—"

He doesn't finish that last thought.

His voice sounds so far away, but I know he's right behind me on the floor instead of in his own bed across the room. I don't know why. I don't want him anywhere near me.

Thomas and Johnathan dropped us off at home. We're back in our parents' shitty apartment. But with an abusive father who has sick friends and even worse enemies he owes money to, and a mother who drinks to escape, we're not much better off here. We're no more than a means of payment.

No one will protect us. No one cares.

I blink and wipe the tear that runs down the side of my face before it can soak into the pillow.

"We're going to make them pay for everything," Ash resumes. "We're in this together, Mace. You and I."

He doesn't reach out his hand—doesn't try to touch me. And I'm glad. Because in that moment, I don't know what I'd do. In that moment, I hate him.

<hr>

I hate my brother.

For no other reason than them picking me out of the two of us.

Of course I hate them, too, for what they put us through, but they're no longer breathing, so that only leaves him.

The resentment toward Ash is always there. Slumbering. Some days, the hatred flares so hot I can't even look at him.

Like today.

We sit in the break room at lunchtime, but I'm not hungry. I can't even stand the thought of food right now.

His phone buzzes where it lies face down beside him on the table. It's been going off all morning, and he didn't say anything, but I just know it's her.

It's Ash's turn to pick Em up from the diner—his turn to have her to himself—and it makes my stomach ache. I'm nauseous thinking of the two of them alone.

Glaring at my lunch, I catch the sound of the keys as he replies to the text. Elbows propped on the table in front of me, I brace my forehead on my hands. The fingers of my right hand are stretched around a clenched fist, flexing every so often as images of my brother's paws on her form in my mind. Of her on his bike, her thighs spread around him.

"You okay?" he mumbles around his sandwich.

Before I'm forced to respond, the door swings open.

My head lifts to see Isaac walking in, the travel mug in his hand his only source of sustenance at the shop. He usually goes home for lunch.

Acknowledging us with a curt nod, he pivots toward the counter to get a refill from the fresh coffee I put on. It's all I can keep down.

My eyes follow his motions, ignoring Ash's obnoxious chewing in my periphery. Isaac sets the glass pot down, fastens the lid then swings around.

I'm not surprised when he pulls out the empty chair to my left and joins us at the small round table that really only seats three. Even though he doesn't eat here, we use this time to chat.

I push my sandwich away and cross my arms on the table, facing him. "Have you found a replacement for Tatum yet?"

His daughter has made plans to move away with her fiancé after their wedding in a few months. Other than managing sales, she has no interest in running the shop, which is why he's considering leaving it to Ash and me.

Isaac lowers his mug, stretching his legs out as he leans back in the chair. "I got a couple of applications, but no one feels right yet."

"I offered," Ash cuts in. "You know I can multitask."

Isaac arches a brow, tipping his travel mug toward him. "I'd prefer someone with better people skills than you."

Ash shrinks back. "What's wrong with my people skills?" He throws up his palms in defense.

Isaac shakes his head and laughs. "I know you're good at charming your way into a girl's pants, but I require some professionalism in the storefront. 99% of our clients are male."

"And you don't think I can charm my way into a guy's pants? I bet I could have them eating out of my hand."

"I'd almost pay to see that," Isaac mutters, raising the mug back to his lips. "Almost."

Just then the door handle dips again, and Tatum pokes her head in.

"Oh, hey guys," she chirps in her usual, carefree tone. A soft smile stretches her lips, finding its way to her golden-brown eyes. "Sorry to bother you on your break, Dad, but can I borrow you for a moment?"

"Sure thing, sweetheart."

Isaac rises and follows her out, leaving Ash and me alone.

The man isn't wrong about her being hard to replace. Besides being great at her job, she's the first person to make contact with customers entering the shop, and she leaves quite the impression. Blonde curls frame her face, and as far as I've seen, she always carries a positive attitude. It's infectious.

"Hey man," I poke at Ash, "maybe you can rekindle things with Tate and get her to dump her fiancé for you. That would take care of our replacement issue."

She had a casual thing with him a little while back. Before she met *Mr. Right.*

The last bit of his sandwich pauses midair. His eyes narrow into slits, and he glares at me. "You'd like that, wouldn't you?"

Stifling a grin, I challenge him with a shrug.

I know there's no way, and I'm happy Tate found someone to get serious with, but I still like poking at my brother. 'You don't screw the boss's daughter.'

But that's Ash, putting his dick where it doesn't belong, breaking rules, changing deals. And Isaac doesn't know about the fling either. He treats us like sons. For 10 years we've worked here.

Ash takes a swig of his water bottle while I continue burning a hole into his forehead. He thinks he's so slick he can get away with anything. Just someday I wish his shit would catch up with him.

He crushes the sandwich wrapper into a ball and shoots it in a high arch from where he's sitting into the trash bin by the door.

His phone buzzed again.

He tips it up to give the screen a glance, then refocuses on me. Crossing his arms on the table, he mirrors my pose and smirks, a glint in his eyes.

"I'm taking her out after work."

Heat shoots up my neck. "Taking her out?" I parrot, knowing he's talking about Emily now.

"Yeah. Like a date."

A date? Something snaps inside me hearing that word, and then I remember it's her night off.

My lips twitch under the friction of my teeth as every muscle in my body flexes. I draw heavy breaths. I want to explode. I want to rip Ash across the table and fight it out with him right here.

But I know whether she does or doesn't give it up to him tonight isn't up to me. It's her choice, and there's nothing I can do about it.

Bracing my palms on the table, I push to my feet, swiping my lunch up as I turn to leave.

Or at least not much, I think, balling the paper around the sub and dumping it into the trash on my way out.

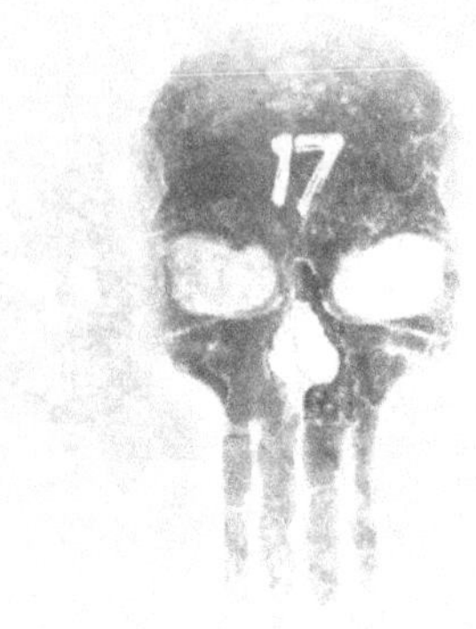

Em

I zip through my apartment to put on the finishing touches and give my hair another fluff in the mirror:

Volume—check.

Makeup—check.

Outfit—double check.

I'm wearing a black tank top, paired with black combat boots and a short, pleated black and pink skirt. I want to feel Ash's bike against bare skin. I know it's reckless in case we crash, but lust has overwritten my common sense.

I give my fashion choice a light laugh. I look more like a punk now than I dared to back in high school.

What a difference 10 years can make…

But it's really the last month that has made such an impact on my confidence. I have no one but myself to answer to. No guilt. No inhibitions. It's everything I ever wanted.

I like to think it's my newfound independence that brought it on, but I know it's more than that, and when the pounding knock on my apartment door jolts my heart up into my throat, it's the confirmation I can't deny.

Someone must've let him into the building.

A giddy grin forms on my lips. For a moment, I *do* feel like a teenager again.

"Coming!"

I swipe the hoodie from my bed before rushing down the hallway, but when I open the door, it's not Ash's familiar smile I encounter.

"Mason!" I yelp in surprise, my fingers clenching around the sweatshirt in my hand.

The one he's wearing is not the same black one he had on in the alley—this one has the auto shop logo on the front— but I can still tell him apart from his brother.

"I thought Ash was taking me out." Did they pull a switch on me again?

"He is."

Mason takes an uninvited step inside as I half-stumble backward in shock. My mouth hangs open.

"But that doesn't mean I can't fuck you first." The door slams shut behind him, and then he's on me, bearing down on me with his staggering height.

My mouth goes dry as I can't seem to close it while my accelerated pulse chokes my breath.

His eyes drop down, and he tips his head, teeth pinching his bottom lip.

I follow the motion as his hungry gaze drifts down my body, taking in every inch of my bare legs in slow, scrutinizing detail.

His attention makes my skin prickle.

"Look at you, baby girl. All dolled up," he drawls with a suggestive lilt, stepping into me.

But I'm not game. I press my hands to his chest, stopping him from making further advances. "Am I just a number to you?" I bark, annoyed by the generic term of endearment. "Interchangeable with all the other 'baby girls' that came before me?"

I guess, unlike Ash, Mason can't be bothered with remembering the names of his many hookup's.

"No, Emily. You're not," he says with a sigh.

I scoff, unimpressed. "I'm surprised you know my name." He's never used it. "I assume Ash passed that on to you, like everything else I told him about me."

"No." He releases another sigh, his hands coming up to clasp my face, and his stunning green eyes holding mine. "I read your name on your doorbell when I followed you home that first night."

My stomach drops.

And just like that I *do* wish he got my name from his brother instead of stalking me all the way home without my knowledge.

I stare at him blankly.

But my chagrin fades when he lowers himself to me. His mouth melts to mine as his hands shift and broad palms cradle my head while his fingers dance through my hair, pulling it lightly.

My body arches into him, compelled by the growing need to feel him against me.

With his tongue teasing mine in slow, exhilarating strokes, there's something else that's distinctly him:

Sandalwood and spice.

I recognize it from the bandana Ash blindfolded me with. It wasn't the detergent or dryer sheets. It was Mason's cologne.

The scent heats my chest and winds a slow path down to the empty space between my thighs.

I ache for him to fill it.

My hands slide up his chest to link behind his neck as I draw more of him into me. His body pressed to mine, Mason follows my lead, kissing me deeper, and winding me up with the slick curling motion of his tongue.

He feels so different from Ash.

They might look identical, but there's something sinister about Mason. He never really smiles.

Ash is uncomplicated: what you see is what you get. But Mason? Mason is an abyss of mysteries that pulls me into its depths.

His darkness already has a hold on me.

His right hand skates down my front, rolling my hard nipple with his thumb as he squeezes my breast briefly.

I moan against his lips. I'm not wearing a bra under the ribbed tank, and the friction of his touch is sweet agony.

My anticipation builds with every inch he sinks lower down my stomach, and I feel the slickness gathering between my thighs. My clit hums with the heightened sensation from the soaked material now covering me.

A soft chuckle weaves through his voice. "I like the easy access."

Mason's hand reaches the flared hem of my skirt and dips under. His fingertips rise slowly along the inside of my thigh, inching my skirt higher in the process.

He slides his fingers in at the side of my underwear, his knuckles tracing my slick seam. "Who is this for, Em?" He flicks his tongue at me, taunting. "Tell me."

"For you," I reply.

"Me… who?"

"Mason. For you, Mason," I moan his name more desperately.

"That's right. *Mine!*" he growls in satisfaction. "All of it."

Then he pulls away, undoing his pants and shoving them down before taking my left leg and hiking it over his hip.

Hands at the back of my thighs, he opens me up, aligning himself, and then thrusts into me.

Oh God! Pinning me to the wall, he spears me in one go.

I grip his shoulders as he stretches me to the max, my breath caught in my throat by the sudden invasion. My legs tremble.

Mason retreats, then fills me again, just as smooth and steady as before. His left forearm braced against the wall beside my head, he rails me hard and deep with each thrust, the ladder piercings along the top side of his shaft stroking my clit on every determined drive.

He winds us up, we climb fast, panting as our bodies meet again and again. I feel the tension cresting. That tingling in my core. I'm so close already.

"I want my cum dripping out of you when you spread your legs for him," he rasps.

I hear the rumble of Ash's motorcycle as he rolls up outside, and realize I never heard Mason's. Where did he park it?

We're still in the full swing of things in the hallway when he knocks on the door.

He's right there waiting for me to answer.

I can't call out.

I'm so fucking close.

Oh God… I'm going to—

"Tell him you're coming," Mason's rough whisper dares me.

My mouth opens as my orgasm explodes so deep in my core I think I might black out. But Mason's hand clamps down over it to muffle me as he thrusts his hips into me faster and harder, pounding out his own release.

His breath hot and ragged at my throat where his face nestles in the crook of my neck, he spears me one last time then stills with a shudder I feel through the connection of our bodies.

"I want to see you in that skirt again." He presses a kiss to the corner of my jaw and releases me before stepping back.

I sag against the wall, my legs weak. The last I see of him is his silhouette disappearing out of my bedroom window down the hall.

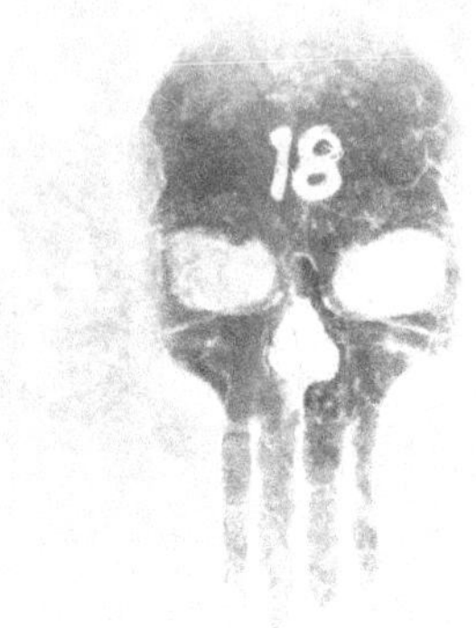

Em

Ash takes us on a 20-minute-ride to a bar outside the city, and the first thing I do is excuse myself to go to the bathroom. I have to clean up.

I answered the door, cheeks flushed and my breaths panting like I ran a marathon—and that's exactly what I felt like—but somehow he didn't look suspicious. He had no idea Mason and I were going at it on the other side.

Hands braced on the edge of the sink, I glare at my reflection in the mirror. I need to get Mason out of my head. This isn't fair. I'm on a date with his brother for fuck's sake, and all I can think about is him railing me against the wall.

I frown at the flattened condition of my hair. I don't even know why I bothered with the volume. It's all gone now after wearing a helmet.

But hey, at least he saw it blown out first. I hope it made an impression.

I give my head a shake and walk out to find Ash at the bar. He looks so hot in his dark blue, lightly distressed jeans and a black button-down with the sleeves folded up his tattooed forearms.

He went home after work to change and shower while Mason rode his bike straight to my house, buying himself a few minutes with me.

The whole outfit looks so effortless and yet sexy as hell on him.

How the fuck do guys do that?

And of course, *his* hair is on point, just the perfect amount of tousled, begging me to run my fingers through it.

Ugh! I want to sit on his lap while I do that. The way he straddles the barstool so casually, slightly slouched, and those strong thighs propped up on the step drives my fantasies wild. I can just feel his big hands cradling my ass.

Alright girl, reel it in. You got your head in the game now. I roll my eyes and approach on his right, sliding onto the empty seat beside him.

Elbow on the counter, bracing his chin on his left hand, he tips his head toward me. He bites his bottom lip, but I can see the crooked grin dangling there as he takes in my outfit again. I carry the hoodie in my hand to grant him another full view of the entire ensemble I put on just for our date. I accessorized with bracelets, a necklace, and dramatic eyeshadow of course.

I left my lips bare for fear of smudging, and I'm glad that I did, although I can't for the life of me recall why. I'm all in the moment now. With Ash.

"What can I getcha?" the bartender asks me.

My eyes flash to him, and then to the glass of water in front of Ash. "I'll start off with a water, too. Thanks." I give the guy a curt smile and refocus on Ash.

I notice that he shaved before meeting me. There's no 5 o'clock shadow darkening his jawline.

"If you're thinking about ordering a salad, I'm taking you back home."

"No." I give a soft laugh. "I was thinking a burger and fries, but I'll take whatever you recommend." I'm starving, and my surging libido tells me I'll need the calories.

His eyes light up. "Burger and fries it is," he says with a grin.

I try not to think of Laura's remark about his big hands squeezing the buns.

We order our food, and I add a Strawberry Daiquiri while Ash sticks to water. I have to admit, I'm equally surprised and relieved that he doesn't consume alcohol since both our lives—and the lives of others—depend on it.

"So how long have you been working at the auto shop?" I ask, lowering my drink.

I'm hoping to needle Ash with more questions. He might be more likely to open up than his brother.

He sets his burger down and sucks some juice off his thumb before reaching for his water. Turns out, he's a one-handed guy when it comes to food. His right hand is braced on his thigh as his body faces mine.

He takes a sip and swallows. "Since we were 18."

His reply stumps me briefly. That's right out of high school with no previous hands-on training unless they grew up in a garage and learned from a parent or relative.

There was a workshop setup at the house, I remember.

"And your house, is that your family's home? The one you grew up in?" It looks brand-new, though. Or at least very recently renovated in a modern style.

"Nah." He shakes his head. "We didn't have it that nice growing up. We took off once we turned 16."

A fry pauses on its way to my lips as I choke on the last bite. *On their own since they were 16?*

"What happened to your parents?" I wonder apprehensively.

He shrugs. "We kept checking in with our mom off and on. She passed away three years ago."

Ash doesn't go on, leaving me hanging without the rest.

"And your father?" I cue.

His brow furrows as if with bitter memories. "Prison, probably." He lifts one of his fries to his mouth. "Haven't seen him in over a decade," he adds, taking the bite.

So not a happy childhood, I conclude.

I change the topic after that to something a little more uplifting, and we share a few more laughs about my own pathetic life story. It's not bad, just very plain.

I finish a second Daiquiri and feel the buzz on another trip to the ladies' room. When I return, Ash has already taken care of our check.

My fingers clench around the wallet I have tucked into the front pocket of my hoodie. "You paid last time," I remind him with a light scowl. "I wanted to cover this one."

He slides off his seat and straightens in front of me, shoving his hands into his pockets. "That was never going to happen," he tells me, his chest so close it brushes mine.

A hint of warm vanilla tangles through the darker notes of amber and oak I recognize as his cologne.

My nipples harden as I stare up at him. I'm sure he can feel it. I don't know whether it's the effect from the alcohol or him, but my skin is suddenly heating all over. The hairs at my neck prickle.

"Why?" I force my tone steady so as not to reveal how desperately I want him to touch me right now. "Because you're old-fashioned and don't believe a woman should pay for dinner, or because she's required to pay the guy back in other ways later?"

The deep, sensual green of his eyes pins me. "I wouldn't let you pay, because *I'm* the one who asked *you* out. The only requirement of you was to show up. And you held up your end." He frees a hand from his pocket, reaching up to touch my face. "I don't expect anything else in return, Em."

My gaze drops to his lips at the sound of my name, and my eyelids grow heavy.

Ash's fingertips skim my jawline, searing a path directly to my core. The pulsing between my thighs increases with each beat while my breathing shallows.

"But tell you what," he prompts, tipping my chin up, and drawing my attention back to his eyes. "Next time, *you* ask *me* out, and I'll let you pay. How about that?"

"Next time?" I raise my brows at his bold presumption.

"Yeah." The corner of his mouth turns upward. "Next time."

I match his grin. "Deal."

I drop my eyes as I slide my free hand up the thick bulk of his bicep, feeling his shirt glide smoothly against his bare skin underneath.

My voice takes on a hopeful tune. "What else do you got planned for us tonight?" I ask, raising my heavy gaze back to him.

The tip of his tongue comes out to wet his lips, and his teeth do a slow rake across the bottom before his grin turns up another notch. "Put on your hoodie and find out."

I don't miss the sparkle in his eyes when he nudges me toward the exit, and I pray he has something more private in mind. I remember our unfinished business at the park. The view was spectacular there.

Ash pauses before stepping outside to let me get dressed, then slides his hand into mine.

My right palm fuses to his left. It's not warmth that spreads through my body but scorching heat, setting me ablaze all at once.

"I thought I recognized the bike."

Both our heads snap around at the remark. It's spoken with a contemptuous edge, and the hairs on my arms and neck immediately bristle in alarm.

I turn toward the street where a guy is leaning against Ash's motorcycle that he parked next to the curb. He's about Ash's height, with an indication of a light muscle bulk beneath his dark sweatshirt.

Around him mobs a small posse of four guys with similar builds and threatening facial expressions. Two of them have their hoods up like their leader, and all I can think is that they look like some street gang, and we're about to get jumped.

Ash tugs me closer to his side when the guy by his bike dips his chin in a curt greeting, his hands buried in his front pockets like he might be concealing a weapon there. "Ash."

"Vince."

Oh shit! They know each other.

Something feathers over Vince's expression, and his lips quirk in amusement. "That's a nice piece you got there," he says with a tilt of his head.

An icy chill creeps over me as his curious gaze takes me in. He's not talking about Ash's bike.

"Looks like a comfortable chassis," he adds with sickening appreciation. "Made for a good ride, I assume. Those legs…" He makes a whistling sound instead of finishing his sentence.

"What do you want?" Ash barks, cutting him off.

"I was just wondering if you and your brother are going to show at the race in Sierra Valley next weekend?"

"Why? Did you already make plans on how to spend the prize money in case we don't?" Keeping me close behind him, Ash strolls up to the guy, goading him. "Everyone knows that's the only way you'd win. Always the bridesmaid, never the bride," he taunts with a sneer.

Vince's face retains its animosity. His eyes narrow and his mouth gives a cynical twitch. "You can't *always* win, Ash," he grinds out, then arches a brow.

"Maybe your girl here would enjoy the show." He pushes off Ash's bike and takes a leisurely step to the side, seemingly surrendering his post without starting a fight.

But I'm not fooled.

"You should bring her along," he tacks on offhandedly. "She looks… *fun.* Are you two passing her back and forth?" He gestures vaguely between Ash and me. "She knows there's two of you right?"

His left hand still linked to my right, Ash leans into him, leveling his chest with Vince's. "Just prepare yourself for third," he sneers, jabbing the guy with his forefinger. "As usual."

Then he nudges me toward his bike, handing me my helmet and getting on first.

Vince cocks his head. "You and Mason… always in competition." He *tsks*, giving my body another suggestive once over.

I climb on behind Ash as he revs the engine like a threatening growl.

We watch the group of guys part in a somewhat reluctant pace, then take off.

The tension in Ash's muscles never lessens. Even at the stoplight, his upper body remains flexed through and through. Vince's words must've triggered a nerve. Are he and Mason really that competitive?

I hug my arms tighter around his chest. I want him to know that I'm here. Not just on the bike with him, but also for emotional support. I care. And I'm not bothered by what the prick said.

Before the light turns green again, I feel his sigh, and all at once, his tension loosens, like a weight falling off.

His gloved fingers give my hand a quick squeeze, then return to the throttle to accelerate, but I know, in this brief moment, something that doesn't need words passed between us.

I lean into his body on the bike, my legs spread around his, the engine roaring between my thighs. Each time we ride, I get more confident. My curves are very familiar with his contours by now, and it's not awkward to touch him so intimately. I no longer find the closeness daunting. I revel in it.

And I trust him.

Even when he takes us on an obscure path through the woods.

Ash decelerates to weave through the trees until they open to a jaw-dropping view of a lake, completely hidden away by the dense forest vegetation.

A gasp leaves my lungs as the moonlight glitters across the black glass surface. "Holy shit!"

I catch Ash's pleased chuckle before he cuts the engine and silence takes over. Not even a breeze whispers through the leaves.

I scan the shore. The lake isn't very big, and yet I can't make out a single house in the distance. There's no one but us for miles. I'm guessing it's a natural feature, not man-made.

I dismount and take the helmet off. "How in the world did you find this place?"

It seems the perfect dumping ground for a body, I muse to myself. There's not even a boat dock that suggests anyone visits this spot. Ever. The path we took was tough on the bike—more manageable with a car, I guess—but weeds and brush going up to the water are thigh-high. They tickle my legs up to the hem of my skirt.

Kind of idyllic, though.

"Mace and I used to go hiking in this area," Ash says, removing his gloves, his helmet sitting on his lap. "Even camped out here on warmer nights. Anything was better than being at home."

His voice grows somber, and I look back over my shoulder at him. This place must hold some pleasant memories for him then.

Is that why he brought me here? To add happy memories?

I stroll back to him still straddling the seat of that fierce machine, my fingertips weaving through the tall weeds. I'm glad I'm wearing combat boots and not heels.

The glitter of moonlight reflects in his eyes, making him look utterly irresistible even before he catches on to the extra sway in my step. Those dimples deepen with his roguish grin, and a heatwave rushes me.

I reach for the bottom of my sweatshirt, pulling it off and tossing it into the grass without much care.

Ash does the same with the helmet on his lap, and I hear it land with a soft *thump* before I swing my leg over the bike's middle, facing him.

His boots are firmly planted on the ground, keeping us steady when I link my arms around his neck and scoot my ass closer, legs dangling on either side of him. My skirt fans out without restricting my movements.

Strong hands clasp the back of my knees to jerk me toward him that last bit, and then his hungry kiss crashes down on me.

"This outfit's been driving me crazy all night," he rasps, his mouth slanted over mine.

His tongue explores me. His arms coil around my waist to lift me onto his lap, and I follow his cue, wrapping myself around him with growing need.

Ash's kiss is smooth. It's deep and bold.

Straddling him, I rock against the enlarged bulge at his fly, my fingers running through his longer hair on top, tugging at the root.

"You got me so fucking hard, baby," he groans, his hands kneading my ass encouragingly while I roll my hips to grind down harder.

Teeth graze my bottom lip, nipping and tugging with erotic greed that feeds into me. I feel the charge tingling under my skin.

Ash's hands slide under my top. He relinquishes his claim on my mouth to plant feverish kisses along my throat with more sucking and biting while stroking me.

I tip my head back, eyes closed. His touch is everywhere.

"Lean back," his panting voice urges.

A jolt rocks through me. "Aren't we going to tip over?"

"I got it," he assures me.

My hands unlink from his neck, and Ash lays me out on the gas tank. I can still feel him hard against me with the angle of my hips, my legs draped over his thighs as he keeps the bike steady.

Grinding the thick ridge of his shaft into the already soaked material of my underwear, he pushes my top up to expose my breasts.

"Fuck, you're beautiful, Em."

The breeze tweaks my hardened tips, and with the way the moonlight carves his features, I see the strained expression on his face matching the rough edge in his tone.

"Touch yourself for me." The bike rocks as he shifts to undo his jeans and shove them down. "Let me watch you."

I don't even hesitate at his demand. Both of my hands dip under my skirt, one pushing the cotton aside to tease my clit and the other sliding two fingers along my wet seam.

My eyes roll up at the sensation. I've touched myself so many times before, but with him watching me, everything is heightened.

I refocus my sight on Ash, a fist wrapped around his hard cock.

The silver piercing glints with the faint light from above the lake, and a slick bead sits ready at the tip.

There's no sly grin curling the corner of his mouth. He appears too fixated to be gloating. Left hand on my hip, he stands tall over me, stroking himself as his eyes rivet to my movements.

I arch off the gas tank, spasming under the pleasure. I'm so close. My leg muscles jitter.

"Fuck! That's it. Come for me, baby girl."

I hear him speeding up, the wet sound filling my ears, and right when I'm about to come, he rips my hand away, replacing it with his thumb as he thrusts his fully enlarged cock into me.

I splinter apart on impact. He impales me with every inch he has at his disposal, and I can't stop my descent. My body contorts on the bike. My muscles twitch. I take his ruthless pounding as my walls squeeze his throbbing length until Ash rears back from his own release.

"Fuck!" he bellows into the night.

Then he collapses down on me, his face buried in my neck. "That was so hot."

A laugh bursts from my chest. I've never felt so high on sex.

Ash presses a kiss to the side of my throat. His hair tickles me, and a light sheen of sweat coats his neck as I run my nails along his nape.

"I hate that I have to take you home," he groans resentfully. "*Your* home, I mean. I'd love to take you back to *my* place. But, you know…"

Yeah, but his place isn't just *his* place. It's *their* place.

"You got work tomorrow?" I can't remember if he said the shop is open on weekends.

Ash pulls out. "*I* do." He lifts off and straightens, his eyes finding mine. "We're open half-day on Saturdays, which Mason and I alternate since Isaac doesn't need both of us."

"Isaac's your boss?" I ask as we both tuck our clothes back into place.

"Yeah. He owns the shop. Built it from the ground up."

"And Sundays?" I prod.

The lightness in Ash's demeanor returns with a hopeful grin. "Closed." Then his hands slide under me to pull me up.

I'm grateful for the boost. My abs are sore like I did 1000 crunches.

His arms slide around, holding me too him as he kisses me again, slow, and deep, but with the initial hunger sated for now.

I still love every second of it.

And if he didn't have to get up early, I'd invite him to stay the night.

Ash watches me from the curb as I walk up to the apartment building, fishing my keys out of my hoodie's pocket even though I don't know why I bother with it. He told me that apparently the main door doesn't latch properly, which is how he'd gotten in when he came to pick me up.

My eyes drop to the lock as I find the door slightly ajar, the mechanism not catching, and when I pull it open, I notice tool marks. The damage was deliberate.

Dammit!

I make a mental note to call the super in the morning, but the chances of me reaching anyone and getting it repaired over the weekend are slim to fucking none. I won't be able to sleep, knowing there's a strangler on the loose. Both victims had dark hair and were close enough in age to me. I fit his pattern.

On the danger of sounding like a total girl, I admit I would've really liked to have Ash stay the night.

The fading roar of his bike tells me he's gone shortly after I let the door fall back on its busted latch and start stalking down the dark hallway toward my apartment.

I switch keys. Sliding the right one into the lock, I twist it and step into the secondary void beyond. It's not until I turn around and shut the door that the presence of a large mass registers behind me.

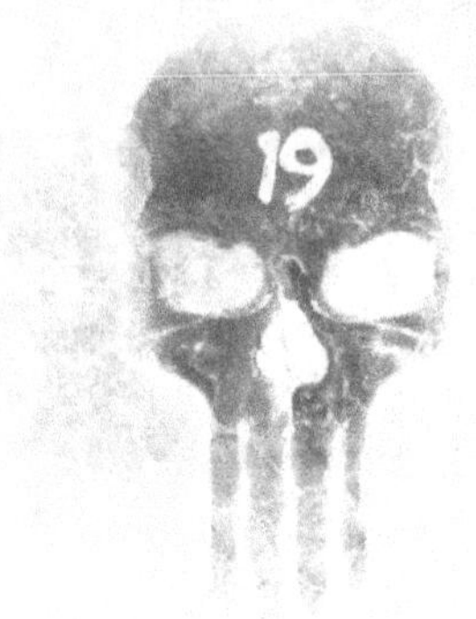

Em

I drop my sweatshirt in a panic. Two large hands seize me, one clamping down over my mouth, the other around my throat as he crushes me against his chest.

The feel of him is like steel.

With his arms ensnaring me, his fingers flex in a tense grip, digging into the hinges of my jaw, his palm at the front.

But he's not choking me. Sharp breaths shoot from the little gap he left below my nose.

He tips my head to the side, and I squeeze my eyes shut on reflex even though it's too dark to make out anything in the hallway. Maybe if I don't see his face, he won't kill me.

My pulse is rampant. The coarse stubble lining his jaw scrapes my cheek as he inclines his head.

That's when I smell the sandalwood and spice.

Mason.

"Gotcha!" his voice grates into my ear. "How fucking aroused are you right now? Touch yourself and tell me."

I roll my eyes in annoyance but make no motion to free myself from his hold.

Keeping his right hand around my throat, he skates the left one into my hair. He gives a pull, twisting my head and forcing my chin up until I can see his face fully.

Dark, hooded eyes rivet to my lips as he cradles my skull possessively.

"How was your date?"

"Oh God," I groan, "you didn't follow us, did you?"

His fingers fan through the hair at my nape while he delays his answer. It's a reasonable question, considering his track record for stalking and the repeated B and E.

Did he break my window again? I just had the super fix that.

"No," he replies gruffly.

Thank God. I feel a drop of relief. I don't want to imagine him watching us at the lake like he did before at the park.

His fingers curl into a fist in my hair with an air of jealousy that carries into his voice. "How many times did he make you come?"

My thighs give a twitch. "Three times," I blurt.

I don't know why I lie. Maybe I want to provoke him. I like him handling me roughly with his hand around my throat.

His grip tightens, making my pussy throb so hard I vibrate. I imagine his hand there, working me just as harshly.

Fingers flexing around my jaw, he lowers himself, his mouth hovering over mine. "I can beat that."

Oh fuck!

My lips part, and I suck in a clipped breath before his tongue dives in, bold and demanding, swirling around mine.

He curls the tip along the roof of my mouth on his retreat. "And I wasn't kidding, Em," he says with another skilled flick of his tongue. "Slide those fingers up your tight cunt, and let me hear how wet you are."

His mouth crushes back down on mine as I gasp at his crude language, but I can't help that it only arouses me more.

And then I do as he wants.

My right hand skims down the length of my skirt, dipping underneath the pleats while my left reaches up for his arm to steady myself.

I slide in at the side—for the second time tonight—and shudder. Slick, warm flesh meets my touch, readily welcoming the friction.

I ache.

I move my fingers in and out in a smooth motion, building on the cresting surge in my core. I feed into it. My hips roll in sync, grinding back at him.

My eagerness earns me a moan, and Mason's heavy hand on my throat shifts, stroking me encouragingly.

The sound of his praise resonates in my chest. He fuels my climax without touching me. He's in my head.

Sloshing sounds carry to my ears with the suction. I'm knuckles deep, my palm curved over my clit, but *he's* the one taking me there, *his* demand, *his* voice.

"More!" he growls. "Let me feel you come."

My muscles clench around my fingers as his words push me over the edge, and for a few seconds, I stop breathing entirely. My body convulses.

"Good girl." His right hand gives my throat another praising squeeze, but his fist relaxes in my hair. "That's one down."

Then his grip locks around my wrist, and he tows me to the bedroom.

Mason whirls me around him, backing me up toward the foot of the bed before his hands seize the hem of my top. He rips it over my head, then does the same with his hoodie and T-shirt in one go.

Stepping into me, one strong arm looped around my waist, he urges me backward onto the bed.

The mattress creaks with our combined weight when his mouth dips to my breasts. He suckles one, then the other, swirling his tongue around the pebbled nipple.

I whimper, arching in pleasure against his hold on me while scooting my ass toward the headboard to give him room.

His free hand slides up my thigh. With his other arm bracing my back, he pulls my underwear down one-handedly before settling fully between my legs.

The only thing I got left on are my skirt and combat boots.

Mason releases my nipple. Keeping up the assault with his tongue, he licks a trail along my stomach. His eyes flit up to meet mine, the dark green appearing almost black as he circles my belly button slowly.

I don't miss the wicked glint. His hands slide under my ass, and I bunch the sheets at my sides to brace myself for his dive under the pleats.

A high-pitched yelp breaches my lips. His firm hold keeping me from squirming, he seals his mouth to me, hot and wet while he lashes out with his piercing.

Holy fucking shit! I shatter almost instantly, my hips bucking off the bed in spastic motion, fists clenching the sheets.

Mason lets me ride out the shivers against his tongue before rising. "Fuck, you look hot like that, baby girl."

Moving up, he sinks into my shape. "You're a man's wet dream," he groans, lowering his mouth to mine.

He rocks the hard bulge of his fly against my tender parts but then stops and lifts abruptly. "I want you to see what I see, Em."

Mason rolls off. Propping himself up at the headboard, he pulls me back against his chest, spreading my legs.

Oh God! He has us facing my floor-length mirror across the room.

"Watch!"

As his left hand slides around the front of my throat, he takes my right hand, lacing our fingers, and guiding them to my awaiting pink flesh.

His coarse stubble scrapes along my jaw with intent. "That's mine, Emily," he declares, his breath hot at my cheek while teasing me with a soft touch.

Leading me, he traces my seam front to back, spreading me open.

"And you'll remember that every time you come." Then he pushes into me.

I draw in a breath as I stretch around our combined fingers. Mason moves them in and out, catching the sensitive bundle of nerves at the cusp on each stroke.

"Do you feel my brother's cum inside you?" he asks, thrusting deeper. "Mixing with mine?"

A sense of panic prickles over my skin. Mason's voice is cold and hard, lacking any form of amused teasing.

"But I was there first," he tacks on.

Mason speeds up. He's rough—much rougher and faster in his pursuit of my orgasm than I was earlier.

"And I'll be there last," he grates out, one hand squeezing my throat, the other one crushing mine as he pumps in and out of me relentlessly.

Oh God. I was right. He really *is* jealous. It's not an act. They *are* competing over me.

But I can't stop my climax. It rushes me like a tidal wave, and my body contorts in his hold as I cry out.

"Fuck, you feel so good." Mason flicks over my clit one more time, making me jerk, then locks his arm around my middle.

"Are you ready for the big finale, baby?" he asks before releasing my throat.

The bed shifts under his movement. "Cause I am." Keeping my ass flush with him, he pulls his legs in and hauls me onto my knees.

Mason positions himself behind me, his straining hard-on rubbing against my bare skin insistently as his palm between my shoulder blades shoves my face into the mattress. Hands braced on either side of me, I can't get up. He's holding me down.

"I want you head down, ass up, baby girl."

He bends over me, his fingers threading into my hair to pull my head back a little. My eyes lock with his in our reflections across the room. "But that doesn't mean I don't want you to watch," he rasps low in my ear. "Eyes on the mirror, Em."

Mason straightens slowly behind me. Knees spread in a wide stance and chest flat on the bed, I watch him undo his belt, utterly mesmerized by the sensual movements of his hands.

When he pulls it out through the loops, I wonder whether he's going to spank me with it.

I imagine the burn it would send across my flesh. The back of my thighs. My ass.

Heat flares with the acute throb between my legs, and I squirm in anticipation, my fists clenching the sheet.

Fuck! I want him too.

The curve at the corner of his lips that meets me in the mirror tells me he knows.

"You sure?" He arches a brow.

A nod is all I manage.

"Say, 'Please, Mason, spank me with your belt.'" His long fingers slide along the black leather, folding it into shorter sections.

"Please, Mason," I echo, a whimper chasing the words. "Please spank me—"

WHACK!

Ffuuuckk. Mason doesn't hesitate. With a swift motion of his arm, he sweeps the rigid strap through the air. The leather streaks across my ass, the skin flaring white-hot.

Another whimper breaches my lips, and I start to tremble. The pain that follows the intense sting is exquisite.

My gaze rivets to his reflection in the mirror. To the way his muscles flex in the dark. To the exhilarated rise of his chest. Sweat glistens on his skin. He's just as aroused as I am.

"Again?"

"Please yes."

WHACK!

He swings again, smacking me on the opposite side, and my legs quiver. My knees sink. My hips undulate stiffly. I need to come.

WHACK!

The third strike catches the back of my thighs, and my orgasm explodes. I shatter into a million pieces.

My rushing pulse thrums in my ears, but I still catch the surprise in his voice. "Did you just come?"

"Yes!" I blurt to catch my breath.

Mason clicks his tongue with a note of amusement. "Bad girl, Emily. I wasn't ready." He tosses the belt to the floor and then fumbles with the rest of his fly. "You get that one for free," he says, shoving his jeans down his thighs.

One hand at my waist, he teases me with the slick tip of his cock, nudging in just far enough to spread me open and letting me crown him, then retreating. I can't take it. Tears spear into my eyes from the torture. It's too much. I need him inside me.

"Please, Mason," I cry, begging him to fill me.

He acknowledges my need with a grunt and stretches me around the thick head again. Then both hands are on my waist. Gripping me tightly, he yanks me into him to impale me on the first thrust.

I bury my face in the sheet and moan as the sensation rocks through me.

Mason's left hand leaves my side to thread back into my hair, curling into a fist. "Eyes on the mirror, baby girl," he reminds me. "I want you to see how beautiful you are when you climax. I want you to own it. Watch how much you love coming for me."

And then he delivers. He pulls back to plunge his engorged length into me repeatedly, hard and deep, pummeling me with his thrust.

I take all of it. He feels so good pounding his hips into me.

Sparks flash in my vision with his fierce, unrelenting pursuit, and when his breaths turn jagged, I know he's close. I watch his face in the mirror, his beautiful features twisted in pleasure that I bring out in him.

Then I climax too, right there with him, my body gripping his pulsing length as he spills himself into me.

Mason rears back, face toward the ceiling, highlighting the erotic curve of his throat and Adam's apple with a roar. Every muscle is flexed, his hips still jerking.

A smile curls my lips. *I did that to him.*

He pulls out, letting himself fall onto the bed, and I have the feeling he won't be getting up any time soon.

I turn around and collapse beside him. I need a few moments to recover before I can manage to take my skirt and boots off. I'm not even sure I have the strength to get up and brush my teeth.

My gaze trails over Mason's relaxed face, eyes closed, and breaths deep. He didn't even bother tucking himself away.

I chuckle. I guess I can muster up the energy to give him a hand with his clothes. At least, I don't have to spend the night alone after all with a murderer at large.

My head turns toward the curtains, and a frown creases my brow.

I don't know how he got in this time. The bedroom window looks untouched, and I didn't see a crowbar anywhere either.

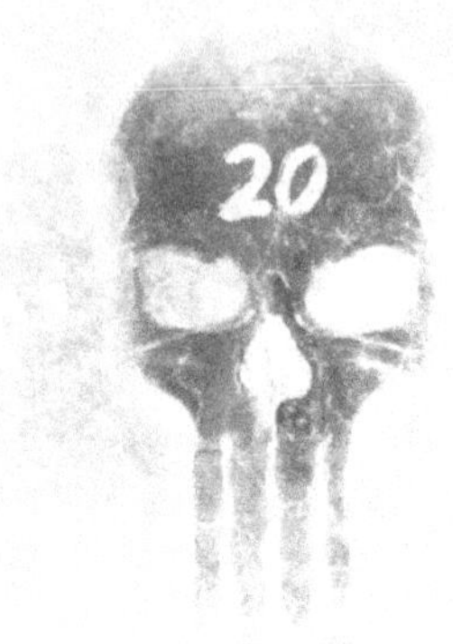

Mace

10 years ago.

Leaning against the building's brick exterior, I stand watch as Ash picks the lock—not that anyone is going to come snooping around; people here don't give a shit. Even if they hear a scream. Or maybe especially then.

Ash is crouched low beside me, his back toward the street. His hood is raised, with a black fleece balaclava-type ski mask underneath, the face shield down like mine. We don't raise them up just yet; they're for dramatic effect later.

Fidgeting with my hands in my pockets, I glance left then right. Everything is quiet, but I'm itchy. I wanted to do this. I've been planning this night for too long.

Damn rock. Every other time Ash would play scissors, but today he throws paper?

"Tada!" he whispers, a grin on his face as he opens the door without a sound.

Showoff!

I roll my eyes and sneak past him. "About time," I sneer over my shoulder. I could've done it just as well.

Maybe faster.

Breaking and entering has become one of our specialties. Sometimes it's to steal, sometimes to leave something; it's whatever Mr. DeMarco requires of us. We sneak in, we sneak out, without anyone the wiser until morning.

If at all.

But tonight, it's a bit more than that. And we're not here under the boss's authority, either. This one is a personal matter to us.

We ghost up the stairs and down the dark hallway. It's been three years since we've stepped foot into this wretched place, but we still remember every turn... every stain on these walls.

Cold fingers tease up my nape when we reach the apartment door and repeat the spiel on the lock. It feels eerie to creep back in here after all this time. I wonder if they'll even recognize us.

Adjusting his mask over his mouth and nose, Ash takes the lead. I raise mine up too and check the dial on my watch. It's 4:26 a.m. when we breach the threshold.

A heaviness settles over me with the first step in. The apartment looks exactly the same, sucking me instantly back into my memories.

My muscles freeze.

I close my eyes and force the lump forming in my throat down, taking a moment to mourn the innocence of our childhood that was ripped from us here.

My breaths grow deeper, but my hand still trembles when I draw my knife from my back pocket and push on.

My boots whisper along the dark living room carpet. It's quiet. Save for the subtle snore coming from the Lazy Boy's direction.

I recognize Jonathan's baritone timbre, but I know Thomas is around too, even before I find his feet hanging over the side of the couch.

Assessing the room, Ash nods toward the recliner, and we go for the man sleeping there first.

He leans over him when I come up beside him, his left hand braced on the armrest. He taps a gloved finger to his forehead to rouse him, and I can picture the satisfied smirk curling under his mask. It's the same one I'm carrying. We finally get to take our revenge.

Jonathan's limbs jerk as his eyes open to the shape hovering over him. But he flails for only a split second before Ash's knuckles collide with his throat, crushing his windpipe so he can't scream to alert the others.

With his ass still planted in the recliner, his hands fly up to the injury, eyes wide in shock. He gasps for air, clawing at his jugular, but we know he doesn't have long.

Ash straightens calmly next to me, mimicking my stance, and I wonder if Jonathan's oxygen-deprived brain is catching on yet, or whether he thinks he's seeing double—same black clothes and masks, we look identical.

In my periphery, Ash reaches for his mask. He slides it down slowly, drawing out the suspense until his full face is revealed underneath.

Jonathan's expression reaches another level of terror, and his eyes dart from Ash to me, finding the same green there, glaring at him through the hole in the fleece. I don't need to lower mine. He knows.

"He's all yours." I look at my brother, then back to him before making a motion to leave.

On a last, desperate burst, Jonathan's hand shoots toward Ash. He makes an attempt to get up, his mouth flopping like a fish to call out to Thomas only a few feet away.

Ash takes a step back, his chuckle carrying to my ears as Jonathan drops to his knees, the air in his lungs depleted.

But his wide stare remains on me when I turn toward the door on my right.

"Hey! Over here," I hear Ash tell him. "Eyes on me, asshole."

I catch the flick and the faint sound of his knife plunging into soft tissue, chased by more slicing of fabric, but I don't turn to watch my brother's mayhem.

Walking past the couch, I leave Thomas to Ash, too. I have only one target in mind.

My right grip clenches around the steel handle of my knife, the blade still sheathed inside when I reach for the bedroom door. I pull it toward me, rotating the knob silently from the wrist, then push.

Ely doesn't stir. I find him sprawled out flat on his stomach, a blanket covering him only from the waist down.

Slipping the flex cuffs out of my hoodie's front pouch, I straddle him from behind and grab his wrist.

"What the fuck?" His head jerks up, but before he even knows what's happening, I have his hands restrained at his back.

"Who the fuck are you?" he bellows, his body bending to look over his shoulder at me as he tries to wrestle me off.

He's bigger than me still. He twists and squirms under my weight, but I made sure I'd keep the upper hand.

Pressing my forearm into his back, I lean down, and flick my blade open. "Time to pay up, Ely." I wag the tip in front of his face. "The devil has come to collect your soul."

"What?" His voice is hoarse, and I catch the deep crease between his brows as his eyes lock with mine. He doesn't understand what's going on yet.

But he will.

"Johnathan and Thomas are dead, and you're next," I clarify, listening to the muffled screams coming from the other room as Ash is carving up Ely's second henchman.

My guy hears it too. His eyes swing to the open bedroom door before returning to me, and I see a glimmer of realization sparking. He knows I'm not bluffing.

But he still doesn't grasp the reason I'm here. "Why?" he has the fucking nerve to ask.

I stab my knife into the pillow beside his head. Rage shooting through my veins, I rip my mask down and growl, "Remember me?"

Ely refocuses on my face, then his eyes widen. "M-Mason," he stammers.

I reach into my pouch again, getting out the garrote. I don't want this to be quick. I need him to suffer.

Gripping the little wooden handles at each end, I loop the wire around his neck and pull.

Ely's muscles jerk as the line draws tight, and I cut off his carotid artery. I want to feel the life drain out of him.

My tension on the garrote jitters under the force I'm putting up with every second that ticks by. The wire slices through the skin at his jugular, and blood stains the white sheets before he loses the fight and goes limp.

Unwinding the line, I tuck it back into my sweatshirt and lift off his body to flip him around under me. I switch into autopilot. I can't stop myself from ripping the knife free and plunging it into his chest.

Again and again I stab him, my gloved grip slick. All I see is red. I can't stop.

I hear a shot go off but ignore it still stuck in my blind rampage. I'm drenched in Ely's blood.

Then Ash is beside me. "Mace…" He yanks on my shoulder. "Mace, stop! That's enough. He's dead."

I turn and see him shove a hand gun I've never seen before into the front of his waistband. Then both his hands are pulling me. "Let's go."

I sheath my blade and climb off Ely's mutilated corpse to follow Ash into the kitchen. When we pass the other two bodies in the living room, I notice the bullet hole in Thomas' forehead.

"Where did you get a gun?" I ask, reaching for the bottle of cheap vodka on the counter.

Is it the man's own? I don't know if he was packing or where Ely stashed his.

"DeMarco."

I pop the cap on the liquor as Ash continues his rifling. Drawers and cabinets slam. "You know they can match that shit, right?" It's why I prefer knives. We leave nothing behind.

"Relax." He sets down two more bottles he found tucked away. "It went right through. I picked up the slug and the casing too. The cops won't match shit."

I pour a trail from the kitchen into the living room, dousing the bodies there for good measure while Ash stuffs rags into the two additional bottles.

"Here." Meeting up with me, he hands me one.

I pull out my lighter and watch the rag catch fire before launching the bottle through the open bedroom door. My aim ensures it smashes against the wall to disperse the flammable substance properly.

Ash does the same with his, propelling it toward a wall in the living room on our way out. Pulling the door shut, we leave it all to burn.

We hurry back down the stairs the way we came. I don't turn over my shoulder. I don't look at the carnage in our wake. They deserved everything.

My hands tremble and my knees go soft as we make it across the street to safety. Only now can I manage to face the aftermath of my plan.

With Ash beside me, I swing around to look up at the angry flames flickering behind the third story windows and the smoke rising. But I don't feel guilty. I don't feel relieved.

I only feel sick.

A shutter roils through me, and bile burns my throat. Lunging toward the closest trash can, I hurl.

Hunched over with my head in the bin, somehow Ash's laugh finds its way to my ears. "You know they can match that shit, right?"

FREAKS OF NATURE

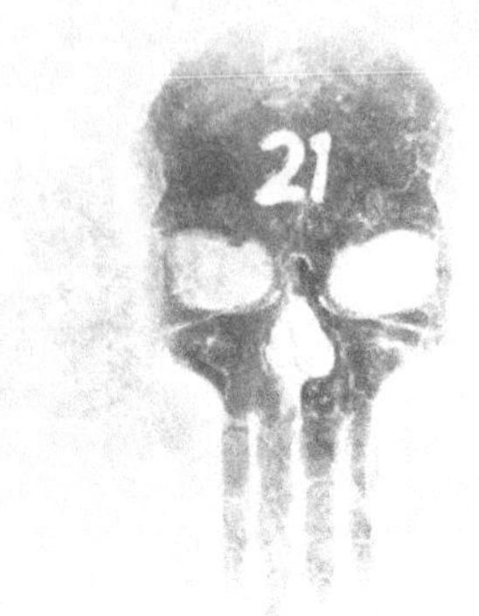

Ash

I stand over her bed, the LED mask covering my face as I watch her sleep. She's curled up on her side, her features relaxed and holding a serene beauty.

A few black locks fan out over her face and shoulders, calling my gaze to travel her contours everywhere her smooth skin is exposed.

It lingers on the visible muscle tone of her tanned thighs, and my mouth waters behind my mask. I want to run my tongue along every inch, licking her with the desperation of a starving man and feeling her soft flesh melt against my mouth.

She must've kicked the blanket off in her sleep, as it's now bunched by her feet, showing off a strappy black top and purple boy shorts that stretch over her curves.

Unlike yesterday, when I sneaked in a little after 1 p.m. to surprise her and found her naked, limbs entangled with my brother, both still passed out cold.

What the actual fuck.

He doesn't do that. *Sticking around after sex? Cuddling?* Neither do I, but I still had the urge to wrap my hands around his neck and choke him out.

Mason comes up to stand beside me, watching her sleep too. A pleased hum carries to my ears from under his own mask.

My fingers curl into fists as I picture him with her, lying in bed. I can share her with him when we fuck, but not like this. Not this intimacy. I don't know why, but *I* want that with her.

Turning my eyes back on Emily, I give her peaceful form another detailed scan. The pulse behind my fly turns urgent as my thoughts trace those smooth, toned legs I had the pleasure of running my hands over Friday night.

My palms tingle with the memory. *So soft and warm...*

My restrained cock gives another punch to the zipper before I let the image loose. I remind myself that I'll have her soon enough.

Emily had to walk home alone after her shift last night because Mason and I had an errand to run for Mr. DeMarco that required both of us. More of a pickup and dump than a drop-off, and that gave me an idea.

"Wake up, baby girl," I whisper, bending over her, my thumb trailing the curve of her cheek. Her skin is like pure silk.

She stirs, and her lashes flutter briefly before her sight locks on to my mask. Her eyes fly open wide. Emily flinches back, arms and legs flailing in an attempt to scurry away.

She has nowhere to go.

Her panicked stare darts back and forth between us to make sense of what's happening.

"Time to roll," Mason says, pulling the cloth hood in his hand over her head.

I watch the material get sucked in with a sharp inhale where her mouth is before I flip her onto her stomach.

Straddling the back of her thighs, I grind my swelling cock into her ass while securing the nylon rope around her wrists.

I take my time. She feels so good as she struggles to get free, the friction only makes me that much harder.

I flick my eyes to Mason standing right beside the bed, watching. I can't see his face under the mask. *Is he still grinning?*

I swing my leg and lift off. As I throw her over my shoulder, Mason grabs the keys of her car from the nightstand.

Then we're out.

I put her in the trunk of our Impala, a secondary ride we keep on hand, while Mason follows us home in hers.

I open the garage and back the car in. There's just enough room with our bikes occupying the same space, but we don't want the neighbors to get nosy when we carry a restrained female through the driveway.

I pop the trunk and get her out without waiting for Mason to pull up to the house. I lost him a few stop lights ago; not entirely by coincidence.

Tossing Emily back over my shoulder, I trap her thighs in a firm hold against my chest and carry her down into the basement.

I don't flick the light on. The street lamp shining through the small window on top illuminates the space enough to get around.

I slide her off my shoulder, dropping her at the short side of the pool table, facing me. Her chest rises and falls rapidly despite knowing it's us who took her.

Her fear is real.

Unlike the bandana that first night, the cloth hood serves a deeper purpose than simply depriving her of sight. It restricts her air flow.

I want to fuck her like that. I want to hear her gasping for each precious breath as she stretches to fit me.

And I want Mason to watch.

She continues to struggle with the restraints around her wrists, thinking she could get them free.

It's cute.

One hand clamped around her upper arm, I lift the other to the hood over her face. "You're gonna be a good girl and play along, yeah?" I prompt, my thumb stroking her cheek through the cloth. "I promise we'll make you feel good."

Another juddering breath pushes from her nose and mouth, billowing under the hood.

I yank her top up to free her perfect tits, then whirl her around to face the pool table before I bare her ass, too. I slide the skimpy shorts down her thighs, my cock swelling with every inch I expose.

I catch a glimpse of her soft, pink flesh, and my stiff length is in my hand when I push her down on the rough green felt of the table. I want her to feel it chafing her nipples as I thrust into her from behind.

Her breaths pant in anticipation. I align the head at her wet slit and drive it into her with a grunt.

Just then I hear the door slam upstairs, followed by Mason's boots pummeling the wooden steps.

My sight catches on his tight fists. His mask is down, but I don't need to see his face to know he's seething, finding me already balls deep in her. His shoulders are squared like he's braced for a fight.

The corner of my mouth twitches with the rush of mirth shooting through my veins.

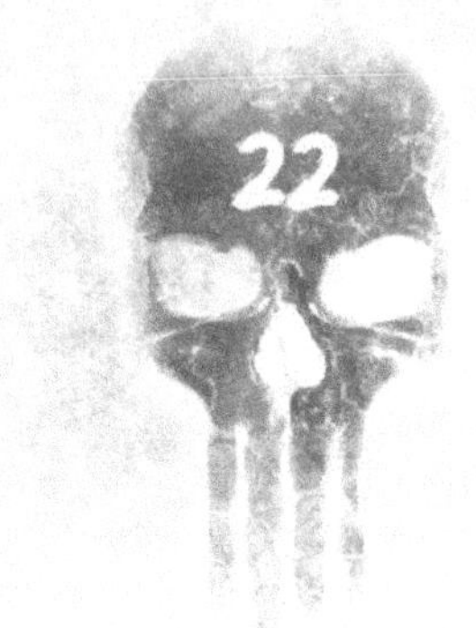

Mace

Ash pulls his hips back and sinks into her again, slower this time, his eyes on me as she moans under him.

It's a provocation, I know, but I won't admit that it's getting to me.

I unfurl my fingers, and he gives her another lazy thrust, then pulls out, dick in his hand when I come up beside them.

I ignore his smirk and the proud stroke he gives himself at his accomplishment. Turning my attention on Emily instead, I slide her shorts to the floor, then straighten her with gentle hands against my chest.

My left palm finds her naked breast, my light squeeze coaxing a moan from under the dark cloth. "Why don't you tell my brother how good you taste on him?" I suggest, slipping the hood off her head as she's facing him.

Her hair is tangled, and her cheeks are flushed. She looks breathtaking like that.

My hands nudge her shoulders, and she follows my cue to get on her knees. She's so fucking perfect.

"Open your mouth for him, baby girl," I tell her as she stares up at him sliding his mask back down over his face.

Her breaths shake. It doesn't matter that she knows it's us. It's the kink of being fucked by two masked men that has her on edge.

Emily complies. Her lips stretch around his shaft, and her throat jerks to adjust.

"Relax," my voice reminds her. "Breathe through your nose."

She swallows, saliva making her seal slick, and I watch her take him, her wrists still tied behind her back, so submissive, so trusting.

"That's it," I praise. "Good girl."

Ash's hand settles at the back of her head, and I sink onto my knees behind her, freeing my aching cock.

The feel of her is sublime. Skin on skin, I stroke her breasts, kneading them in my palms while she grinds her ass into me. The flexing of her muscles with the undulating motion of her body has me tipping my head back in ecstasy.

With Ash pumping steadily in and out of her, Emily molds herself to my shape, so needy to have me fill her too.

"You ready for me, baby?"

I know she can't really answer, but I accept her muffled groan and adjust the grip of my left hand around her upper arm. My knees on either side of her, I guide my cock through her slick seam.

Emily's muscles tremble like she's about to come, and I can't fucking restrain myself any longer. Gripping her tight, I sink into the hilt.

Unlike Ash, I have no patience to go slow. After our hips meet on my first thrust, I rail her hard and fast.

I feel her orgasm cresting and figure my brother is close too when he increases his pace, a fist in her hair.

Her body jerks on a gagging sound. Her walls clamp tight, and I know I'm done. And so is Ash. He bends at the waist with a roar, thrusting forward a final time.

My hips lock into her. Emily swallows all of him down while the pulsing of her greedy little cunt chokes me as well.

I grant her every drop. Lazily, I rock in and out of her until the last waves of her climax subside.

I'm still at half-mast when I unsheathe myself from her heat and don't have to look at Ash to know he can go another round shortly too.

I put my cock away for now and untie one of her wrists before pulling her up.

"I hope you don't think we're done," I say, laying her out on the pool table. "We're just getting started."

Then I dive between her thighs.

She comes for us on command as we take turns. We have her on all fours, with her knees spread wide on the floor, and bend her over the couch in various angles before returning her to the pool table to finish off.

Well, I already had the pleasure when she gave me head after riding me. Now I'm just waiting for Ash to get his.

"I'm watching, Em," I tell her, her upper body cradled in my lap as I perch on top, one leg bent underneath her, the other dangling over the side.

With her ass off the edge, her body is laid out across the green felt. Ash's hands grip the back of her knees to work himself into her. Each thrust shakes through the table.

My left fist holds the cord that's still tied around her wrists, only now in front, with her arms up by her head. Her black top is bunched around her elbows, leaving her fully exposed and subjected to my depraved gaze devouring her.

"Your ex is a fool for not treating you right, baby girl. Your body is sublime." I stroke my thumb across her plump bottom lip, the same lips that stretched around my engorged shaft only minutes ago.

"He might've been too ashamed to admit it, but I bet he had filthy thoughts about you," I speculate. "About shoving his dick down your throat and watching you choke." My thumb nudges past her teeth with the insinuation, pushing up to the second knuckle.

She works a swallow to adjust.

"I know I have," I confess, sliding over her tongue, the languid back-and-forth motion encouraging her to suck me.

"That first night I saw you, I wanted those luscious lips wrapped around my cock and taking me deep. I knew it'd be heaven." With the slick heat of her mouth enclosing me, my thumb presses down on the back of her tongue.

A prolonged moan vibrates up the entire length of my arm.

I feel myself getting hard for a third time. Her heavy lashes flutter, but her gaze lifts to mine, utterly captivating me.

Her breasts jut up as she arches off the table, and I fantasize about taking the hardened tips into my mouth, suckling her with the same fervor I imparted between her legs.

Ash's grunts cut through my thoughts, and he pushes out a few more thrusts to finally finish.

When I slip my thumb free, my eyes rake over Emily's features. I don't think she came this time. She's exhausted.

I untie her wrists and remove her top while my brother straightens his clothes, then I scoop her into my arms.

She weighs nothing, but the moment I let go of her to hand her over to him, I feel a void in my chest.

Watching him carry her away, I try not to think about him taking her up into the master bathroom off his bedroom to shower and run his hands over her some more. She'll end up in *his* bed, not mine.

Clenching her shirt in a fist, I pick her cute, little shorts off the floor and follow upstairs to clean up too. I got my own shower across from my bedroom; there's also a guest-bathroom and one more downstairs. The basement has a small kitchen and could house a third roommate.

Emily, for example.

Didn't I make it clear her apartment can't keep anyone out? I tampered visibly with the main lock to scare her, but I was careful not to leave any marks when picking the one on her apartment door. I wanted to give her a false sense of security before I struck.

What a rush.

Not quite as good as the look on her face from the dramatic effect of busting through her window, but a close second.

Lathering the body wash up, I give extra attention to my throbbing cock. *How the hell am I so hard again?*

The second my fingers close around the stiff length, her face pops into my mind, her lips parting, eyes on me.

And I recall the suction of her mouth.

Fuuuck! I let my forehead drop to the shower wall…

…but my grip doesn't let go.

Swelling against my palm, I stroke myself to the image of her going down on me.

But it's not the same. It's not enough.

No matter how good it feels, I know I can't finish like that. Not by myself. I never could again after that night.

I rinse and dry off. A towel wrapped around my waist, I grab something from the dresser in my room, then sneak into Ash's.

The door barely creaks as I open it. With the black-out curtains drawn, it's dark inside despite daylight hours.

I find Ash fast asleep, lying on his chest, his head turned, but Emily is face up, the blanket only covering her partially. A bare leg is sticking out, and her glorious breasts are on full display. I can even make out the pink of her nipples.

A smirk curls my lips. I drop my towel beside the bed and tug the sheet away.

Lowering myself down on her, I feather my forefinger over her sealed lips. "Open your mouth for me, baby girl."

Her eyes shutter, and I only see white for a second before her sight focuses on me.

"Mas—"

"Shh." I press my finger to her lips to cut her off. "We don't want him to hear," I say, nudging her mouth open with my bandana.

Emily catches my intent and complies, parting her lips for me to feed her more to keep her quiet.

Her breaths come strained, but she remains relaxed, drawing air through her nose.

"Just like that." I let go of the cloth and open her legs to me. "I don't want him waking up while I'm fucking you right here next to him in his bed."

A whimper carries around the cloth as I slide my cock along her pussy.

I press a kiss to the hinge of her jaw. "Are you sore?" I ask, not indifferent to what we put her body through.

She shakes her head *no*, and I continue trailing more tender kisses down her neck, taking in the feel of her breasts against my chest.

I rock my hips slowly, breaching her opening with only the tip to get her ready.

It's maddening.

I want to sink every inch into her, but I also want to feel her come. I can't rush her body.

Mouth at her throat, I slide my palm to her ass, angling her hip better. "Spread your legs more for me, Emily," I urge as I slide a little deeper this time before retreating again.

Emily releases a soft moan. Tongue swirling across her pulse point, I absorb every tremor my thrusts spur.

The motion of her hips meets mine until the glide turns smoother, and I know she's ready to take me.

I pull back and give her a full thrust.

Another tremor rocks me. Buried to the hilt, I hold my breath, because I don't want to miss this sound. Every time I plunge fully into her, she makes a little choking noise as if still taken off guard by the size of me assaulting her tight passage. But on my next harsh thrust, her body welcomes me, soft, slick, and ready to be claimed with a most primal need.

I speed up when I feel her fingertips scrape across my skin, digging in. "I love your nails on my back," I growl, my face tucked into her neck.

Her muscles take on that preceding tremble before her climax, and a moment later her walls grip me tight, pulsing in an erratic rhythm around my cock.

She's still coming when I pull out and flip her over. Hauling her onto her knees, I plunge into her again from behind, my rough fingers at her clit to keep her orgasm going.

I'm so fucking close.

"Don't stop coming for me, baby girl. Squeeze my cock like you own it."

Her tight pussy strangles me, and I relent. The lightning bolt shoots through me, sending ripples through my groin and thighs as I jerk into her.

Her smile meets me in the dark when I flip her back and pull the bandana out of her mouth.

Emily wraps her limbs around me, and I mold my body to hers. I don't want to leave. I pretend that my brother is not right there. That it's just us.

"How come Ash gets the bigger room?" she prompts, running her fingers through my hair and down my buzzed nape.

Tipping my head to the side, I hold her curious stare. "What makes you think his is bigger?"

"It has the adjoined bathroom. It's a master suite, isn't it?"

"It is." But our rooms are nearly the same.

"So, why does he get the upgrade?"

Because unlike me, he occasionally has a girl over.

I shrug. "Older sibling clause, I guess. I never really cared before."

I roll my hips into her, then drawl in her ear suggestively, "My bed's the same size, though."

"Yeah," she says with a laugh. "I figured."

Emily turns her head to the bunched bandana beside her. "He used your bandana."

She's referring to the night Ash blindfolded her, so we could trick her into having sex with both of us. He said he took it out of the laundry when really I handed it to him as I waited in my room.

"How do you know?" I wonder.

"It smells like you."

A genuine smile forms on my lips. "That's my girl," I say, my fingers tracing the curve of her cheek.

Refocusing on the cloth, I pick it up and loop it around her neck. "Now it's yours," I declare, tying it at the front of her throat.

I like to leave a little reminder for Ash that I was here without him witnessing the deed. I like having her to myself.

Emily's eyes study my upper body, and I know what they're zoning in on in the faint ambient light: my tattoos...

"Are those cigarette burns?"

...and the other marks.

I drop my eyes to her shoulder. Our father added just as many as his *friends*. We got the ink to cover them up, but could never escape the scar tissue underneath.

"I noticed them on Ash too," she elaborates. "You didn't do that to yourself, did you?"

I shake my head listlessly.

"Was it your father? Ash mentioned something."

I bristle. "What did he tell you?" I know he wouldn't say anything. But...

"Only that he thinks he's in prison."

I release a shallow breath of relief.

In the silence that follows, I feel her studying my face. Then her hand reaches for me.

"What happened to you, Mason?" She clasps my cheek, with a touch so tender, so caring... I can't stop the words from spilling out.

"Our father wasn't a good man, Em," I say, meeting her hazel blue eyes. I know if I averted her scrutinizing stare, she'd only dig deeper.

"He was a gambler; dog races mostly," I go on in a blithe tone. "But he couldn't always pay up. We were a way for him to clear his debt. He would lend us out to the loan shark he owed." I shrug a shoulder like the past is long buried and has no more hold on me.

But it does.

It made me what I am.

"You! Mason," Ely's gruff voice prompts where he sits in a chair.

They know how to tell us apart—something I'm not even sure our father can, and definitely not our mother on the rare occasion she's lucid.

I assume they do by our wounds, the scars they leave in our skin. Ash has a cigarette burn on his left clavicle Ely put there himself a year ago.

"Take off your shirt," he orders me, dropping the cigar from his mouth.

It's not the first time, and I do as I'm told, pulling it over my head, and tossing it onto the table between us.

Rap music plays from a speaker in the corner while a pungent mix of alcohol and cigar smoke fills the room.

I watch him narrow his eyes, then cock his head thoughtfully. I assume he's considering where to burn me this time.

His fingers twist the cigar in a loose hold, and I get the feeling something is off before his words hit me.

"Drop your pants."

What?

"What?" I feel Ash flinch beside me, our twin minds mirroring each other.

"You heard me. Whip it out. Give it a stroke." He motions at me with his cigar. "Show us what you're working with."

I don't get it. He wants me to jack off?

I watch him slouch in his chair, raising the cigar back to his lips like it's a casual request.

But I know better.

My stomach churns with dread as I go for the button on my fly and release the zipper. My breaths shake. My hands tremble. But I don't let my fear show. Hooking my thumbs into the waistband of my boxer briefs, I shove them down along with my jeans.

"Well look at that!" Ely exclaims, facing his friends with a nod toward me. "You might got yourself some competition here, Tom. Boy's not even fully grown yet." He takes another drag, expelling a white plume of smoke. "Barely hit puberty," he adds with a laugh before stomping the cigar butt out in the ashtray to his right.

Straightening in his seat, he refocuses on me, fingers laced as he leans forward excitedly. "Go on then. Don't be shy."

Shutting my eyes, I blow out a shallow breath. It's not the first time I've touched myself for the purpose of pleasure, but never with an audience. I don't want to see their faces staring back at me.

My fingers start trembling even more when I close my grip, and I swallow hard, pretending they're not there to get myself through this.

I drag my palm up and down from head to base in a steady motion, the smooth skin shifting beneath my touch. More blood immediately rushes to my dick, rippling through my thighs and swelling the stiff length in my grasp.

It feels so good.

"Stop."

My eyes fly open at the command, and I'm confused for a second. He doesn't *want me to finish?*

"Oh, we're not done here," Ely clarifies, reading the hint of relief on my face.

His eyes are two black pits staring back as his next words shatter me.

"Bend over."

My skin catches fire. My lungs seize. I can't breathe. I've never been so scared in my life.

The men exchange nervous looks. They don't appear to have expected this either.

Ely's eyes drift from me to Ash.

"You sick fuck," I hear his barely audible voice.

"Ely," Jonathan interjects. "They're brothers for crying out loud."

"Give him the toy to use on him, then," he says, motioning to the other man. "And lube it up. It's his first time after all." A dark chuckle trails his comment that scrapes like nails down my back.

"No!" Ash bellows as arms seize him to my left. "I won't. Fuck! I won't fucking do this." His shoes scuff against the ground to fight against Thomas' hold, but we both know it's futile.

Jonathan returns from another room, something in his hand as he comes up to Ash. I can't turn to look.

"Do it," Ely's deep growl challenges my brother when he doesn't take it. "Or one of us will," he drags out.

His lips twitch, and there's a sadistic flicker in his eyes. Ely gets off on his power plays, but it's about more than simply having me raped. He knows how close my brother and I are. He wants to break our bond.

I hear more shuffling of bodies beside me. Ash is as scared as I am. He doesn't know what to do. He can't protect me.

"Perhaps a bit more motivation," Ely prompts, his right hand disappearing to the small of his back beneath his loose fitting shirt.

When he brings it back around to the front, he's clutching the grip of a gun. He casually raises it toward Ash and levels the barrel at his head. "What's it gonna be, boys?"

I'm still just standing there, frozen, my dick in my hand, staring across the table at Ely. I try to swallow the lump in my throat. I know he and his guys won't let us go until I do what I'm told. Until I finish.

My brother falls silent, all fight abruptly drained from him. No, he can't protect me from this, but I can protect him.

So I make the choice for us. I release my grip to push my boxer briefs and jeans further down. Bracing my palms on the table, I bend.

"Good boy." Ely's dark eyes pin me as he lets out a coarse laugh.

I grind my teeth and swallow the building rage in my chest. One day, I tell myself… One day, I'll make him pay for this.

Bowing my head, I screw my eyes shut again and wait. I train my ears on the heavy beats of the music, drowning out everything else around me.

My fingers twitch.

The pressure meeting me is timid at first. Then cool and slick as the object sinks deeper and retreats, stirring a whirl of emotions in me.

I expected to go soft at the foreign sensation, it's wrong, but fuck it feels good. I don't want it to stop.

And I hate myself for it.

My hand wraps back around my throbbing hard-on, and I stroke the entire length slowly, getting the rhythm going.

I should be embarrassed that my dick swells against my palm. That I'm so stiff I ache for the release. But I'm not. Braced on the table, I speed up, gripping myself harder to the point where it almost hurts. Then I let my inhibitions go.

I drop onto my forearm as my orgasm wrecks through me, my legs barely supporting my weight. I can't tell if my eyes are open or shut. For an instant my vision goes black.

When the table underneath me comes back into focus, my sight catches on my brother's left hand braced next to mine.

Deep shame sears a path through my insides.

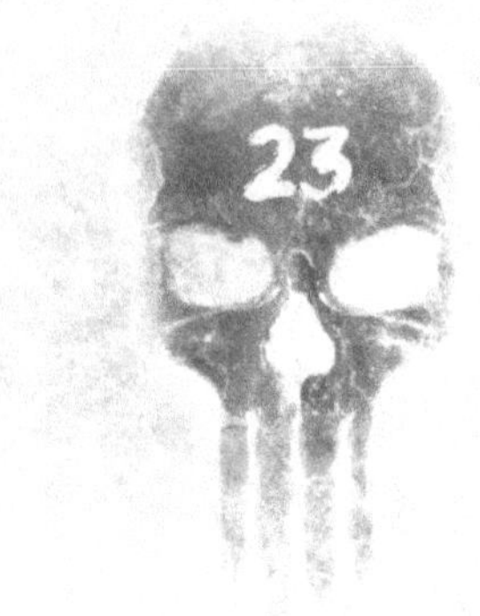

Em

I stand in the guys' kitchen, clutching the jingling bundle Mason tossed me with both hands. "My keys!"

Even without being able to see, I knew the trunk they stuffed me in was way too large to be my compact's.

"We put you in the trunk of ours," Ash supplies. "Mason drove yours. We didn't want you thinking you were forced to rely on us to take you home. And it's not like you can take the bus in your PJs," he adds with a wink, popping another bite of bacon into his mouth.

PJs, which I'm waiting for the dryer to finish after Mason ran them through the laundry. I'm currently wearing one of Ash's T-shirts, feeling the breeze around my business.

"You mean after you dragged me out of bed in the middle of the night?" I point out, watching his grin stretch with glee. "How thoughtful."

And it really is. The guys even woke me with breakfast, despite it being four in the afternoon. In front of me on the kitchen counter is a homemade spread of scrambled eggs, pancakes, and, of course, bacon.

I crane my neck to look out of the window over Mason's shoulder as he leans back against the sink, sipping his coffee, gray sweatpants hanging low on his hips. "Which one's your car?"

"The Impala out front," Ash mumbles around his food.

"Nice. I expected something else, considering the flashy bikes."

He lets out a laugh. "I like the trunk space," he says with a wink.

Taking a seat at the counter beside him, I scan over Mason's tattoos for the first time in daylight. The theme and style of his ink are the same as his brother's, but I see now the skulls are in different positions and depicted from alternate angles. I totally missed that the night the guys pulled the switch on me.

Bastards!

I finish a plate of scramble and two pancakes, plus my own mug of coffee, but it doesn't do much to increase my energy. I can't keep my eyes open.

I know it might have something to do with the two guys who broke into my apartment at 4 a.m. to kidnap me and haven't let me sleep all day—not to mention the physical ache of what they put me through.

Okay, I'm not really complaining about that, but I still feel drained. How am I supposed to make it through my shift?

"Call in sick," Ash suggests, reading my mind when I drop my face into my hands on the counter. "Stay another night."

"I can't." Brushing my hair out of my face, I straighten on my stool with a sigh. "I've never called in sick before. And I need the money. I can barely get enough together for rent as it is."

"Then they're overcharging you," Mason chimes in. "That place is a shithole, and you know it."

"But it's all I can afford at the moment. I've applied to twenty-nine different companies. No one's hiring." At least not me. They want someone with experience in PR or marketing. Something I lack because nobody is willing to give me a chance.

"You should move in with us until you find a new job."

"Right," I scoff and meet Mason's level stare with a note of humor. "And whose bed would I be sharing?"

"Mine," they both reply in one voice.

I laugh. "That's what I thought."

"Fine," Ash groans, setting his elbow on the counter to prop his chin up with his fist. "You choose. We'll take turns."

"Sure you will."

"You don't have to share a bed with either of us if you don't want to," Mason assures me. "You'll have the basement to yourself. The couch is pretty comfy."

Ash tips his head to one side. "How about going into sales? You have people skills, don't you? Being a waitress and all."

"She has a college degree. She's not gonna want to work at our shop," Mason argues, raising his mug then adds, "She'd have to deal with your ass all day," under his breath.

I stifle a grin at the jibe. It's the first time Mason has shown a slice of humor.

I like it.

Pushing off the stool, I let out another sigh. "I'll think about it. But I'm not calling in sick. I'll manage somehow."

———

"Meanwhile, women across the city fear for their lives as the killer remains at large," the blonde reporter stresses with a note of disappointment into her mic.

The case of the strangler continues to dominate every news channel as still no arrest has been made. I can't blame her for being angry at the poor results of the investigation.

I watch the screen of Drew's TV switch back from the on-screen reporter at the police station to the crew at the studio, then turn to discard my apron.

"That cute boyfriend of yours walking you home tonight?" Laura asks.

"No. He cancelled." Ash texted that something came up. I'm low-key glad. I need a break from all their *attention*.

"But it's alright," I assure her, clocking out. "I swear I won't dilly-dally or talk to any strangers." I wink and give her a grin over my shoulder before I push through the back door into the alley.

15 minutes later, I slide my key into the fixed lock of the building's entrance, and another 45 seconds after that, I shut myself up inside my apartment.

I sag against the door for a moment, sighing heavily as I take inventory of my body's aches. I wish I had a tub to soak in. My legs feel like cooked spaghetti.

The conversation in the guys' kitchen this afternoon has been playing in my mind on a loop. After Ash made that first comment about my apartment being unsafe, Mason must've felt compelled to prove his point by breaking in.

Or perhaps he simply enjoys scaring the shit out of me.

I know they aren't wrong. The building is old, has rusty pipes, drafty windows, and sketchy wiring, but it isn't as dilapidated as they make it sound. Power has only gone out here once since I moved in.

It was so easy for him to gain access, though.

A chill of dread prickles over my skin. What if it had been someone else?

Like the one who's been strangling the women... I shudder.

Yeah, I need a better job, and then I need to get out of here, I determine.

I push away from the door and wobble into my bedroom, ignoring the latest rejection letter I received in the mail lying on my nightstand when I drop my keys there.

Despite the mattress calling my name, I want to take a shower first to get the diner stink off me.

Stepping under the lukewarm spray, I remind myself that *I* made the choice to leave an easy ride behind. That I'm here because I wanted to be independent and not rely on others as a crutch.

Ash's offer is not a handout, though; even if it's not exactly what I'm looking for. It's still a job. A better one. With a job at the auto shop, I wouldn't have to work nights anymore. That would be nice.

But moving in with them?

How could I not feel like I'm prostituting myself for a safe roof over my head? For a heater that works consistently? For a hot shower with water pressure? For a fucking bathtub?

Right! I'd much rather give it up for free. *Gotta keep your pride, girl.*

Dropping my forehead against the tile, I let the soft drizzle from above wash away the tears that threaten to well up.

It's not until I open my eyes again, that I notice I'm standing in the dark.

A growl builds in my throat. "Great! Just. Fucking. *Great.*"

I shake my head and shut off the water before snatching the towel from the hook.

At least I already rinsed my hair out.

I give myself a quick pat down to dry most of the water dripping from me, then secure the towel around my chest. With my wet hair hanging in messy streaks down my back, I feel my way into the kitchen where I keep a flashlight and candles.

The hallway is pitch black. I clutch the towel tighter to my body, and my heart rate picks up a notch. I can't see my own hand as my fingertips brush the wall to my right for guidance.

The floor gives a creak under my bare feet.

As I come up to the corner, faint light penetrates the kitchen curtains from the street lamp outside.

I try one of the switches, hoping they might run on a different circuit that isn't affected, but nothing happens. The apartment remains dark.

Another creak from the hallway has me spinning around to face the door I just came through.

Someone's in my apartment.

A freezing cold rushes my skin as I realize I might have walked right past him in the hall without knowing.

I stare at the dark void beyond the door frame, my voice trembling with a flicker of hope. "Mason?"

Oh God, please let it be him.

But I don't get an answer, and when I creep a silent step closer on my toes to peer around the corner, I can't see a thing.

But I hear him breathing.

His gravelly chuckle travels through the darkness directly to my core. "I never said I was going to play fair."

My pulse punches up my throat at the sound of his gruff voice.

The fear is irrational. I know nothing bad is going to happen when he catches me. Just like in the alley. Of course, I remembered his threat. It was all I'd been thinking about since he left my bedroom that night.

Perhaps I was taunting him by walking home alone after work.

And yet I'm so fucking scared.

Mason terrifies me in a way that arouses me. He takes control, and I have no idea what he will do next. His play leaves me an aching, whimpering mess.

"You feel that, baby girl? The hand around your throat stealing your breath… your heart racing?" he taunts. "That's me."

My clit answers with a pulse, and my nipples harden in our standoff. With the rough terry cloth shifting against my skin, I recall the feel of the brick wall in the alley chafing through my T-shirt as he pinned me.

Mason dominates the darkness of the hallway. There's no escaping him.

And I want him to catch me.

Clutching the towel, I lift my chin and step into the hallway—the devil's domain.

Another wicked chuckle commends my courage, rippling through me like all the other times he praised me.

Through the whisper of his clothes under light motion, I recognize the unmistakable flick of his knife, but I don't see his hands. I think he's wearing his black motorcycle gloves.

Then I catch a glint of the blade from who knows where. He wags it in a beckoning gesture.

I swallow, weighing my options. It's a long hallway. He's standing somewhere toward the end by the bathroom and my bedroom, leaving only the front door on my left accessible.

I'd rather be caught dead than locked out of my apartment in nothing but my towel.

I consider diving past him to make it into my bedroom and lock the door. Would he kick it down to get to me?

Since he broke in without making a sound, I'm starting to believe he has a key to my apartment. Would he justify causing that kind of damage?

Where does he draw the line?

I take a timid step, the cold slickness that meets me from below reminding me of my lack of underwear.

Mason mirrors my movement, challenging me, but I still can't make out his face in the dark as he flips the knife in his grip, blade going back instead of out toward me. I assume it's so he won't accidentally stab me.

"You know I don't need to touch you to get you wet, baby girl," his voice reminds me. "You can already feel me fucking you."

Yes, I can feel his greedy hands mapping my curves, nudging between my thighs.

My clit throbs more vehemently. His words hit their mark. He'd hardly have to touch me, and I'd come apart in his hold.

Making my move, I feign right, then lunge left and duck under him—

But Mason is faster. His arms lock around me from behind.

He laughs, mocking my attempt. "Did you really think that was gonna work?"

It's only now that I realize his voice is slightly muffled by something.

"Fuck, you smell good," he groans, nose-diving into my damp hair.

Mason tightens his embrace, and every solid ridge of him from his chest to his hips presses into me.

Then he lets me slip his hold, but not without the cost of my towel. A breeze hits me when he snatches it from my body as I tear away from him and spin around, facing him fully naked, mere inches apart.

That's when I finally see his face.

Or his head at least. His dark blond hair is tousled. His eyes are dark. A black cloth mask covers his nose and mouth with the bottom half of a skull.

Fuck me! He looks so hot.

Mason's breaths fall heavy through the face shield, his intense eyes scanning over every inch of my bare skin.

An inferno rages low in my belly as I watch the heaving of his chest, shoulders lifting and dropping with the motion. He has me questioning my sanity. Every inch of my body screams for his coarse touch… for his hands to squeeze me and his mouth to kiss, bite or suck.

He tips his head, holding up the towel. "Dropped something?"

"Keep it." Without taking the bait, I whirl around to make a second run toward my bedroom.

I don't make it two steps.

I shriek as Mason's hand cuffs my upper arm. He hauls me around and slams my back into the wall.

Alarm bells of a new level ring in my ears. I catch only a glimpse of his masked face before the knife's blade plunges into the drywall up to the hilt right beside my head.

I tremble with the vibration. "Oh God, Mason, stop!" Fear has me in a chokehold. He's taking it too far.

He rips his mask down. "What if it wasn't me?" he rasps, leaning over me. "What if someone else broke into your place to get himself a little piece of you?"

I suck in half a breath before his mouth crushes to mine, his tall muscled body flattening me further against the wall at my back.

He claims me like a hurricane. Unyielding. Unapologetically.

When his hands wrench my legs apart to thrust his hips at me, I bristle in anticipation of his jeans stroking my bare and still-tender flesh.

But instead of meeting the rough texture of his fly, my body melts against his boxer briefs.

Fuck, he's hard under the soft cotton.

Panting and grunting, he grips the back of my thighs to grind himself into me, fast and harsh, every thrust catching my clit. He's close.

God! Fuck! So am I.

His open mouth slanted over mine Mason pants down my throat, "You're so hot and wet, baby. Soak me. Let me feel you come."

I unravel fully under his demand. Meeting his fierce movements, I climax from the most intense dry humping of my life.

Mason follows me over the edge only a second later, the jerking of his hip against mine drawing the last shivers from me.

Lowering my legs to the ground, he rests his head at my temple "Fuck, that was so hot."

I almost laugh at his words. It's what Ash said right after we had sex on his bike in the woods. *Twin minds really work alike.*

"Where's Ash?"

I regret asking the second the question slips out. His brother's name is probably not the first thing he wants to hear out of my mouth after what we just did.

I feel his body tense before he says, "Work." Then he straightens to zip himself up and readjust his sweatshirt.

"At the shop?" *At this hour?*

"No." Mason hesitates, looming over me but no longer touching. "A different job. We freelance."

They have second jobs?

The way his eyes darken before they pull away suggests I don't want to know what it entails.

Perhaps *this* is the job that really pays their bills. The bikes. The house.

I slide my hands up his neck, pulling him back into me. "You are so different from your brother," I remark. *Despite the occasional slip of the tongue.*

He traces my cheek with his gloved fingertips. "And that's a bad thing?"

"No. But…"

"But Ash goes down smooth where as I am an *acquired taste?*"

"Yeah," I agree with a soft laugh.

"And do you?"

"Do I what?"

He lowers his mouth to mine. "Like the taste of me?" he asks, the words feathering across my lips in a murmur.

"Mmmhm."

His eyes drop to the source of my hum. Mason angles his head more, his nose brushing my cheek, and I expect him to kiss me, but instead he straightens.

"Here's your key," he says, fishing the small metal object from the front pocket of his jeans. "After your shift tomorrow, get your ass in your car and drive to our place. Don't make me come get you."

He plants a quick kiss on my lips and stalls for a heartbeat, our eyes locking, a grin pulling at his mouth.

When he swings around and rips the door open, I note that it wasn't locked. Did I forget to turn the bolt, or did he really make a copy of my key?

I wouldn't put it past him to sneak in while I'm asleep.

"Wait!" I straighten off the wall. "Are you just gonna leave that there?"

Hand on the door, Mason's brow furrows, and he looks at me like he doesn't know what I'm referring to. Then his stare shifts to where mine gestured beside my head.

I swear there's a flicker of confusion on his face as to how his knife ended up in the wall in the first place before he steps forward and yanks it free.

I can see the effort it takes in the tension of his body. He really jammed it in there.

"Sorry about that," he says, retracting the blade and storing it back in his pocket. "I got carried away." He shrugs, then spins around to take off.

Carried away and then some, I muse.

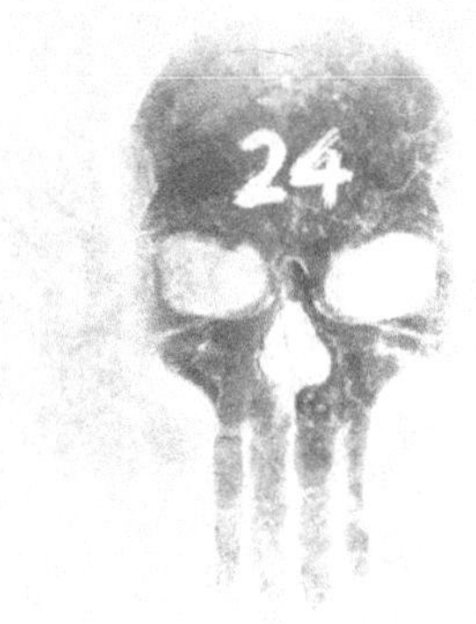

Mace

When the fuck did I draw the knife?

I weave in and out of traffic, my heart racing. It's not the first time I've done something I can't recall—not the first time my hands have acted on their own. If my mind blocked out that part, what else is missing?

I walk my memory through the whole thing again, from cracking open the electrical box outside to finding the one for her apartment to cutting the wires… The knife was in my hand for all that, but I put it back in my pocket before picking the locks.

I *know* I did.

Then I saw Emily, creeping out of the shower, wearing no more than a towel, and then nothing at all. I felt my hand clench into a fist.

Fuck. Fuck. FUCK!

I DIDN'T FEEL THE KNIFE!!!

My fingers squeeze the throttle, and I feed the machine more gas. I still remember the first blackout I had. Or at least what happened before and after the episode.

We never told our father the extent of Ely's *games*. He didn't care what we had to do to clear him as long as it kept him out of trouble with the man.

Ash and I dealt with it on our own. As always. Mostly by staying away.

We hardly spent any time at home anymore in fear of them catching us there when our father's bills came due again.

His luck actually turned around for a while.

But we knew it wouldn't last forever, and 6 months later, they broke down our door and dragged us out.

I rub a hand over my temple. My head throbs. Jonathan's fist hit me so hard I collapsed and saw stars before he grabbed me.

I heard Ash yelling for me to run from the hallway, but I couldn't leave him.

I turn my head toward Ash, sitting next to me on the couch, as Jonathan pours him another shot.

But either he can't hold his liquor as well as I can, or they drugged him because not five seconds after downing it, his body goes limp beside me.

I watch the glass drop.

Ely lets out a little laugh from across the room, and my eyes drift to him apprehensively, my neck too stiff to move.

He gives a nod to Thomas who grabs me by the arm and pulls me to a stand. I feel light headed at the rush of movement, but I catch Ely turning and opening a door before stepping inside. I stumble after him as his guy half-drags me into the next room.

My eyes snap to the bed and I panic. Everything starts spinning when Thomas shoves me toward it. My feet trip. My knees go soft. I fall.

I collapse onto my hands, but whip around in time to see the door slamming shut…

…leaving me alone with Ely.

His black eyes focus on me in a cold, menacing grin, and all blood drains from my face with a tingling sensation.

I scurry back on the mattress, my fists clenching the rough comforter underneath me. Shallow breaths shoot in and out of my lungs. My heart is racing.

"You liked it, didn't you?" Ely starts, his voice like a scrape down my back. "I bet you're going to think about how it felt every time you wrap your hand around your dick to rub one out."

I can't open my mouth to respond. I'm too scared. I'm petrified.

Ely turns and paces a step. My chest heaves as I watch his tall, dark shape move through my blurry vision.

"See, Mason"—*he tips his head over his shoulder, looking at me*—*"pretty little boys like you and your brother could make me a lot of money. If you just…* behaved.*"*

"Behaved?" My eyes narrow. He means complied.

"You know, play nice. *No fighting."*

No resisting.

"Trouble is," he prompts, holding up his forefinger. "I don't think Ash has it in him to submit to anyone. He doesn't cave. He'll be a problem."

Ely stops pacing right in front of me at the side of the bed, his shins touching the edge.

"But you…" he lets his words drift, setting one knee down, then the other. "You know how to play along, don't you, Mason?"

Bile rises in my throat like acid. The mattress pivots. His hands grab my legs.

Flipping me onto my chest, he leans over me, his sickening voice right by my ear as he grates out, "Because what's to keep me from holding a gun to his head again?"

My body goes still. I don't struggle when his hands fumble with my jeans and shove them down. I don't listen to the clanking of his belt and the sound of him spitting into his hand. I don't even feel his hands or the weight of his body on me.

"So tell me," he draws out. "Are you teachable, Mason?"

I don't know what happens after that, I don't pass out, but my mind shuts down to block out the memory. I can't remember anything. The next thing I know is Ely walking me out of the bedroom to find Ash still passed out on the couch.

"Fuck!" I groan, rubbing my hands over my face. I know from the moment I wake up to the sound of rain that I'm going to have a shit day.

And it's not just a little drizzle. A downpour pelts the windows at a sideways angle under the wind, which means I can't ride my bike.

I pound on Ash's door, knowing that unlike mine, his alarm won't go off for another 10 minutes; I like to get to the shop early. "Get up, bitch. It's raining. You got five minutes, or I'm leaving without you," I bellow.

A grin dances around my lips hearing him swear through the door. He's going to have to miss out on his morning shower. Lucky for me, I prefer to shower at night. And I'm considering skipping a shave just to light a fire under his ass.

He knows I mean it. I've done it before, and I already have the engine running when, four minutes and some odd seconds later, he dives into the front passenger seat of the Impala to escape the downpour.

Despite me being as wet as he, I'm brimming with glee as I pull out.

The car is usually parked at the curb. I want the garage space for the bikes. Could I have backed up into the driveway to save him the trip through the rain? Sure. But if I had to make it, so does my brother. He could count that as a shower.

We make it to the shop before Isaac. I get a pot of coffee going first, then pick up where I left off last. I assume Ash does the same. We don't need much directing.

By lunchtime, the rain has let up a little. I hand him the keys so he can go out to get us food while I keep painting through our break. I'm working on a personal project, and I'm not really hungry anyway. My stomach is still in knots about last night.

Keeping my hands steady, I focus on my line work with the fine brush. I'm always meticulous, but this one is special. I'm personalizing Em's helmet.

I don't get to finish the little details in my free time before I have to go back to what I get paid for, so I decide to take it home to put the final touches on with my setup in the garage.

When we close up shop, Ash drives while I finish what's left of my lunch. I've had a few bites in between paint jobs to tide me over.

Music is playing from the car stereo, but we don't need to talk for me to know what's on both our minds.

"It turned out really sick," he says, nodding toward the backseat at the helmet. "She's gonna lose her mind over it."

We're both equally good mechanics, but I've always had more artistic skill than him. I prefer to paint.

"It's not finished," I reply. "I don't even know her favorite colors."

I went with a dark purple and gold theme over matte black, because I think it suits her. Regal, feminine, but also badass.

"Still." He throws me a sideways glance. "It's kinda personal, no?"

That's the point. "Jealous because all you can offer her are finger paintings?"

"Hey, no girl ever complained about me practicing my body painting skills on them," he counters, wiggling his digits in the air between us.

I laugh, because I bet it's true. And because it's for exactly this quirky side that I needed him to get me close to Emily.

It reminds me that I'm the creep. A voyeur. Because all I want to do is go home to get my bike, so I can sit across the street from the diner and watch her through the window while she works, fantasizing about the things I want to do to her on those tables. I don't even care that it's still raining. I'll imagine pushing her jeans down her thighs… her body bending for me… her needy, wet pussy welcoming my throbbing—

"Is she going to come over after her shift?" Ash's voice slices through my daydreaming.

My jaw clenches as I stare through the space the wipers cleared of raindrops on the windshield. If she does, I'll have to share her with him.

"I don't know," I say, becoming aware of the crumbled wrapper in my fist.

Putting my elbow up on the window, I brace my head on my knuckles and scoot lower in my seat.

We stay quiet for the rest of the drive.

When we get to the house, Ash marches inside while I plug in my earbuds and set up my workspace, so I can add the missing highlights.

After the final clear coat, I let it sit to dry and check the time on my phone. Emily is just starting her shift.

Luckily, the rain has stopped completely, and I don't need to change into waterproof gear before heading her way.

My head snaps up from the screen when Ash walks out.

I cut the music. "Where the fuck are you going?"

"I thought I'd stop off at the diner, grab some dinner, and maybe flirt with the cute waitress there."

My shoulders square on reflex, fists balled down at my sides, the right one clenched around my phone. "The fuck you are."

"Why not?"

"Dammit, Ash." I take a threatening step toward him, my right hand coming up between us. "Stay the fuck away from my girl." I can't figure out why he hasn't lost interest in her yet. He should be looking for new pussy to screw by now.

"*Your* girl?" He tips his head back on a laugh. "You keep calling her that, but she made it clear she's not *your* anything. Especially when she's screaming out *my* name. '*Oh, Ash… don't stop*'," he taunts in a feminine lilt, turning to his bike.

My eyes flick to the phone in my hand. *Has he been texting her?*

I have her number too, but only through him. She never volunteered it.

A growl ripples up my throat. "I'm warning you."

He gives me another cold laugh. "Make me," he counters, slipping on his gloves. "Or better yet. Let's race for it. Winner gets to eat out." He reaches for his helmet, not waiting for whether I'll take the bait or not.

With my feet momentarily rooted to the ground, I watch him put his helmet on, then jump into motion grabbing my own.

He turns his back and swings his leg over his bike as I match him, fastening the straps on my gloves. But when we start the engines my phone vibrates in my pocket.

I pull it out to check the screen and see it's a message from Christopher—I have a job.

"Fuck!"

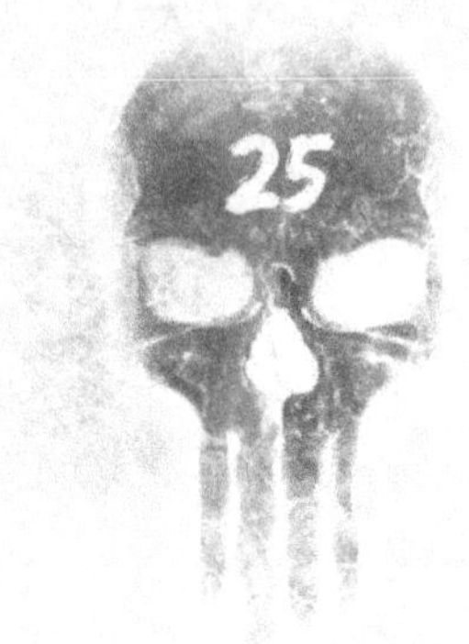

Ash

"Hey, pretty girl."

"Ash!" Emily's bright smile greets me as I slide my ass into a booth.

The diner is packed, and I'm lucky to get the last seat in her section. I was prepared to take on the elderly lady ahead of me, had she not turned to find a spot on the other side.

"You look hungry," she says, sliding a menu across the table.

I back up against the window, my body angled toward her and my helmet on the bench beside me. "Famished." I grin.

"Is Mason not with you?"

I try not to take it personally when her eyes flick to the door to check for him before I can reply.

"He wasn't hungry," I tell her. "He had a late lunch."

Not a lie. But I also saw his text about the job for Mr. DeMarco.

I put my elbow up, leaning toward her across the table. "And I wanted to say sorry again in person about not making it yesterday. I feel really bad for canceling on you last minute."

Emily shrugs. "Don't worry about it. I told you I don't expect a nightly escort. Not by you or Mason." She nods at the menu in front of me. "So, whatcha in the mood for?"

"You!" I meet her eyes, holding her stare. "And eating you out on this table right here."

Fuck! My dick gets hard saying the words out loud. I've been thinking about her wet pussy all day.

A blush shoots into her cheeks, and I watch her throat bob as she swallows back her shock at the shamelessly audacious statement. I bet she felt her little cunt twitch at the remark too.

Embarrassed, she covers her face with a hand and shakes her head.

"Fine." I slide the menu across the table and lean back against the window. "I'll settle for the house burger, medium-rare, side of fries, and iced tea... *for now*," I add presumptuously.

That last part draws a smile from her before she snatches the menu up and leaves to put in my order.

She returns a minute later with my drink, her cheeks still flaring. But as much as I enjoy the pink color on her, I don't want her to ever feel embarrassed about sex. I love her confidence. I want her to own that passionate side of her and the pleasure she gains from it.

I take out my phone to pass the time. As I scroll through the images of scarcely dressed girls the social media algorithm keeps feeding me, I wish I had photos of Emily in provocative poses.

Like when I watched her masturbate on my bike.

The memory of her sprawled out with her legs hiked around me lives rent-free in my mind, but having a live video would come in handy whenever she's not around and I need to take care of things myself.

When she brings my food, I stall her again. "I wanna make it up to you," I prompt, catching hold of her wrist before she can pull it away. "How about I stick around until your break? You can sit with me. Keep me company. I'll buy you dinner."

Her button nose scrunched with a laugh. "My meals are free, Ash."

"Then I'll add it to your tip." Anything to get her to sit with me. I need to convince her to come over tonight.

Emily puts up her hand. "Oh my God, stop. I will *not* accept your money in exchange for my time. I feel bad enough for even considering your guys' offer to stay at your house. Mason shouldn't have given me the key."

"What!" I sit up a little straighter. "When?"

"Last night. When he came over," she clarifies. "He didn't tell you?"

He told me he watched her walk home. He didn't say he went inside her place. *Motherfucker!*

"Of course not." Her head gives a shake, reading my surprised expression. "Here!" Then she digs into her front pocket like she's going to hand me the key back.

"No!" My palms shoot up. "Keep it. I *do* want you to come over," I affirm her. "*Tonight!*" I stab the table with my forefinger. "Or I'll be back here tomorrow for the key *and* the pants you keep it in."

I'll rip them right off her body.

"Alright," she agrees with a soft laugh. "But no waiting for me. I won't have my dinner break for another hour, and I can't stand the idea of you hanging around, watching me while I work."

Oh if she only knew...

"Do you want a second order of that to go?" She motions at my plate, her stance pivoting to leave.

I hesitate for a moment. I don't know when Mason will be back.

"Just the burger. No fries," I decide.

It will be cold, but it's better than nothing, and if I wasn't constantly reminding him, he'd probably forget to eat.

I finish my food. Emily sets the bill in its faux leather holder upright on the table and lingers.

"Can I interest you in dessert? It'll be on me," she tacks on in a teasing lilt.

Oh this woman...

I count out the cash—plus tip—and put it in the holder before handing it back, but I can't keep a straight face as I slip out of the booth. "Raincheck."

Rising to full height in front of her, I tilt her chin up. "But I'll be cashing that in later tonight... and you'll be on the menu," I stress, my thumb caressing her as I add, "with a whipped cream topping."

At the edge of my view, her chest rises as she draws an excited breath, but I don't lower my eyes to her revealing cleavage from my vantage point. Biting my lip, I drop my gaze to her mouth for a second, letting her speculate whether I intend to kiss her.

"Text me when you leave here," I say, then my hand falls as I turn away, leaving her hanging.

———

Right after leaving the diner, I texted Emily to make sure she has the address. I've taken her to the house on my bike twice, but I don't want her to get lost driving out here on her own.

Mason still isn't back. I kept the door to my room open as I fell asleep on my bed. Instead of the sound of his bike, it's her text saying she's on her way that wakes me a little after 3 a.m.

I grab a bottle of water and the blue aerosol can from the fridge in the kitchen. Back in my room, I open my music app, then turn the volume up on the Bluetooth speaker next to my bed to prevent falling asleep again.

20 minutes later, I hear the key in the front door.

My lips curl.

I snap the first shot of her when I see her stepping into the hallway.

She catches the sound of the shutter. "What are you doing?" she asks, moving toward me, a timid grin twisting her mouth.

I'm only wearing a pair of boxers, and with my body facing her as I stretch out on the bed, I'm sure she can tell how hard I already am.

"Taking pictures of you." I hold the phone at a height where I can see both versions of her, the one on the screen and the one coming closer.

Fuck. My cock twitches in response, and she thrives on the attention. She even adds a little sway to her hips like she's modeling on a catwalk. She's so goddamn sexy.

"Make love to the camera, baby," I tell her as her hands come up to her head.

She plays with her hair, fingers dancing around her sensual lips like it's the most natural thing. Mouth slightly parted and eyes hooded, she's a vision of pure lust and seduction.

My hips roll on reflex watching her. Turning sideways in the doorway, she arches her back against the frame, using it to accentuate her curves.

My hands turn sweaty as my skin heats. She's still wearing the skin-tight black tank with her tits bubbling out on top, her jeans hugging every inch of her bottom half.

I want to see her body bend like that naked.

"Strip!" I cue. "Slowly."

I snap more pictures as she moves to the music, teasing me with the gradual release of her zipper and the shimmying down of her jeans.

I love how much she's enjoying this.

I toy with my tongue piercing behind my teeth and answer the urge to reach into my boxers to flick the barbell there.

Moaning, I arch off the bed.

Emily's eyes never stray from me. She's the epitome of confidence as she raises the tank top overhead, and her long black locks tumble down around her face.

I follow the path, mapping the full mounds of her breasts with the distinct hard tips and along her toned stomach down to the gap between her thighs. I take it all in, the rigid length in my grasp stiffening further at the sight.

When her hands and knees hit the mattress and she crawls up to me, I almost drop my phone; my fingers are so slick.

Letting go of my aching shaft, I lie back as she straddles my lap, thighs spread wide for me. She grinds her hot pussy down on my cock, her body undulating with the rhythm of the music, making my head spin.

Her breasts bounce in the lacy black cups that match her bottoms, and my thumb keeps tapping the screen. I can't stop. She whips her hair, dancing for me like she's a professional at a strip club, and I have her in the back room all to myself.

Only it's better because I'm allowed to touch.

Her eyes finally catch the blue can on my nightstand.

"Extra creamy, huh?" She gestures at the Reddi Wip I got from the fridge along with the water bottle.

"My favorite," I note. "Since I got to pick dessert."

A wicked twinkle flickers in her eye. "Are you sharing?"

I grin when I reach for the aerosol can, holding it up. "Knock yourself out."

Emily bites her bottom lip, and my toes curl when her fingernails tease the waistband of my boxers, tugging them down slowly while backing up.

Enjoying the view of my insistent hard-on, she takes the can and gives it a shake. I keep my phone ready. I don't want to miss this.

Her left hand stands me up, granting me a few lazy pumps in her firm grasp. I have to use all my self-control to hold my hips still at the feel of her touch.

With her hungry eyes studying me, she tips the can upside down and aligns the nozzle. But she stalls. Her thumb flicks the metal ring going through the hypersensitive skin below the head.

The anticipation is killing me. More blood pumps into my cock, letting me feel the thrumming pulse against her palm.

Engaging the aerosol can at last, she draws a thick, white line from the piercing across the entire tip of my dick as if to mark a path for her tongue to follow, because in the next beat, she dips and traces the line up.

Holy shit, she feels good. I clutch my phone, my eyes nearly rolling back as her tongue lolls around the head, flicking and swirling with a ravenous passion.

She draws back only to top me with whipped cream again.

Her mouth sinks down over the most sensitive part of the head, and immediately, the heat engulfs me. Her cheeks hollow. She sucks the cream off, then retreats before sliding lower along my shaft.

Ffuuuckk! Instead of taking a picture, this time I hit record. I'm going to want to play this back over and over.

With her lips forming a slick seal, her head bobs up and down, drawing me deep down her throat each time while keeping the suction.

Her hand falls into rhythm, adding to my high.

"Fuck, Em… Don't stop… I'm so close."

My free hand threads into her hair, clasping the back of her neck to go deeper and harder as I pick up momentum. I fuck her throat raw.

My camera is still rolling when my orgasm slices through me. My hips buck off the bed, giving a last thrust so deep she gags around me. I feel the friction at the tip.

My muscles spasm as I relent every last drop down the back of her throat before pulling out to let her swallow.

Stopping the recording, I release her neck and pick up the can.

"Open!" I tell her, readying the nozzle at her mouth. "Tongue out."

Tipping her head back, she does.

Her throat bobs to keep up as I fill her.

"Fuck yes!" I hover over her open mouth, squeezing the can more in my grip. "You look so perfect."

Watching her swallow the mouth-full of whip, I drop the phone and can to pull her back down on me.

Her lips are sweet and sticky. I devour her, one kiss after another, working my tongue in her mouth with the same devotion she granted me.

My arms tighten around her waist. I roll us over, my hips still grinding into her with unrelenting fervor. The strip of lace covering her is drenched, and I'm eager to answer her need.

My hand skates up her back to unhook her bra. "My turn," I rasp, releasing her lips.

Kneeling between her thighs, I straighten and slide the bra off before reaching for the can on the bed again.

I shake it.

With the button pushed, I make two circles, one around each dark pink nipple, then connect them in a curve like a smile across her sternum.

"It tickles," she says as I add another line of thick white along her stomach.

I stop at her panty line and lose the Reddi Wip for a moment while lowering my lips to her. My tongue swirls her nipples first. Then, meticulously slow, I lick and suck all traces of cream down her front to the gap between her thighs.

I pause.

My eyes lift to her, and a guttural sound swells in my throat when I meet her anticipating gaze before I dip.

Em whimpers as I kiss her through the lace. I draw her in, feasting on the sweet scent that's all her. She smells sublime.

But I need more.

I need a taste.

I hook the front of the delicate black material with my forefinger and rip it down in one go. Eyes riveted to her face, my hand recovers the aerosol can blindly.

I don't stall. I can't. The sight of her so ready robs me of patience. I cover her pussy in whipped cream and dive in.

The first curl of my tongue has her squirming against my mouth. I hook my arms around her hips to keep her still, but she bucks like a wild horse as I start to suck her clit.

I hold her tighter, flicking my piercing at the bundle of nerves, then thrusting it up into her slick seam again.

Emily splinters apart against my mouth. I straighten and push my cock into her to feel the last pulses of her climax.

Reaching for my phone on the mattress beside her, I press record again.

I go slow. I want to draw this one out. I'm not going to blow my second load so quickly.

Soft moans tangle in her breaths. I capture every sound, every little whimper my movements force from her. She can't hide it from the camera. Can't hide it from *me*.

Her hips roll to meet my lazy thrusts, her heels pushing off the bed to urge me into a deeper angle, thighs trembling.

I hold back.

I want the friction edging her, but I don't want her to come yet.

And then I pull out.

"Show me how in control you are, Em," I say, taking her hand and guiding it to her pink pussy. "Masturbate for me."

I wrap a fist around the head of my pulsing shaft, squeezing it in my palm as my eyes follow the path her fingers lead.

I match her rhythm. Stroking my entire length from tip to base back and forth, I give her control over my pleasure.

And fuck, she's good. When her middle and forefinger dip into her soft flesh, it ignites a ball of lightning in my stomach. I want to speed up.

"Faster, baby," I hear my own voice say over the rushing sound in my ears.

But Emily's already on it as if she read my mind. In and out she moves her fingers, stroking her clit in the process. She knows how she likes it. Her spine arches, her perfect tits jutting up and her hips bucking to chase the high. She's close.

Her head flings backward, eyes screwed shut and lips parted giving sound to the most exquisite cry of euphoria.

I record until the spasms subside. My fingers are sticky as I click around the screen.

I chuck it, watching it bounce on the mattress in my periphery when I bring her fingers to my mouth and suck them clean. "Fuck, you taste delicious."

I roll her onto her chest and go for the can of Reddi Wip while hauling her hips up.

"Have I told you dessert is my favorite meal of the day?" Shaking the canister, I nudge her knees further apart. "You're about to find out how gluttonous I am."

And then I unload the whipped cream.

My tongue wets my lips. Squeezing her left cheek in my palm, I spread a thick white streak right down the middle just as generously as before to eat it out of her from behind this time. Not a speck of pink is left.

I drop to my stomach. Em arches her back, throwing me a shocked look over her shoulder. "Oh my God, Ash… you're not going to—"

But her words cut off when I trace her seam in one long lick.

A heady moan replaces her alarm. Gobbling up the sweet cream by the mouthful, I dive in between her lips, swirl my tongue, and retreat to make another pass. My sweeps are thorough. I clean every last bit.

The can has rolled off the bed, and I use both hands to open her up to me.

"Ash!"

The sound of my name rings on in my ears, and I feel her pucker against my tongue when I drag the tip up the crease of her ass, but I won't be denied.

"Oh God…"

Her cry coaxes a growl from me. With light pressure, I circle her rim, squeezing her ass harder before I dive into her slit again.

Em squirms. Her legs tremble.

I flick my piercing over her clit and seal my mouth to her as my teasing triggers another climax.

I pull back, then push up behind her.

Straddling the back of her thighs, I bend over her and cuff her wrists. With most of my weight braced on my forearms, I rock my hips into her ass, my dick perfectly nestled in the crack. She's slick from the oily residue of the cream, and my skin slides against hers as smoothly as if I were already inside her.

She grinds back, countering me.

"Does my girl want to get fucked some more?" I drawl, my voice hoarse against her cheek.

Her affirmative murmur hums through me like a tuning fork. "Mm-hmm."

"Let me hear you beg for it."

"I want your cock, Ash."

My head gives an amused shake as I chuckle. "That doesn't sound much like begging, baby girl." *More like a demand.*

"Didn't you want me to show you how in control I am? Well, this is me… *taking control.*" She wiggles her ass underneath me to emphasize her point.

She's not wrong. And I kinda like it.

"Alright." I lift off, my right hand reaching for my phone. "Let me see you take it then."

I'm keeping this video for later use too.

I spread her legs into a wider stance and adjust my own knees for balance. Aligning myself at her entrance, I push in just the tip, then press record on the screen.

A breath bursts from her lips as her tight cunt welcomes me back. With my left hand at her side for leverage, I thrust my hips at her, my cock spearing her up to the hilt.

Emily trembles. Every time I retreat and plunge in deep, I force more whimpers from her.

But she *does* take it.

Her body readily absorbs the ruthless assault of my thrust, and fuck, does she feel good.

My grip on her waist slips from my building momentum. She's so fucking slick everywhere.

My hand leaves her side. With a turn of my wrist, I settle it at the base of her spine.

When my thumb traces the crease of her ass down, she reads my intent.

Her voice trembles. "Ash…"

I can't tell if it's disapproval in her tone or her heightening arousal.

I circle the hole greedily with more pressure, holding my breath. "Yes or no?"

"Yes," she groans, clutching the sheets in her fists. "Fuck. Yes."

I exhale. "That's my girl… taking it in both. That's my good fucking girl," I praise, nudging my thumb into her.

The glide is smooth, lubed by our combined arousal and the cream that dripped down her cunt. Her body makes it easy. Her tight rim stretches to swallow what I give.

Emily's muscles twitch. Her movements grow stiff, and her breaths turn to short huffs. She's going to come.

But the moment her walls clamp down on me and her lungs release that exquisite cry of ecstasy, it's not the only thing I hear.

My ears catch the sound of a distinct roar.

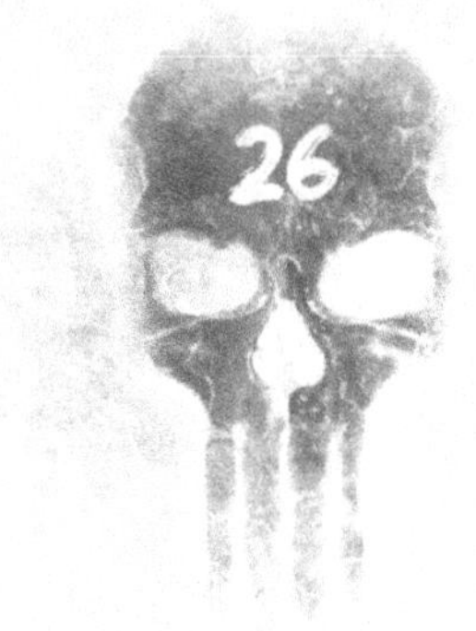

Mace

Since we're on call for Mr. DeMarco at all hours, I always have a mask and a lock-pick kit in my backpack ready to go, not to mention my knife, but this job couldn't have come at a worse time.

After stopping off at the club to get instructions from Christopher, I'm on my way to a remote location at least 45 minutes out of the city through rush hour, and to say that I'm pissed about it is an understatement.

Why couldn't it have been Ash to get the job?

Following the GPS into the woods in the middle of nowhere, I close in on the coordinates ahead of me—a single two-story house surrounded by trees. I can tell from the distance it's neither extravagant nor dilapidated, and my first thought is that it's a temporary safe house of sorts.

I creep closer. I don't see any visible security cameras, and only one vehicle is parked out front. A black Jeep Wrangler.

I dismount and transfer what I need to the smaller pack strapped to my thigh before scoping the place out.

According to Christopher's intel, there's supposed to be one guy on the second floor guarded by a security detail, but

I never know what I'll find once I get inside. I need to be prepared for anything.

With my black Hayabusa hidden out of sight and mask in place, I ghost through the trees. My directions are to drop the man upstairs and pin a note to his chest, then get out without being seen.

Easy enough.

My eyes scan over the drawn curtains. The top floor appears dark, but there's a light on downstairs.

Dropping to a crouch, I watch the windows for signs of movement, my ears perked.

Other than the occasional hoot of an owl, it's quiet.

I decide to make my move. Staying low, I sneak around back to find a point of entry away from what I assume is the living room. With my boots no more than a whisper across the grass, a man's heavy snore reaches me over the indistinguishable mumble of a TV where the only light in the house is coming from.

I pass some basement windows and keep the option in mind in case I don't find the access I'm looking for in the rear. I'd rather not go through the entire house, guard sleeping on his watch or not.

But as I clip the corner of the cabin, I'm in luck. My eyes travel up to a small balcony approximately 15 feet in the air, and my heart gives an excited kick behind my ribs. It'll get me straight to the second story.

I throw another quick glance over my shoulder, then back away from the house a few feet and take a running start at the exterior wall. Pushing off the ground, my left boot meets brick first, immediately followed by my right as I keep going vertical.

On the last step, I kick off my right foot to push myself left toward the balcony. My fingers reach just high enough to catch the bottom ledge. With a better running start on concrete, I could've managed more altitude.

Swinging my legs, I pick up momentum to launch my body higher, and this time my grip finds the railing.

With my toes secure on the balcony's ledge, I straighten and climb over while training my sight on the window. There's a gap in the curtains, allowing me a view into a dark bedroom.

On closer observation, I determine it's empty. The man I'm looking for must be in another.

When I move silently toward the sliding door, I notice the two lights hanging on either side. They're turned off, but I reach up and unscrew both lightbulbs just a tad to make sure they won't come on to put me on display.

Slipping my hand into the pack strapped to my thigh, I retrieve my tools and drop to my knees in front of the door to pick the lock.

I feel it turn over more than I hear it. I'm all about touch, which is why I work so well in the dark.

As long as my mind doesn't disconnect, that is.

I slide the door open and squeeze in before tugging it shut again behind me, but before I can take another step, I catch movement in the hallway.

The door to the bedroom is open to the second-floor landing, where a shadow slithers along the ground.

My pulse remains flat. I've done this too many times. There's no thrill to it anymore.

I creep closer to peek around the corner, my hand hovering over my pack. A man matching my mark's approximate height and weight moves from the room next door toward the stairs, his back to me, but I can't tell for sure he's the guy. I need to see his face.

Completely hidden in the darkness of the room, I watch him round the banisters, and when he turns to descend the steps, I get my confirmation; he's the target from the surveillance footage Christopher showed me—Alexander Bates, aka the snitch.

I linger in the spare bedroom until I know he's reached the bottom.

As I take a step into the hallway, I hear him yelling at the sleeping man downstairs. Under the disguise of the argument's volume, I slip into the bedroom my target vacated and plant myself behind the open door to wait for him to return, however long it might be.

I listen to the fridge opening and closing, chairs being dragged on the hardwood floor, dishes moving. It's an agonizing wait.

At last I hear his steps ascending the stairs.

My fingers flex around the cylindrical shape ready in my fist as his footfalls draw closer. I briefly consider the possibility that he's carrying a sidearm he could shoot me with. My standard knife is sheathed at my back, but I have a second, smaller one inside my boot. Other than my hands, those are my only weapons.

I watch his shadow grow in the faint ambient light of the hallway. The moment he steps in and slams the door shut, I jump him.

With my left arm over his shoulder, I pin him to my chest and stick the needle into his neck.

He never even sees me.

As I push the plunger down, I rely entirely on Christopher's information regarding the contents of the syringe. If it's anything other than a sedative, he might not go down at all or just drop dead in front of me.

I'm fully aware of the risks. Every time I do this, there's a chance Mr. DeMarco plans to set me up for murder or have me killed in the process. I know too much to be taken in by the cops.

Ash and I never exchange details about our individual jobs. I don't know whether they call him for different tasks than what they require from me, and that might be the reason I'm here instead of him.

Would he take a blind chance with the syringe and put himself at risk like that?

Bracing the unconscious man's weight, I lower him to the ground quietly, to not alert his guard downstairs with the sound of a body dropping.

I give him a shove to roll him onto his back and retrieve the note with the message:

Still think I can't get to you?

The pin I'm using to attach the paper to the man's shirt is one from Mr. DeMarco's personal collection. The sender of the message is obvious.

I push off and retreat the same way I entered. Slipping out through the balcony door, I screw the light bulbs back in before sliding down the brick wall.

As I take off toward my bike, I glance back at the lit first-floor window. There's no sign of motion. No sign I was ever here other than the note on my target.

After gulping down the bottle of water I keep in my backpack, I put my helmet on and push my nearly 600-pound machine a little bit further until I'm sure I'm out of earshot.

Before starting the engine, I pull out my phone to text Christopher that it's done. I set it to silent with even the vibration turned off so it wouldn't distract me or give me away. I'm surprised to see that it's lit up with texts from Ash.

I open the app.

Heart pounding out of my chest, I stare at the words, 'Thought you wanted to be included', along with several pictures.

And one 42-second video.

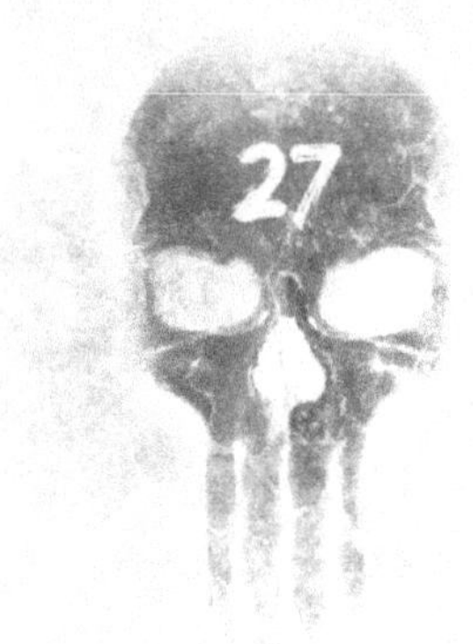

Em

A sh throws his phone onto the pillow and whips us around until I'm on top straddling him, my hands braced on the mattress by his head.

The swift maneuver has me crashing into his chest while it takes him no time at all to align himself. In one thrust he seats his cock inside me again.

I've barely drawn a breath.

His splayed hands on my ass spread me open as his hips come up, pumping his stiff length into me with the efficiency of a piston. He's in full control, and all I can do is take it as he holds me steady.

At the angle he keeps my hips locked, he pounds my G-spot at a quickening pace. I'm going to come again. The pressure builds so rapidly.

"Ash!" His name bursts from my lungs as forcefully as the orgasm ruptures in my core.

"Yes, baby. Come for me," he pants, the punishing force behind his thrusts unyielding.

My walls squeezing him, adding to the slick suction linking our bodies despite his pace tapering down.

Still going deep, Ash shifts his hands. He flattens me to his chest, an arm like a vise around my middle.

His wandering touch prowls up and down the crease of my ass until his fingers linger where he's not filling me yet.

He pushes in.

"That's two fingers now, baby girl," he says, the hoarse texture of his voice scraping along my jawline. "Do you think you can fit more?"

I'm almost ashamed to admit.

"Yes," I moan, rolling my hips in anticipation.

I feel him stretch me with a third. He moves them in and out, working me open further.

"You're a needy girl, aren't you, Emily? You like the pressure. One cock filling your cunt isn't enough."

I tip my head back, getting pulled under by the exhilarating sensation of his play when his voice drones on, "Can you take another?"

My ears stop tracking Ash's words. I hear a sweatshirt drop, and then a second pair of hands is on me, kneading my breasts, demanding to be filled. His fingertips delve into my flesh.

"We'll make it fit, won't we, baby girl?"

Mason! My breath hitches.

Pumping steadily in and out of me, Ash trails hot kisses along my jaw. "You will let us fuck you at the same time, won't you, needy girl?" he groans. "You want to feel both of us."

My ears perk to the sound of Mason's movements as his hands leave me: the unfastening of his belt and fly, the whisper of clothes sliding over skin.

Oh God! What am I doing?

I ball the sheets in my fists and respond with an apprehensive nod. I know they don't intend to hurt me, but I'm not sure I can do this.

Ash ceases his thrusts and retracts his fingers to give way for his brother, his broad hands settling their grip at the outside of my thighs instead.

Mason's thumb circles me with purpose. "Did he get you ready for me?"

I whimper under his persistent teasing. His touch is cool and slick—slicker than the residue of the whipped cream. He's using lube.

Repositioning his hand at my hip, he aligns the thick head of his cock and enters me.

I tense. My body stretches to adjust to his respectable size, but I'm scared. He can't possibly fit all—

Mason gives another languid push, and a cry weaves through my juddering breaths as my muscles tremble to accommodate him.

But he has no intention of retreating. Bending over me, weight braced on the mattress by his right arm, he drops his forehead on my shoulder and sinks gradually deeper, inch by thick inch.

Ash feels the shift too. His mouth hot at my throat, he groans underneath me, the matching size of his hard length already filling so much of me.

They're too big.

"Oh God, I can't."

"Easy," Mason's voice rasps across my skin. "I told you, you're made to take me." And then he gives one more smooth push, seating himself fully inside me with a final grunt.

I bottom out. My mouth opens, but no air moves in or out.

"Breathe, baby girl," he reminds me.

Mason doesn't move. Feathering kisses along my shoulder, he waits for me to relax.

I draw air into my lungs, and my tension flees on the exhale.

Rocking in and out in a slow rhythm, Mason's hand leaves my side to rove my breast while Ash keeps a firm grip on my hips, guiding me over the length of his shaft. Each drive strokes my clit.

His back arches to force his thrusts deeper, and I don't miss his amused lilt. "Do you feel full now?"

A snicker chases Ash's question, but as they use my body for their own pleasure, they give so much in return. I bend to their whim—to their demands of me—and with the friction of both of them working in tandem sliding along my walls, they edge me toward my climax. They feel so good; I can't fight it. My muscles stiffen.

Mason rails my tight passage with more urgency. "Fuck! Em… I'm so close," he pants, his body trembling like mine. "Come for us. Let us feel you shatter, baby girl."

The timbre of his voice bursts the dam holding me together wide open. I cry out on his command, convulsing as I let the waves of ecstasy crash over me.

A curse under his breath, Ash's hips buck, and then Mason too locks into me with a roar that lights me up from the inside before it ricochets off the walls.

It wouldn't surprise me if the neighbors heard that.

Half collapsing onto Ash and me, Mason drops his forehead back on my shoulder for several breaths, his skin slick with sweat and bangs drenched.

Then he pulls out.

His pants are back in place before he lifts me off Ash, and I don't think I could walk if he gave me the option, but gathering me in his arms, Mason carries me into the shower.

He doesn't bother with the switch by the wall. Mason drops my feet to the ground while keeping one arm wrapped around my waist until he gets the water temperature right. Then he ushers me in.

Steam rises in my vision. I back up but don't shut the glass door. The bathroom window's foggy texture lets in just enough light from outside, and I watch him undress with growing excitement. His well-defined muscles flex under his movements, stirring the ache to touch him.

My hands come up as he joins me. With the hot spray slicking his skin, I run my palms over his chest, his broad shoulders, his back. I draw him to me.

Lowering his lips to mine, Mason sinks into my touch. His contours fuse with mine, soft curves molding to muscles of steel.

We both moan.

One of his hands tangles in my hair while his arm around the small of my back arches me against him. His heated skin sliding across mine is everything I need right now. My knees may never carry my weight again. I feel like I'm floating.

When I link my arms around his neck, Mason angles his head, parting my lips with his and sinking even deeper into my embrace.

Holding me to his chest, he kisses me like he hasn't gotten his fill yet. Like he never wants to stop kissing me at all. He cruises the shape of my mouth with sensual care as if he's studying me.

He drifts lower, nudging my head back to access my throat as more heat builds between us.

"You have to go to work in a few hours. Shouldn't you be getting some sleep?"

I'm sure Ash has already passed out.

Mason straightens, but his dark, hooded gaze doesn't waver one bit in its intensity. "Sleeping is the last thing on my mind right now."

He reaches for Ash's body wash, and my arms fall from his neck as he squeezes some onto his palm.

After lathering it between both hands, Mason returns his attention to my naked state in front of him. He starts washing me. Tracing the shape of my breasts, he leans into my body, skating his touch over me slowly with such care and reverence I didn't know he could impart.

I grip his shoulders.

His lips hover over my cheek as his head leans against mine. He's not kissing me, and yet it feels like his tender caress is an extension of his mouth traveling my skin.

And then his fingertips dip in between my thighs.

I suck in a breath when his soapy touch slides over my flesh to stroke my clit in deliberate little circles. Each new smooth glide of his finger incites a tremble before I come apart for him once again.

The pleased hum emanating from him vibrates through my chest. "That one was just for me," he declares with a dark edge.

Then he retracts his touch.

Gripping himself, he pumps a lazy fist over his invigorated hard-on with the remaining body wash.

"Am I going to get to watch you rub one out this time?" I muse suggestively.

"No."

"Why?" My shoulder gives an easy shrug. "All guys do it."

"I don't!"

There's a bite to his voice when he says it, but then his tone softens. "I got girls for that," he adds.

I don't doubt that.

Mason reclaims my mouth, and then his hands slide over me again, gripping the back of my thighs to brace me against the wall as his hard length fills me in one thrust.

Soap suds make our skin slick. He works himself into me over and over in smooth motion that grants me all the friction of his top ladder piercings while I cling to him.

His ragged breaths drop to my throat. With my limbs wrapped around his flexing muscles, I welcome everything he gives.

It's beautiful.

It's perfect.

And when we both climax together, I don't want to let go. I want him to hold me like this… in his bed… our bodies entwined.

Mason pulls out and sets me down, his panting breaths evening out before he rinses us off.

I guess he's ready to catch those *Z*s now. He grabs a towel for himself from the cabinet, then hands me a second that's a matching shade of dark blue.

I shut the water off and take it, wondering for a second whether the ones in his bathroom are a different color—black probably. Like his wardrobe.

Wrapping the oversized terry cloth around my chest, I step out and let him sweep me up into his arms again.

A chuckle winds through me.

As Mason carries me from the bathroom, I catch a glimpse of Ash in the dark, sprawled out on his stomach, and, of course, fast asleep.

He's also still buck-ass naked.

Stifling another grin, I refocus my eyes on the door instead of his rear. But Mason's grip on me shifts before I realize what's happening. He bends over his brother's bed to lower me down beside him.

Confusion stuns me as the mattress dips with my weight and his arms pull away. He doesn't even meet my eyes before he straightens and walks out.

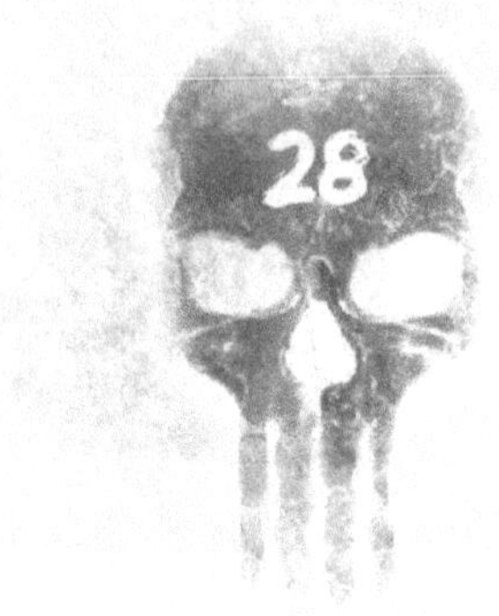

Ash

I drop my backpack by my feet and slam the metal door shut.

Mason's fist comes flying at me the second I turn around. I narrowly dodge its trajectory by ducking. It crashes into the locker behind me instead.

"What the fuck is your problem, man?" I straighten and square off with him. *I'm only 10 minutes late.*

But who can blame me after finding Em naked in my bed this morning? *Totally worth it.*

Mason seizes the front of my shirt and yanks my face toward him. "You know damn well what my problem is," he grates out.

I chuckle. "What, you didn't like the pictures?" I figured since he couldn't be there in person. "You seemed to get there just in time."

"Argh!" Mason's eyes flare with his roar as he shoves me back against my locker. His fists flex. His jaw twitches under tension.

"Get your fucking fill already and move on," he snarls.

His grip releases me, and I stare after him as he storms out.

What the actual fuck?

Charging at the door, I catch it before it slams shut. "Hey, maybe you should consider taking a half day and go home to sleep it off!" I shout after him. "And when was the last time you ate?" *Cranky-ass bastard.* His food from the diner was still sitting in the kitchen this morning. Untouched.

Mason's arm swings back, and he raises his middle finger at me as he keeps walking away.

I shake my head. He doesn't want to share? Fine. But *move on?*

I have no intention.

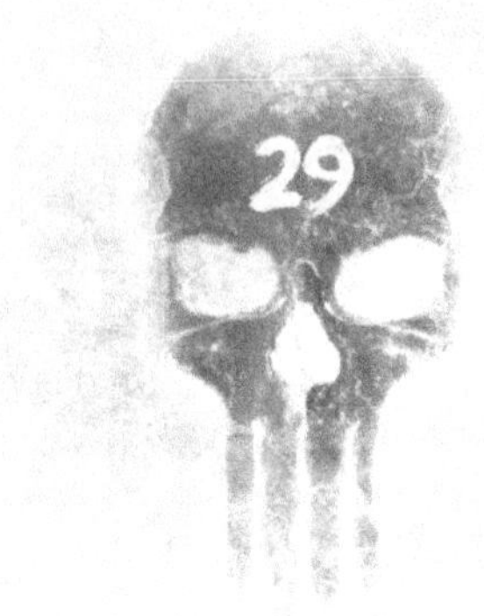

Em

"No, Mom. I'm fine," I groan into the phone for the millionth time. "Really."

My mother's call woke me shortly after Ash left for work. She's heard about the recent string of murders on the news and wanted to make sure that I'm not being reckless with my safety walking at night.

I couldn't confirm the 'not being reckless' part, but I *did* assure her that I was safe, and luckily she didn't press for details. I didn't want to mention that instead of *one* guy watching out for me, I have *two*.

I catch a rustle through the speaker as she adjusts the phone by her ear while shuffling around the kitchen. A pan sizzles over fire. She's cooking breakfast.

"I ran into Nate the other day at the farmers market," Mom chitchats on in a merry tone. "He was with his new girlfriend."

I hug Ash's comforter closer to my naked body, feeling suddenly exposed. "Good for him," I reply. "I'm glad he's moved on."

I harbor no ill will toward Nate. It took me a long time to realize we weren't a good match, and calling our engagement off was as much for his benefit as mine. Still, I feel a twinge in my stomach.

"Her name is Sarah. Lovely young woman. She owns a pastry shop in town."

My mother's words come out offhandedly, but something strikes a chord. I wonder if she considers me a failure. I'm broke, I live in a crappy apartment, and I'm stuck in a minimum wage job with no prospects of getting out any time soon.

"I invited them over for dinner this weekend."

The fingers of my free hand curl toward my palm involuntarily, bunching the soft fabric in my lap as I swallow the bitter taste in my mouth.

I force my voice soft. "How nice."

I think I'm gonna be sick.

"Soooo," Mom drawls inquisitively, "What about you? Are you seeing anyone?"

I knew the question was burning on her mind, but I won't disclose my current situation with her. I know she will disapprove and think I'm a whore for my choices.

Was I seeing someone? Yes. But…

"I'm not dating anyone," I reply on reflex.

"Oh well. I'm sure you'll meet someone soon. You've only been there a short while," she reasons. "Are you coming home for your birthday? We would all love to see you."

My shoulders sag with a long sigh. I shake my head. "I don't know."

My birthday is still a few weeks away, and I haven't yet decided whether I want to take a few days off to make the long drive.

Especially now that my parents have replaced me.

I sit up straight. "Listen, Mom, I gotta go," I tell her to end the call.

"Oh, okay, honey." Her hair whispers into the phone with the abrupt shift in her posture. "Call soon, alright?"

"I will. Love you."

"Love you too."

I hang up and drop my phone into my lap. It shouldn't have surprised me. My parents have always loved Nate and treated him like a son. Even without me by his side, they still consider him family.

I was the broken one.

They resented me for calling things off. There had to be something wrong with me. In their eyes, he was perfect—handsome, polite, successful. Why couldn't I make it work?

Maybe there really *is* something wrong with me, I reflect, but I'll be damned if there isn't someone out there who can match my freak.

I swing the comforter off my legs and slip out of bed to get dressed even though I still have hours to spare. Since my mother's call woke me early, I figure I can take the opportunity to do some sleuthing.

I still haven't seen Mason's room.

Gripping the handle, I pause briefly in anticipation of it being locked, but it isn't, and I'm somehow relieved that he doesn't feel the need to hide things from me. He knew I'd be alone here while they're at work.

I swing the door inward and meet the darkness beyond like it's an extension of him. It's one thing I expected of Mason.

But the first thing I notice after the thick blackout curtains and black sheets is that it's very clean. Even tidier than Ash's room.

I give air to a little snort. A *neat freak* is not what I took him for.

I don't switch on the light as I enter. I have a feeling he doesn't either, and I want to see it the way he does.

Mason wasn't lying when he said his room matches Ash's in size. My eyes sweep the space. He has several shelves with books, ranging from the mechanics of cars and motorcycles to various styles of art, but there are also volumes of classic literature. A soft grin teases my lips, and my finger tips the spine of Mary Shelley's *Frankenstein* affectionately before I let it fall back into place.

Everything is sorted by type and alphabetized. Very organized indeed.

I turn toward the open door of his closet. The walk-in is also spacious despite it not being the master suite. Various pairs of black boots and dark cargo pants as well as jeans fill the space.

I flip through the hangers of shirts. From what I can see, his style is the same as Ash's, though Mason's attire is distinctly darker. His brother wears colors other than black.

As I exit the closet and give the room another browse, it strikes me that there are no drugs of any kind that I can see. Not even a bong. No alcohol either.

My eyes land on the yellow and red bottle of cologne on the dresser to my right. I pick it up, brushing my thumb over the Creed logo on the front.

I recall the first time the fragrance licked through my airways—how it invaded my senses and overrode my inhibitions. The man owned me before I even knew who he was.

I pull the cap off. As I lift the bottle to my nose, heat rushes my body. The distinct scent of Mason pulls me into an embrace, and I instantly feel myself melting.

My body begins to throb fiercely with the memory of him filling me everywhere. The empty space between thighs aches for his touch, and while I'm still clutching his cologne, my free hand answers the call.

Leaning back against his dresser, I stroke myself over my jeans. I consider taking care of my need right here in his bed. He would never know.

My fingers hover over the button. My eyes catch sight of the plastic LED mask on his nightstand, and an idea forms in my head.

But I have to stop off at home for a minute.

251

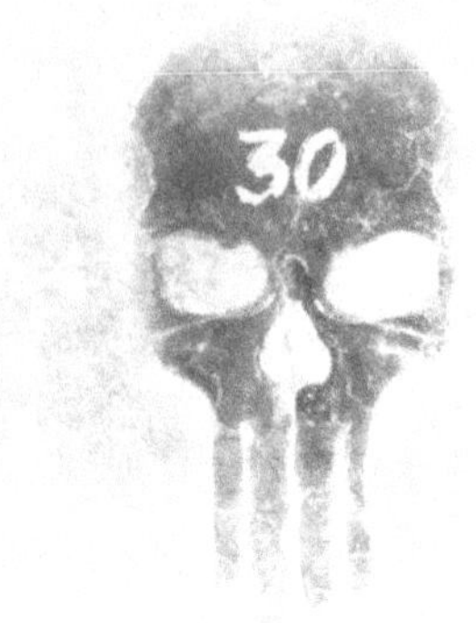

Mace

I head out for lunch to get away from my brother. It's a miracle I lasted this long in the same building with him, but getting his food?

Fuck that! He can get his own.

My anger threatens to surge again at the reminder of last night… the pictures… the video.

I've never felt so possessive over anyone. I wanted her out of that shitty apartment, and if that meant she'd be around my brother more, I thought I'd be okay with that. At least she'd be safe.

Until I saw them together.

But I don't get it. Yeah, we've fucked the same woman before, at the same time or on separate occasions, and it's never been competitive. They didn't care whose dick was railing them, and we didn't care whose name they cried out when they climaxed. It was sort of funny. We don't even have the same taste; Ash likes blondes, where I prefer dark hair and bright eyes.

So why her? What makes Emily so special?

A tremble runs up my forearms as I brace my weight on the handlebars, and I ease up on the throttle. It already requires all of my focus not to wrap myself around a tree when I'm driving this angry. Add the lack of sleep, and the chances of my ride becoming a suicide mission double.

I make it to the soba house, a place I frequent more than Ash, in one piece. Shaun, the owner and one of my few friends, greets me from the back and puts in my usual order as I seat myself at the counter.

It takes me mere minutes to inhale my meal. With my elbows propped on the edge, I rub my eyes. I dread having to return to work. Perhaps I should take Ash's advice to head home and get some sleep.

What are the odds that Emily is still at the house?

I shake my head at the thought. My brother's bed is the last place I want to find her.

I drop the cash for my meal onto the counter. Rising from my seat, I say my goodbye to Shaun and leave. My ride is parked in the small lot behind the building that's only used for staff, but he doesn't mind. I prefer to keep it out of sight.

As I make my way around, my thumbs type out a text to Ash. It's only when I feel eyes on me that I lift my gaze from the screen to my bike.

Fuck me!

I almost drop my phone at the sight. Straddling the seat of my Hayabusa is a very familiar girl in a black and pink skirt, a black tank top, and matching combat boots, wearing an equally familiar LED mask.

Mine.

"Look at you, taking a page out of my playbook. You're a bad girl, Emily." I stuff the phone into my back pocket and swing my leg over the bike to slide on behind her.

I tip the mask back to see her face underneath.

A wry smile meets me, sucking me down a rabbit hole I have no desire to ever emerge from. I want to drown in her hazel blue stare.

Em reaches up and draws my chin toward her mouth, her back arching against my chest. "You have no idea how bad," her voice rasps.

Her teeth graze my jaw, and my grip tightens around her middle. "I'm not wearing any panties," she drawls in a husky whisper.

The words carry to my cock before they reach my ears. A shockwave detonates in my groin. *Her sweet, pink pussy is spread out over my bike in public?*

Her admission and that teasing edge in her voice have my head spinning. When the fingers of my right hand dip underneath her skirt in the front to confirm, I nearly tip us over at slick contact. She's already so wet from the friction of riding the seat.

Emily leans forward before my mind can form another thought. "But I'm wearing something else." Lifting the back of her skirt, she bares her ass to me.

Ffuuucckkk! I groan when I see the jewel stud of her butt plug.

"I really have corrupted you, haven't I?" My left hand drops from her waist, my thumb nudging the toy. "Did you think of me when you slid it in?"

"Yes," she moans.

Mmmh. I love the rough sound of her voice.

"Did you imagine it was my cock stretching your tight, little hole?" My dick swells as I grind myself into her. I want to feel her come on my bike like that even if I'm not inside her.

"Yes." Another moan pours from her lips.

"You felt so good, baby girl. I want to fuck you like that again," I groan, my hips rocking against her encouragingly. "I want to bury every inch of my cock in your ass."

Em's slick pussy glides across the leather seat. Tremors carry from her body into mine, edging me to my own climax.

Reaching around her, I turn the ignition but keep the bike in neutral. "Grip the handlebars," I tell her.

Stretched out over the gas tank, Emily's fingers curl around the rubber grips. I can't help thinking of them closing around me instead, a fist pumping the stiff length in a steady motion.

My tongue licks across my parted lips. "Feed it some gas with your right hand," I say, the words catching in my dry throat.

I'm so hard right now. The vibration of the engine between my thighs is going to tip me over the edge.

"Fuck my bike, baby girl," I grit out through my teeth, my jaw tight. "Don't let go."

I grip her ass, my thumb teasing the plug while she grinds her cunt against the leather. I want her all over the seat.

My right hand feeds into her movements. If someone caught us, all they'd see is me grinding on my girl.

I watch the strain working her forearms. The tension in my quads and groin peaks. Em cries out. Her body shivers.

The sound and feel of her coming undoes me. I climax right with her.

The warmth of my cum spreads through my fly as I straighten her. "That's the second time you made me come in my boxers," I point out, crushing her against my chest. "You better believe next time I finish, it'll be inside you," I add, my tone threatening.

Fuck. This woman has me questioning my morals. If it wasn't for Ash and my no-procreating pact, I'd develop a serious breeding kink. But I want my cum inside her regardless.

I kill the engine but make no motion to dismount. I like the feel of her in my arms.

I slide the LED mask off her head, admiring how the smooth, black locks shift against her tanned shoulders before my view drifts down to her low-cut cleavage. Her tits look marvelous from my vantage point.

"Going through my stuff and stalking me on my lunch break?" I *tsk.* "You pick up quick."

"I watched you leave work," she admits, rolling her eyes. "Wasn't that hard."

"How did you know it was me?"

"The kanji on your bike is gray. Ash's is white."

The sound of my brother's name snaps me out. I drop my eyes and dismount.

Em follows suit. She gives me a mischievous smile over her shoulder before leading the way to her car in the restaurant's main lot.

My stare fixates on her ass as I remind myself of the plug. I can't believe her brazenness.

Pivoting toward the driver's side, she reaches into the front of her top to retrieve the key fob I didn't notice nestled inside her bra. She unlocks the door and rips it open but swings around to me instead of getting in.

Her eyes lock on mine. Her mouth opens and closes, hands fidgeting with the key fob as if looking for a way to stall.

So I give her one.

Emily's arms link behind my neck as I take a step, backing her up against the frame. My hands slide around her, palms cradling her ass over her skirt.

My stare drops to her beckoning mouth, and before I know it, I start to sink.

A moan tumbles free when I melt into the kiss, inhaling the sweet floral fragrance of her skin mixed with the cucumber and mint in her hair. My eyes roll back. I'm not above admitting that I could fuck a pillow if it had her scent on it.

With my fingertips biting into her firm muscle, I capture her bottom lip between my teeth and give it a tug. Her content hum vibrates through our connection, chasing a tingling over the buzzed hair at my nape.

My cock answers with renewed vigor. I've never gotten so hard from a kiss.

I ease up on her lips and give her ass another squeeze, feeling the material shift against her skin in my grasp.

Emily's breath feathers over me. "I was thinking," she murmurs, "since Friday is my day off, you and I could—"

"Wait a minute," a familiar male voice hollers. "I know that skirt."

We both turn our heads simultaneously toward the blue Mustang parked in the row behind hers.

Fuck! My teeth clench down.

"You little slut, you." Vince shuts his door and takes in Emily as he swaggers closer. "Getting the twin-action… I fucking knew it. So, you guys taking turns or tag-teaming this chick?"

His eyes flick from her to me, then back to her. "Double the fun, right?" he taunts, and I want to slit his throat with the knife in my pocket when he fucking winks at her.

Stepping in front of her to block his view, I tip my chin over my shoulder. "Get in the car."

"Mas—"

"Get in the fucking car!" I repeat, even more agitated.

This time she does as told, and I slam the door shut as soon as she's clear.

I take two steps, beelining for Vince. My fist clenched, I reel it back and swing.

My hand is still sore from the punch into the locker earlier, and another round of sharp pain shoots up my forearm as my knuckles collide with his jaw. His head flings to the side. The rest of his body follows behind with the momentum.

As Vince stumbles and goes down, I straddle his chest. My hands wrapping around his throat is the last thing I see.

Then my vision goes dark.

259

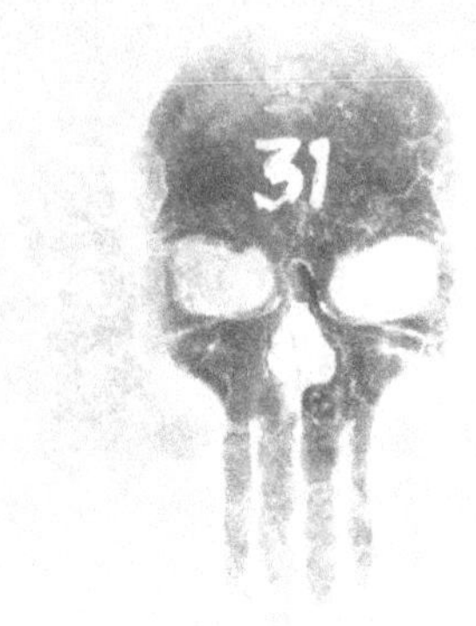

Em

Oh my God!

"Mason!"

I jump out of the car and rush over to where he's pinning Vince to the ground, hands around his neck.

I've never seen anyone get punched before. Not even slapped.

Heaving breaths saw in and out of him. Mason's glare stays down. He's so focused on choking the man, he doesn't even hear me.

I yank on his arm. "Stop it. Let him go."

He doesn't budge. His knuckles are white while Vince's face is starting to turn blue. His legs thrash as he tries to fight Mason off.

I give one more pull. "Please, Mason." And this time the sound of his name breaks his frenzy.

His head snaps around, and his dark eyes find mine, but for a second he looks at me like he doesn't recognize me. His features remain twisted and hard.

In the next moment, his eyes dart over me, and the same confusion from the other night at my apartment washes over him as if he doesn't know where he is or what's going on.

A groan from Vince swings Mason's attention back to him. I watch the tension in his grip loosen, then his hands switch to the guy's shirt to yank his face toward him.

"If you so much as look her way again, I'll pluck your fucking eyeballs from their sockets," he snarls an inch from him, his nostrils flaring with his threat.

He drops him to the asphalt and pushes off.

I take a step back on reflex. I can't believe he laid into Vince like that just for running his mouth. What would he do if someone were to actually put a hand on me?

"Fuck, Mason." Vince rises to his feet, albeit a little unsteadily. "Always with the short fuse, huh?" Glaring at Mason, he straightens out his shirt, then jabs a finger at me.

"She must have a death wish to put up with you," he says before pivoting and marching toward the restaurant's entrance.

Mason turns to me but hesitates to move, wary of my reaction. His fingers twitch down by his sides. His jaw is tense.

I blow out a breath and put his mind at ease.

"What just happened?" I ask, raising my hands to his face. I want him to look at me, and only me. I'm the one who got through to him. That has to count for something, right?

Mason's fingers close around my wrists, the same fingers that nearly drained the life out of a man right in front of me.

"I won't let anyone talk to you that way. You're more than what he implies, Em."

His voice is filled with emotion, and his touch is just as tender—a stark contrast to how he snapped at me earlier.

I half expected him to shove me into my car himself. He was scary. Scarier than hunting me through the alley or taunting me in my apartment. I know he was just playing then, because he promised me I'll always be safe with him; the devil you know, right?

But there's something haunting within the swirl of green that meets me, and seeing him so violent, lashing out at another guy, is frightening. It's a side of him I haven't really given much thought to. Where's all that rage coming from?

And what did Vince mean by me having a death wish?

Mason's throat bobs. His right hand releases my wrist and tilts my chin up. "You're *mine*."

The word is spoken with a soft growl, and as he holds my gaze, I feel his claim on me in my bones. I know he means it with every cell in his body. It's in the way he takes me. In the way he ensnares my very soul.

He nods toward my car. "Now get gone before I prove it right here in the parking lot."

My cell phone chimes in my pocket as I wipe down the table Jake just cleared of dishes. Straightening, I drop the rag and pull it out to check the message I assume is from Ash.

It's not.

> I like watching you bend.

— *Unknown sender.*

My eyes dart toward the large window, and my heart gives a kick to my ribcage when I see the black motorcycle across the street, the familiar rider staring me down through the visor of his helmet. His head is cocked to one side while he slouches on the seat, phone still in his hand.

The sight of him does something to me. He's dressed in all black, per usual, giving him that unyielding air of danger I can't fucking resist.

A tingling sensation chases across my throbbing clit, and I hear his voice in my head, *'I'm already fucking you.'*

The skin at my nape prickles, and I squeeze my thighs together on reflex. Yes, I can feel him inside me, the smooth glide, the pressure, the size of him stretching me, his piercings rubbing my inner walls…

I swallow dryly. My eyes swing over my shoulder across the now-empty diner before I stuff my phone back into my pocket and pick up my rag again.

With a little sway in my step, I'm not at all putting on a show for him when I move toward the last table and turn around, leaning over it with my back arched to grant him a perfect view of my ass.

I can feel his lingering gaze on me. As my hand sweeps over the table with a mind of its own, a heated sensation like palms mapping my body spreads across my skin, and I get lost in my thoughts for a moment.

My phone chimes again. My lips curl into a knowing smile.

"Emily?"

Shit! My spine snaps straight, and I whirl around to face Laura. "Y-yes?" I stammer in shock. Embarrassment flares through me. *Does she know what I was doing?*

I wring the rag in my hands, meeting her nonchalant expression. "What's up?"

"You can take off if you want."

My eyes dart to the clock on the wall behind her. It's 20 minutes till closing.

My posture relaxes. "Oh, okay."

I pass the rag into Laura's waiting hand.

"Have a good night, honey." She tips her head a little, and the soft curve to her lips gives me the indication she's well aware of everything, including the man waiting for me outside.

"You too." I awkwardly wipe my palms on my thighs. "See you tomorrow."

As I walk toward the kitchen, I resist the urge to glance over my shoulder at the window.

I hang up my apron and clock out before finally checking the last message on my phone.

Bad girl, Emily.

Another flare of heat warms my face. I like taunting him.

I push out of the back door and round the building to meet Mason in the front. I sense his grin behind the visor as I cross the street toward him. He's leaning forward, gloved hands working the grips of the handlebars. The engine is already running.

"Waiting for me?" I muse, a hand on my cocked hip.

I feel his heated stare travel over me from my blazing cheeks down my legs and back up, but he doesn't say anything. Then he nods to the helmet on the backseat.

"Woah!" I unlatch the straps and pick it up.

My breath hitches. It appears to be the same helmet, but instead of a plain matte black shell, I'm holding a unique piece of art made specifically for me. Golden filigree designs that remind me of a tattoo swirl along the sides. The words Baby Girl are written in bright purple letters across the front. The details and the shading are insane.

I turn it back and forth in my hands. I remember Ash mentioning the shop's custom paint jobs and wonder if Mason did this himself.

He tips his head over his shoulder as I just stand there admiring it.

"It's beautiful," I murmur.

I've never received anything this meaningful. No one ever *made* something for me. *Bought* stuff? Sure. But this is so much more.

The words choke in my throat. I don't know what to say except, "Thank you."

My eyes linger on the reflective visor, searching for his, and several seconds slip by with us simply staring at each other.

When he revs the engine, I take my cue and straddle the bike behind him, the helmet secured under my chin.

Mason still doesn't speak a word, not even when I realize he's driving in a different direction than the house, and I ask where he's taking us.

His silence is starting to become unsettling.

My fists clench his sweatshirt tighter as we climb in elevation. The trees flanking the highway grow dense before he makes a turn onto a winding backroad, and then lastly onto an unmarked dirt path.

Towering woods press down on us from both sides. My heart drops further into my stomach. It's dark, and sinister, and the mere ambiance sends my pulse racing.

Mason stops the bike in the middle of nowhere. I dismount and remove my helmet before taking a look around. I amble a few feet, wondering why he brought us here.

Sounds of him moving make me swing back around. His helmet is off, but in its place is the half mask of the skull, black eyes trained on me. He looks terrifying.

My breathing judders, and I take a trepidatious step backward. My sight is drawn to his clenched fists. He's still wearing the motorcycle gloves.

He reaches into the pouch at his front, and before I even see the knife in his hand, understanding crashes over me.

I whip around and run.

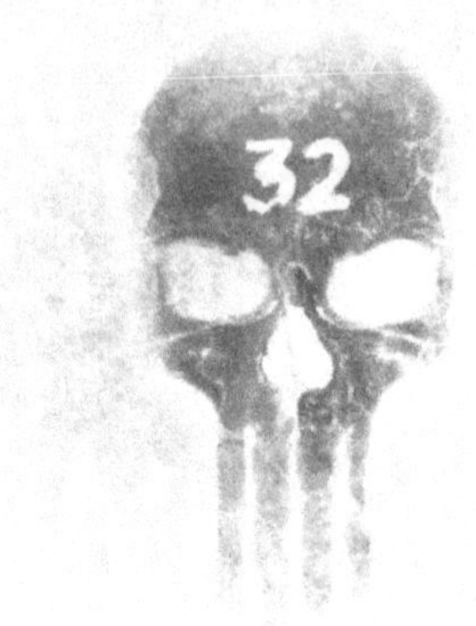

Em

I dash through the thicket, veering around trees and leaping over roots. I have no idea where I'm going, but I'm sure he's right on my heels. I hear the snapping of twigs.

Short breaths burst out of my lungs as I bob and weave to avoid low-hanging branches. I can feel him gaining on me.

"Where are you, baby girl?" I hear him calling after me. "Do you really think you can hide from us?"

Us?

Just then my feet stop, and I shriek as I catch sight of Ash straight ahead of me between the trees. He's dressed in the same all-black outfit and a matching mask.

Fuck! I swing left, pushing more speed from my tiring legs.

Sweat trails down my spine. I stumble blindly in the dark, swatting at the leaves blocking my view. Everything looks the same to me, but I have to assume they know these woods like the concrete maze in their city.

"You can't hide forever," Mason's sing-song voice reminds me. "See, my brother and I have this bet. Whoever catches you first, gets to fuck you. The other one has to back off."

His voice is no longer behind me. He's somewhere to my left as I continue sprinting.

I don't know for how long I manage to evade them. Minutes race by. I feel my strength fading. I can't keep this up.

I stop to catch my breath. My muscles burn, and my chest billows to force air into my lungs. My heart pounds in my ears like a drum. It's all I hear. I catch the sound of rustling too late.

Arms wrap around me from behind. One hand clamped over my mouth to cut off my scream, he whirls me around before his back slams into a tree. I'm trapped, caged to his chest.

My body goes stiff with fear. He tips my head back onto his shoulder. Through the small gap under my nose, I draw in his cologne.

His hard pecs swell against my back. He's panting too, as we both stay completely still, flush with each other.

"Does it unnerve you when we're standing like this?" Mason asks, his breaths easing out through the cloth of his mask.

"When you can't see my face but still feel my breath feathering along your neck, the heat of my body flaring against your backside as both our contours fit together so perfectly…" his voice trails off in a dreamy lilt.

I draw more of his sandalwood and spice scent into me, the ache between my thighs screaming with need.

"It rattles *me*," he stresses. "It sends a need so savage, so primal through me I can't fight the image in my mind of fucking you into the ground."

His graphic language arouses me further. My eyes roll back into my head, and my ass starts grinding into his erection.

It earns me a strained groan. "You're such a tease, Emily," Mason rasps into my ear, raising goosebumps along my naked arms. "Do you need to get fucked hard and dirty?"

I nod under the little movement he grants my neck.

"Undo your pants," he orders.

My trembling fingers fumble with the button. I lower the zipper and push my jeans down as far as my arms reach while he rips his right glove off with his teeth through his mask and stuffs it into his pocket.

Mason's hot breath caresses the shell of my ear. "That's my girl. Always *so* good for me," he drawls, his bare hand teasing into my underwear from the top while his left keeps covering my mouth.

Two fingers trace my seam, stroking me roughly and spreading me open before they plunge into me.

My strained moan leaks through the seal of his grip over my lips as I grind myself into his touch. Heat and slickness well between us.

Mason's rhythm picks up. "Soak these panties for me."

His palm curving over my clit, he adds more pressure with a third finger, thrusting in and out of me faster.

I hear the wetness… the suction…

"That's all mine. I want to drink you like a fucking fountain."

Oh God. My hips undulate, and I open my legs more for him, submitting myself entirely to his desire. *Let this devil take me. I'm his to use as he pleases.*

"You think I can't fill all your holes myself, baby girl?" Mason's voice grates out. "I'm going to fuck my brother's name out of your vocabulary, you hear me? Mine will be the only one falling from these pretty lips."

My hips buck in his hold, and I climax around his fingers right then.

"That's right, squirm for me."

Wave after wave rakes through me at his command as he keeps his ruthless pursuit going. Even once he pulls out and switches his assault to the now-hypersensitive bundle of nerves at my clit. He's so fucking rough that I'm already chasing another orgasm.

His left hand clamps my nose shut, cutting off my oxygen. *No!*

"What do you want, baby girl? Air? Freedom?" he prompts. "Fight me for it. Show me how badly you want to live, and I will grant you both. You're the one in control, Em. Earn it."

Tears fill my eyes. I can't breathe. My nails claw at bare skin where his sleeves have ridden up, and I want to scream at him to stop, but I can't get a sound out.

I'm panicking. I remember how he disassociated with Vince. How he didn't realize what he was doing. What if it's happening again? I can't shake him out of it. I can't call out his name.

Mason' strokes me relentlessly. My body starts to tremble under the tension. I'm so close to coming again. My muscles grow stiff. I feel it peaking—

The orgasm crashes down on me more intensely than anything I've ever experienced. The ground under my feet disappears along with everything else. My vision goes black.

My awareness slowly returns with Mason's coaxing voice. "Come back to me, baby girl."

I feel his thumb brushing my cheek, his hand no longer covering my mouth.

I jerk awake and suck in a breath. Mason's gloved fingers stretch across the front of my throat, but his hold is gentle when he twists my head toward him.

His eyes sweep over my face, and a hint of surprise flickers in them, like he didn't expect me to climax that hard.

The corner of my mouth twitches with amusement. I feel high.

My right hand lifts, and I tug down his mask, revealing a wicked grin.

It only flashes for a second before his lips crash down on me.

"I'm not done with you, Em," he says, his mouth open over mine.

His tongue flicks at me, and his kiss turns fierce, picking up the heat right where we left off when I passed out. "You're going to look so good on your hands and knees out here."

I whimper as the image forms in my mind.

His grip releases my throat, and he nudges me to the ground, my hands already out to brace myself when he settles on his knees behind me.

A heavy palm flattens my chest. With his knees pinning my legs closed, he rips my panties down my thighs.

The cool forest air licks at my wet seam, heightening my sensitivity, and I know it's all part of his strategy. Everything about Mason is primal and raw, and I ache for it. He makes me feel alive in a way only he can.

He proves it with a slap to my pulsing flesh.

I cry out as the strike ignites a sharp sting through my core. My hips rock under the torment, chasing my climax. My legs tremble.

"Not yet, baby girl," Mason chides.

He pumps two fingers into me, then pulls them out.

"Mmmh." I hear him groan as he sucks them clean. "You taste like heaven, baby."

His belt clanks as he unfastens it and frees himself of his restraints. Then the thick head of his cock crowns my opening.

My breath catches in my throat. Mason thrusts into me in one long moan that sends shivers up my spine. The momentum pushes me forward. My knees and hands skid in the dirt, a hot burn flaring from the friction.

He retreats and drives in again, so deep and harsh I can't draw air into my lungs.

His right hand reaches around to my clit, flicking his fingers over the swollen nub. "Whose name are you gonna cry out, huh?"

"Yours, M-Mason," I wail, tears blurring my vision as I jerk into his touch.

"That's right. The devil has come to feast, baby girl. And I'll have my taste. Again,"—thrust—"again,"—thrust—"and again."

He follows up with more punishing thrusts, each one so deep my vision fizzles, and I see sparks. "I should've drawn you like this, baby girl. You're so fucking beautiful on your knees for me."

Twigs crunch somewhere up ahead.

I lift my eyes enough to see Ash leaning against a tree.

"Let's make him watch you come for me," Mason grates out.

His fingers speed up, stroking me almost painfully hard, but my walls only hug him tighter, greedily welcoming his engorged length on each thrust. He has me teetering on the edge.

My nails dig into the dirt. My muscles stiffen. "Oh God!"

"Tell him whose cunt this is."

My orgasm crests the instant the words burst from my lips. "Yours, Mason. It's *yours!*" I cry out.

My inner walls clench around him. With my admission as much as my body's confirmation, Mason reaches his own climax. His hips lock, and he spills into me.

Ash pushes off the tree. "You happy now?" he prompts, ambling toward us. "You got her all to yourself?"

"You heard her." Mason pulls out and tucks himself away before rising to his feet.

Through the haze in my vision, I watch him square off with his brother, leaving me used and discarded on the ground.

A knot twists in my gut.

I catch the sounds of their voices arguing, but the words drift across my mind without substance. My head is spinning as I start to stand.

I pull up my underwear and jeans, swaying on weak legs. My hands tremble. Everything hurts.

Suddenly, Ash's arm is around my waist, steadying me.

"Take your fucking hands off her," Mason growls, a fist clutching his brother's sweatshirt at the neck.

"Or what?"

A tremble surges in my throat. "Stop it! Stop fighting."

My voice is raw with emotion. I never wanted this. I swore I wouldn't come between them.

I wipe my tears with the back of my hand. My palms are dirty. "I can't do this anymore," I decide, expelling a long breath. "Please take me home."

My eyes are downcast as I feel both of them staring at me.

Mason lets go of his brother, then his possessive hand clamps around my elbow.

I flinch. "Not you."

Mason's fingers tense.

"Ash," I clarify.

I don't dare look up at Mason. I feel the icy shift in him at the sound of his brother's name. My rejection cuts him right to the bone.

His hand falls away without another word, and he storms off, leaving Ash and me alone in the woods. I don't move until the sound of his boots fades into the brush.

"C'mon." Ash nudges my feet into motion, and I adhere, curling into his chest as we walk back to his bike.

When he pulls up to my apartment, I dismount and hand him back his helmet. He gave me his since I left mine on Mason's bike.

I also fish out his house key from my pocket to return it. I won't be going back there.

My hand lingers in Ash's. "What's wrong with Mason?"

Ash withdraws his touch hesitantly, like he's trying to figure out how to respond without saying too much.

He sets the helmet on his lap and grips both handlebars. The bike wobbles with the shift of his weight on the seat. "When we were younger, we went through some shit," he replies, his eyes avoiding mine. "We both had it bad, but he never really got over it. He didn't hurt you, did he?"

I shake my head when his gaze swings back to me.

"Look, maybe you should stay away from him." His eyes narrow. "He can be dangerous. I've caught his fist more times than I can count."

I give him a weak nod. I can't say with certainty that I'm not afraid of Mason or what he would do in a fit of jealousy.

277

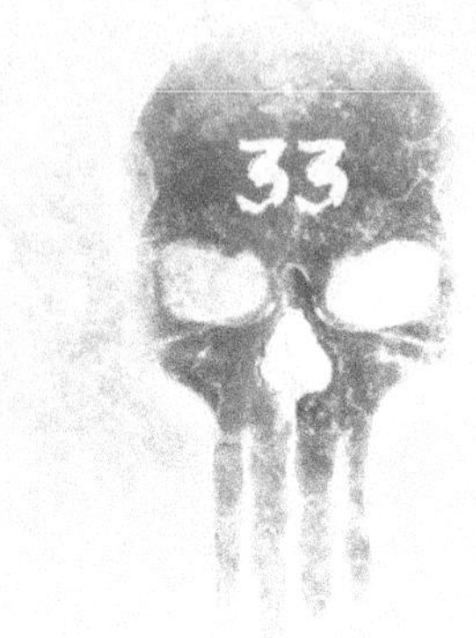

Ash

hat's wrong with Mason?

Now there's a loaded question. What *isn't* wrong with the guy?

Training my eyes on the window to the street, I stab my food and shove some more leftover chicken into my mouth. After everything we've been through, I never thought we'd find ourselves on opposite sides. Not over a girl. He never came home after the woods and even called Isaac to take a personal day off from work just to avoid me.

I'm surprised he's here now.

I put my fork down and go off on him as he strolls in through the garage. "Where the fuck have you been?"

He's still wearing the same clothes from last night. I would've figured he'd stop by to change while I was at work, covering for his ass.

Shooting me a hostile glare, he ignores the question and marches past the kitchen where I sit at the counter.

I push off the stool and charge after him into the hallway. "Would it kill you to answer a fucking text?" I barrel on. "For all I knew you could've been lying dead in a ditch somewhere." I know how he rides when he's enraged.

Mason sneers over his shoulder. "And wouldn't that have been *convenient* for you?" Then his door slams shut.

We've seen accidents happen during races, and he's had several close calls against Vince's Ninja that I lectured him about. *Does he really think I'd want him to crash?*

I hesitate for a moment, grinding my teeth at his remark before going after him.

I rip the door open. "You know, she asked me what your deal is."

"Oh, and I bet you couldn't wait to tell her *all* about me." Mason tears his sweatshirt over his head and fires it toward the dresser across the room. It knocks down his cologne.

His shoulders rise and fall with his heaving breaths, bringing the black skulls tattooed across his chest to life. His fists are clenched. "You've been trying to turn her against me from the start."

I shake my head. "I didn't have to. You did that all on your own." I knew Mason would blow it with Emily sooner or later. "I mean, what kind of psycho chases a girl with a FUCKING KNIFE?"

Mason's eyes flare. He lunges at me before I can counter, and we both fall into the hallway together. We go to the ground, limbs tangled, kicking and throwing punches.

"You don't know her like I do. You don't know anything ABOUT her!" he roars, his right hook coming at my face as he straddles me.

I block the hit, then my own fist shoots out, catching his temple.

I punch him again while scrambling out from underneath him. I manage to get my arm around his neck and lock him in a rear chokehold with both of us still on the ground.

"You've lost your fucking mind, man. Let it go. She's done with you."

Another angry roar ruptures in his throat as he thrashes to get free. He claws at my forearm.

I relent and back off.

Before I can push fully to my feet, Mason spins. His leg kicks out, his steel-toed boot landing a hit to my side.

I collapse against the wall in the narrow hallway.

He straightens, blood trickling out of his nose through labored breaths. "Even if she's done with me, I'm not done with her," he says, chest heaving. "But I *am* done with *you*." He spits more blood onto the floor, then wipes his face with the back of his hand. "You're fucking dead to me."

Mason turns around and slams his door shut a second time. This time I hear the lock engage.

I expel a hard breath. An arm wrapped around my sore middle, I sag against the wall when my phone in the kitchen starts ringing.

"Motherfucker!"

I push off with a groan and hustle down the hallway to answer it.

281

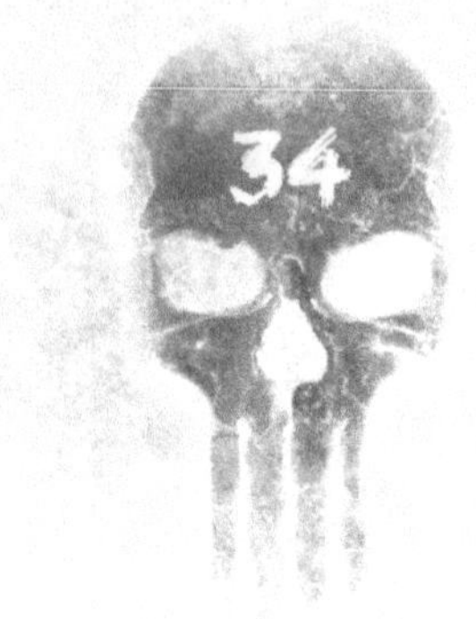

Mace

I stay in my room until I hear Ash leave, then shower and take off again before it becomes suffocating. The motel was a quick fix, but I'm determined to find a new place ASAP. I can't keep living under the same roof as him.

I park my bike in one of the spots up close reserved for security and take the front entrance into the private gentlemen's club.

Ty, the bouncer, gives me a nod and lets me pass. The club is the only place where I can find refuge tonight. I resisted the urge to drive to the diner. I'm afraid of what I'd do if I saw Emily now. I'm still too angry at her. Why would she deny herself what only I can give her? Why would she deny *us*?

I weave through the smoking lounge filled with guys of all ages in pressed suits. It's busy for a Wednesday night, but business here never really slows much between days. In a city like Castle, run by corruption and dirty secrets, Mr. DeMarco has no shortage of customers.

My eyes scan the darkness, skipping over the female servers in their matching 'uniforms', which consist of short black sequin bodycon dresses and red plateau peep-toe heels.

The *Black Lotus* isn't a strip club, though; you won't find the typical stages with poles in the main lounge. If you're willing to drop extra cash, you can, however, book any girl you like in one of the private rooms in the back. Whether it's for a nuru massage, a lap dance, or a little more hands-on and dick-out entertainment, the club's got your needs covered.

Despite the notoriety of what goes on behind doors, jobs at the *Lotus* are highly sought after. The girls make good money, are treated well, and are kept safe by tight security. No means no even here, no matter how rich you are, and you don't want Mr. DeMarco as an enemy. A ban from the club means you're booted from the top of the food chain. Nobody wants to risk that. Membership is by referral only and not cheap either. If it wasn't for the perks that come with working for Mr. DeMarco, *I* certainly wouldn't fly in their circle.

I finally find the face I'm searching for. Jillian sits on the armrest of one of the low chairs, an empty tray in her lap and her long legs crossed. The guy slouching in the black leather has his arm snaked around her hips as he keeps conversation with two other gentlemen across from him.

I know I'm supposed to tread carefully among the rich and powerful, but I simply don't give a shit. "She's taking a break," I say, marching up and nodding at her.

The guy's eyes narrow on me beneath dark brows. I estimate him to be in his mid to late forties; not old enough to make me feel sorry for the girls he pays to fuck here.

He looks me up and down with disdain. It sparks a sense of glee that he thinks I don't belong.

Jillian straightens from her lean against his shoulder. Her hand lingers on his biceps. "Be right back, baby," she tells him, rising from the armrest.

I take the tray from her and drop it on the bar in passing as I lead her back to the private rooms.

Two bouncers stand guard at the mouth of the hallway. They recognize me and wave us through instead of escorting us like they do with the reputable clientele. They know I can find my own way around.

At the fork, I swing right. Occupied rooms have red lightbulbs above the doors. I open the first one on the left that's empty and gesture for Jillian to go in.

A quick glance connects with me over her shoulder. She's twirling a dark brown lock around her finger. "You haven't come by in a while. I thought you forgot about me."

Her tone is sugary sweet, meant to keep up the charade that this is more than a transaction. I can see how some guys would eat that shit up, but I find it nauseating.

Without feeding into her seductive play, I lock the door and meet her where she stands a few feet into the small room.

Black walls close us in from all sides. Only a single dim pillar of light that was triggered when I flipped the lock shines down from the ceiling to illuminate the low platform in the center. A golden pole protrudes from it, surrounded by plush, red seating against the walls, bringing the club's three signature colors together.

I don't have a need for any of it.

Jillian lifts her palms to my chest. "Miss me?" she drawls, her touch skating over me.

I incline my head. Raising a gloved hand to her jaw, I press my forefinger against her lips in a shushing motion.

Her crisp blue eyes stare up at me through thick, black lashes, waiting for my command.

I stall, savoring the moment of control before my right hand lifts a roll of cash into her view.

I don't have to cough up the membership fee, but I'm still required to pay the girls for their time. I chose Jillian because she has a kink for breath play. She gets off on being choked, and that's rare to find in a playmate. I like wrapping my hands around things. Throats in particular.

Jillian takes the money. Tucking it into her bra, she turns around slowly, still batting her eyelashes.

The gesture irritates me further. I'm not here for her for fake affection. She's a proxy. A tool to fulfill a physical need, no more.

She brushes her long, dark tresses off one shoulder and tips her head to the side, offering me all the access I want.

My left hand closes around the front of her throat. My lips dip to her ear. "Touch yourself."

She erupts in soft laughter. "You just want to watch today?"

"Don't talk." My right hand clamps down over her mouth, tipping her head back.

It's bad enough I have to inhale her obnoxious perfume. It never bothered me before, but I fucking hate it now as I'm watching her hands tease the hem of her dress higher. I'm thinking of pink and black pleats and someone else's hands… someone else's thighs… the feel of someone else's tight pussy.

Jillian's ass grinds back against my fly, her hips rocking into me while pleasuring herself. It doesn't feel right. She's too short. She doesn't fit like Em.

Anger swells in my chest. I squeeze her throat, covering her mouth and nose with my other hand. Her pulse beats against my palm in a frantic rhythm. Her body judders. I feel her climax.

I don't let go.

The blackness pulls me under. I'm back in the woods, Emily's body pressed to mine. She squirms in my hold, her cunt dancing around my fingers as I thrust them in and out to drive her higher.

The memory is so vivid, I can feel her pussy squeezing my cock in a slick glide up and down my throbbing shaft. I see her on her hands and knees, taking me. She cries my name. My muscles tremble with tension. I'm about to come.

Boom! Boom! Boom!

"Jilli?"

My eyes fly open at the sound of banging against the door.

"Jilli, are you in there?" a female voice calls from the other side.

I blink, and my vision darts around the room briefly disoriented before my grip loosens on the unconscious girl in my arms.

A long second ticks by.

I hear her sucking in a breath. Her head bobs. Her eyes are hazy as they settle on me.

Fuck! I swallow a mix of shock and guilt. If the knock hadn't jerked me out, I would've killed her.

My chest tightens. I have to get out of here. One arm steadying Jillian, I unlock the door, then practically shove her at the other woman and storm down the hallway toward the back exit, rushing past the two bodyguards in front of Mr. DeMarco's office and another security guy.

Nobody stops me.

I stumble into the parking lot as a whirlwind of emotions floods me—rage, shame, hate… all crashing down on me at once. I know it will trigger an episode.

Letting the door fall shut, I reach into the front pouch of my sweatshirt for my LED mask and put it on. I never leave the house at night without it. Or my knife. They're my security blanket.

The familiar sensation instantly calms my erratic breathing. I tip my head back against the brick wall, my hand dipping into my rear pocket, tracing the shape of the knife's cool grip.

Eyes closed, I relax.

"Well, I'll. Be. Damned."

Fuck! My muscles steel at the familiar voice.

"All by your lonesome tonight, are you, Mason? Does that mean your brother is working your girl over?"

My forearms flex. Jaw clenched, my fingers curl into my palms, and I envision Vince's smug face behind my eyelids.

My fists tremble.

Motherfucker.

289

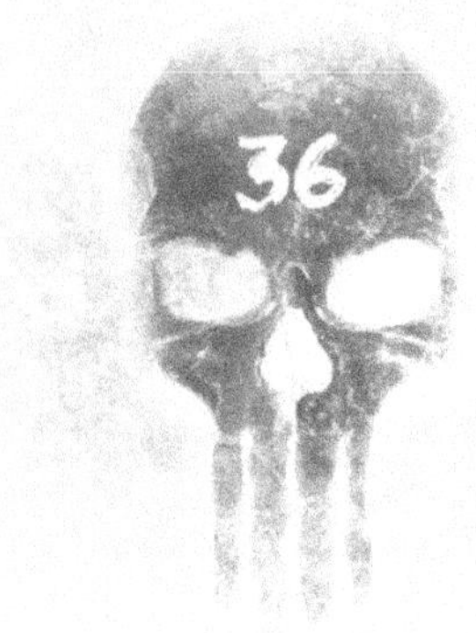

Mace

*F*uck.

I run a hand through my hair, trying to jog my mind about last night as I hunch at the side of the bed, my elbows on my knees.

I only come up blank. I remember leaving on my bike after my fight with Ash, but I don't recall where I went or how I even got home.

Letting the hand drop, I stare at my knuckles in the dark. My finger joints are sore as if they've been clenched in a tight grip for too long.

An icy chill teases up my neck. The last thing I remember is seeing Emily's face. I don't know whether it was real or a figment of my imagination, but I know I held onto those hazel blue eyes like my life depended on it. Like I needed her to save me.

I fear I did something bad if my memory blocked it out.

Without switching on the lamp on my nightstand, I rise to get dressed for work when my eyes catch on the pile of clothes beside my bed. In the faint ambient lighting, I can make out the black jeans and sweatshirt I wore last night. My mask peeks out from the pouch.

I give my head a shake. I don't remember leaving them there either.

I ignore the pile and proceed to the closet, grabbing things blindly from everywhere and finishing with my boots before I make my way to the bathroom across the hallway.

I return to my room for my watch, wallet, phone, and keys on the nightstand when I realize my knife is missing.

My mind drifts back to my clothes on the floor. Crouching beside it, I rifle through the bulk, checking the pockets. I find the knife still in the back and pull it out, but my dread rises as my touch encounters a dampness about the denim.

It didn't rain last night.

I switch on the lamp, and then my feet kick out from under me. I fall onto my ass.

It's blood.

The soaked-in color is indistinguishable from the black fabric, but the red smudges against the white mask are unmistakable.

I gasp in shock. The sticky wetness clings to the front of the hoodie and down a large part of my jeans. The knife is coated with it. It's too much. Somebody died. I *killed* someone.

Bile rises in the back of my throat, and I swallow to force a golf-ball-sized lump down.

My brain kicks into gears as I become aware of my pounding heartbeat. I panic. I roll everything up into a bundle with the blood on the inside and shove it into my backpack, the knife included. I can burn it all in one of the barrels at the abandoned campground. Nobody hangs out there.

I check my watch. Ash's alarm hasn't gone off yet.

Nobody will know.

I take a few deep breaths to calm my nerves, then push to my feet and leave my room.

Before pulling out of the garage, I swipe the lighter fluid and matches we keep for bonfires from the shelf, stuffing them in the backpack too.

Then I'm off.

I haul ass to the campground, burn all evidence, and make it to work only 20 minutes later than usual. Ash beat me for once.

I watch him go in as I pull into the parking lot. I'll be avoiding him for the rest of the day, so there's no need to come up with an excuse for why I'm late.

Isaac, on the other hand…

I would like to avoid him too. I don't know how I'm going to break it to him that I won't be taking over the shop with Ash.

I pass Rob and Jason on my way in. Both of them have been working here for about three years now. Isaac hired them after we started to expand, and we couldn't keep up with the rapidly growing client list.

Just act normal, I tell myself as I stuff my empty backpack into my locker and put on my paint coveralls. I'll be doing a custom full-body paint job on a 1970s Dodge Challenger this morning. I already finished the base coat on Tuesday, and since I took yesterday off, I'm now a day behind.

I check my notes before I start mixing paints and cringe. I forgot it's going to be bright candy apple red—my least favorite color today. This will be torture.

I'm right. The car mocks my memory lapse with each pass of my spray gun. It takes every ounce in me not to throw up. Everywhere I look, I see blood.

A single question repeats in my mind. *Did I really kill someone?*

After finishing the first coat, I take a break. I rip off my mask and unzip the front of my coverall.

I pause before tugging off the gloves. I've washed my hands several times since this morning, but there was never any blood under my nails, which makes me wonder whether I had been wearing my motorcycle gloves. I should probably burn them too just in case.

Leaning back against my worktable, I pull out my phone. I type out a text to Emily, then hit send and wait.

A minute goes by.

And another.

My hands start trembling when I don't get a response. I know she could be sleeping or simply be ignoring my texts, but what if she's not? I was so angry at her in the woods. What if it was Emily's blood on my clothes?

I squeeze the phone in frustration as the sound of a laugh makes me turn. Through the plastic divider between my paint room and the workshop, I catch sight of Ash. His head is down, and he's looking at his phone.

Is he texting her?

Or more importantly, is she responding to *him?*

I can't take the not knowing. I have to see her. I need to make sure that she's okay, that I didn't go to her apartment last night, that I didn't hurt her.

———

Emily replied to my text two hours later, putting my mind at ease about her being alive and well yet rejecting my plea to talk to her.

Fuck that! She's going to hear me out whether she wants to or not.

I decide not to break into her apartment this time, though, and instead ride across town to the diner. Her shift hasn't started yet. I want to catch her before she goes in.

Parking in the alley around back so she won't see me immediately, I remove my helmet and gloves, then dismount to wait.

While I lean back against my bike with my stare on the asphalt between my boots, my mind is grasping at straws.

What the fuck am I gonna say to her?

Pinching my eyes shut, I groan. I really haven't thought this through. When I do recon or run errands for Mr. DeMarco, I make a plan. I know every step. I'm out of my element here.

I vaguely hear the back door swinging open.

"It's Ash, right?"

My head shoots up at the chipper tone I can only assume is directed at me since there's no one else around, to find a scrawny kid with unruly black hair and dark eyes bouncing down the stairs to take out the trash.

I meet his curious stare as he drops the lid on the metal can in front of me. He's the bus boy I've seen sharing Em's shift.

Of course he thinks I'm Ash. She wouldn't tell anyone about me. I'm not the kind of guy you introduce to your friends.

"Yeah," I grumble back.

"I'm Jake. Drew and Laura's nephew."

Drew? Laura? How many times has Ash been here?

"Em talks about you all the time. Nice bike, by the way."

"Thanks," I say as my heart drops another level. *Of course she does.*

Fuck! I blow out a breath and run my hand through my hair. I hate this. It isn't me. I don't fucking beg. I demand! I take!

I should stick to what I'm good at.

"Hey!" I refocus on the kid who's still just standing there. "You mind doing me a solid?" I straighten and grab my helmet. "Don't tell her I was here."

Jake stares at me confused as I put on my gear and straddle the bike in a sudden hurry. "Um… sure," he says uneasily.

But the hesitation in his reply tells me he will.

I let the engine roar and take off.

Perfect! I'll be on her mind all night.

I'm already fucking her.

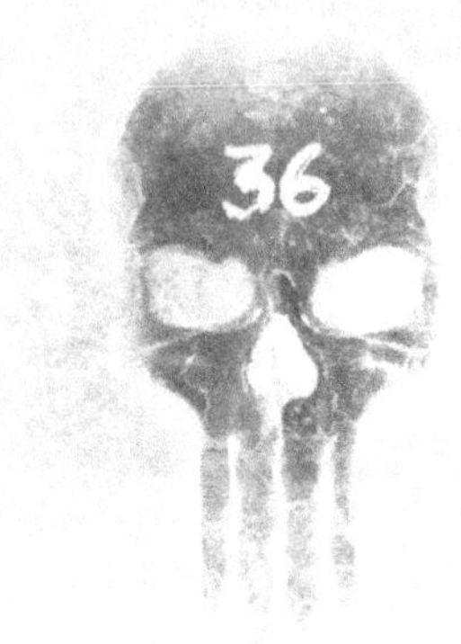

Em

I stir as a dark, rumbling sound of amusement tickles my dormant consciousness. The distinct timbre resonates with familiarity. It warms my chest.

My eyelids shutter. I smell cologne.

Mason's.

It doesn't surprise me that I'm dreaming of him. He's been on my mind all night. Jake told me he saw Ash in the alley, but when he mentioned the gray kanji on his bike, I knew. It wasn't Ash who stopped by. It was Mason.

"You're a heavy sleeper, aren't you, baby girl?"

My shorts are gone. I went to bed wearing them, but in my dream I'm naked from the waist down. I can feel him. *Oh my God,* can I feel him.

"Such a good girl…" His hips pull back. "You come for me even while you're asleep… calling out my name."

His mouth slants over mine, and then there's pressure as the pierced head of his cock enters me.

We both moan.

"Such a good. Fucking. Girl," his coarse voice grates out.

A firm grip claims the back of my knee. Mason retreats and slides deeper, but he doesn't force it. He opens me gradually, drawing a chorus of whimpers.

I give myself over. Thighs spread and my arms up by my head, my hips rock into him. I surrender to the dream.

The friction between us is slick. He feels so good. Each thrust drives me higher, and my toes curl as the sensation in my belly crests. I think I'm actually going to climax.

"That's it, baby." Mason picks up his pace, slamming his hips into me with growing urgency. "You're going to come for me again. I want to feel you."

Come for him again? My hazy mind finally catches on. I taste myself in his kiss. It's too real.

No!

A flare ignites in my chest, ripping me away from the edge of my orgasm when my eyes fly open. My sight comes into focus to find Mason on top of me, my legs hiked up at his sides.

He flashes me a crooked grin. My shirt is pushed up, laying my breasts bare, and I have a pretty good idea where else his mouth has been.

I notice a cut at his left brow that's maybe a day old. *Was he in a fight?*

"What the hell is wrong with you?" I rip my shirt down and scramble away from him. "Leaving that creepy message on the mirror wasn't enough, you had to come back to find out how far you can go before I wake up?"

I reach for the blanket next to me to cover myself. Mason is shirtless but still wearing his jeans. Captivated by his flexing chest and chiseled abs, I almost miss the confused look on his face as he adjusts the waistband of his boxers.

He leaves his fly unzipped like we have unfinished business.

Gripping me by the knees, he drags me back under him. "Don't pretend you didn't like it."

"I didn't."

"Liar!" His fingers grip my jaw, and he squeezes my chin to look at him. "Your body said otherwise," he insists. "You were moaning my name in your sleep. You can't deny that."

I tear myself free. "Well, I guess I'd have to believe your word on that… since I was *unconscious* at the time."

Mason's hands shoot out to lock around my wrists. He drives them into the pillow above my head. "Tell me that you can't still feel me inside you… that you can't taste me on your lips. Tell me that you hate me for coming back to claim what's mine."

"I hate you."

My spunk draws a chuckle. "Say it again," he dares me, a smirk dancing over his lips. "But this time, like you mean it."

With my arms pinned on either side of my head, his face hovers over mine in challenge.

"Mason, stop! Please." As much as I want him, I won't do this behind his brother's back. "Don't put me in this position. It's not fair to Ash."

At the sound of his brother's name from my mouth, something snaps in him. I can see it in the shadow crossing his eyes… in the tension of his jaw… feel it in his grip around my wrists.

His lips twitch, then pull away from his teeth. "You're lying to yourself if you think you'll ever have this with anyone else," he snarls. "Or that you can live without it now that you've had a taste. I know you, Em. You crave this as much as I do, and without me, you will wilt and die. Only I can feed you. Only I can make you feel this alive."

Mason's eyes dart back and forth between mine for several seconds as if searching for something. Then he releases my wrists and sits back on his heels with an air of remorse.

"I wanted you so badly I was willing to throw my brother at you if that was what it took for you to let your guard down."

"And then what?" I sit up too, the pressure behind my eyes rising. "Were you hoping he'd get his fill of me? Lose interest? Is that why you put me in *his* bed instead of your own?"

"Ash doesn't care for a girl once she's spread her legs for him. He only wants you because you're mine."

My voice attracts a quiver. "And how long until *you* lose interest?"

His shoulders drop with a sigh. "Em, I've never connected with anyone like this. There's something in you that wants out. I hear its call..." His hands come up to gesture. "It sings to me. It's the most beautiful song I've ever heard. I'll *never* grow tired of it." He clasps my face. "I see your dark side. Let me show you how beautiful you are."

His words are full of demand, but there's a plea in his eyes he won't voice. I see that he's hurting. That for the first time he let himself become vulnerable.

So I give in. I don't resist.

The moment his lips meet mine, Mason's rage dissipates. It's replaced by something else. *Desperation.*

"You're a drug, Em, better than the high of adrenaline, and I can't fucking breathe unless I'm inside you." The stubble lining his jaw is harsh against my skin. A burn chases the friction.

Mason opens my mouth with his. Pressing his chin to mine, he urges me backward until I'm flat on the mattress, caged beneath the unyielding demand of his body. Every muscle ripples with tension.

His shallow breaths judder as his hands work his boxers down, then in one sweep, the blanket is gone, and he's settled in between my thighs.

Mason aligns himself, never breaking from his kiss. He spears me in a single thrust, his hips slamming into me so sharp and raw, it rips a cry from my throat.

"That's it, baby girl," he rasps on his retreat. "Let me hear you." *Thrust.* "Cry for me." *Thrust.*

A shockwave after shockwave thunders through my body. His left hand curls into a fist at the base of my skull, forcing my head back while the steep points of his fingers dig into the muscle of my ass.

The headboard bangs against the wall. Mason lets me feel every thick inch of his engorged length. Tip to base he comes at me again and again, and with each thrust, he kisses me harder, biting my bottom lip like he wants to devour me.

My fingers twist through his hair. I match the frenzied motion behind his kiss, his panting breaths, the growls and grunts as my nails scrape across his scalp.

I pour every ounce of myself into our kiss, into his hunger, healing the cracks that threaten to shatter him. I give him this last time. I don't care how rough he is. I don't care about the marks he leaves on my skin with his hands or his teeth.

A fist in my tangled hair, his mouth scotches a path along the front of my throat, and his pace accelerates. He hooks his other arm around the back of my knee, pounding into me at a deeper angle as he shifts my hips and folds me.

"You hate this?" Mason thrusts into me so hard and deep that black spots crowd my vision. "You hate how good it feels?"

Tears well in my eyes, but I can't stop chasing the sparks that jolt through my womb with the slick suction. My orgasm peaks, and I know he can feel it.

"Tell me how much you fucking hate me, baby girl."

My joints stiffen. My muscles quiver. My mouth opens, but the words choke in my throat as my arms wind tighter around his neck.

I *do* hate him. For coming back… for giving me this… for reminding me what I can never have with him. I can't be the reason for them hating each other, and I blame him for forcing me into this role. But above all, I hate him for making me fall for him and ripping my heart out at the same time.

The dam breaks. A cry bursts from me, and my hips buck underneath him, milking him into me with every clenching pulse of my core.

Mason gives two more thrusts, then his own climax rushes him as violently as mine. He locks into me, crushing me in his hold.

His hips jerk. His groan vibrates up my throat where his open mouth lingers until the last heat of our ecstasy is extinguished by an icy touch of regret.

Mason removes himself from me, shifting his underwear back into place before my arms even unlink from him.

His dark eyes are downcast. "You *should* hate me," he says, his voice low and hoarse with emotion. "I'm not a good man… and an even worse brother."

I sense some kind of inner torment behind his words fueled by self-loathing, but it doesn't excuse his actions.

When he pulls away from me, I can't hold the tears back any longer. With my vision blurred, I reach for the closest thing on my nightstand. My mind doesn't even catch on to what it is before I strike him with it.

Mason's head flings to the side with the delivered blow. He saw it coming, but he didn't block it. He didn't even flinch.

Blood wells above his left eye where the gash has opened back up. It's deep enough he might need stitches.

Clutching the can-sized Bluetooth speaker, I'm in shock for a long moment, expecting him to lash out and strike back at me… but he doesn't.

Mason pushes off the bed to leave, grabbing the sweatshirt beside him. I notice his eyes swing toward my mirror on his way out, like he's recalling the words he wrote on it using my lip gloss.

My voice trembles. "Don't you dare come back."

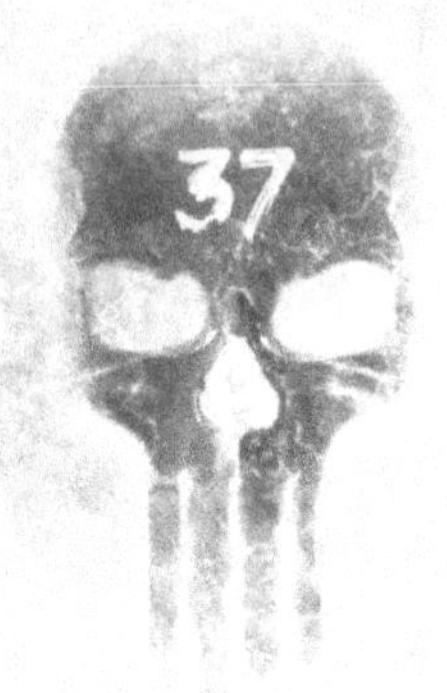

Mace

My fingers clench around my sweatshirt. *WHAT FUCKING MESSAGE?*

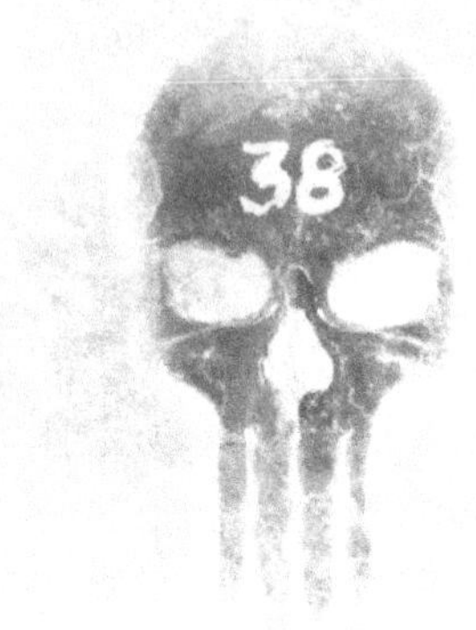

Em

Stretched out on my bed, I scroll through my meager social media feed for a distraction. I haven't left the house all day and barely picked at the late lunch I cooked only to have a reason to get up.

I crawled back under the covers after a few bites.

Mason's cologne clings to the sheets, and I'm utterly at odds with myself. I hate him, and yet I want him.

I never told him that I kept all his sketches tucked into the cover of one of the books on my shelf. I'm not sure why I kept them. As disturbing as they are, I couldn't throw them out. I had the urge to guard them like a secret. A treasure. Not so much because they're images of me, but because with each detail, he poured so much of himself into them. They hold pieces of him.

Fuck!

What if he's right? What if I gave up my one chance to ever feel something more than lukewarm?

Falling for him was never part of it.

Pulling the blanket up to my nose, I close my eyes and fill my lungs with his signature scent of sandalwood and spice when my phone buzzes with a text notification.

Reluctantly, I scan the screen to see that it's from Ash, offering to take me out on my night off.

I read the text in the notification window at the top instead of opening the messaging app. He's been checking in with me, but after witnessing Mason's reaction to his brother touching me in the woods, I've been distancing myself from him, too. I stand by my conviction. I won't be the woman who gets between brothers.

I close the screen without bothering to reply and slide my phone face-down onto the nightstand.

My fingers linger on the case as my sight catches on the wireless speaker again. I can't believe I hit him. I don't feel relieved at taking a stand for myself. It was over, we were done, he would've left… If anything, I'm more afraid of what he'll do next.

I shouldn't have struck him.

I roll onto my back and stare at the ceiling. In my entire life, I've never felt so many conflicting emotions. That look in his eyes, like he thought he deserved it, haunts me.

The sharp buzz of the front door jolts me out of my ramblings. I fling the covers aside and rush down the hallway to answer the intercom in what little I wear.

"Hello?"

"Please tell me you haven't had dinner yet."

I roll my eyes at his persistence. "Ash…"

"Come on, Emily. You have to eat, don't you? I brought takeout. Let me in."

Dammit!

I hang my head in resignation and buzz him in, then race back into my bedroom to throw on a pair of sweatpants and an oversized T-shirt.

I'm back to answer the door right as he knocks.

"See? That wasn't so hard." He meets me with a grin, holding up three to-go bags from the taco truck he took me to on our first date.

I shake my head but can't fight the smile curling my lips as I step aside to invite him in. Motioning toward the kitchen, I relock the door before following.

I grab us water bottles from the fridge. Ash drops the paper bags on the table and goes for the cabinet to pull two plates from it while I take a seat. He found them on the first try.

"What did you get?" I ask, reaching for the closest bag.

"Same as last time." He drops one plate in front of me and scoots the other one across the table.

I unroll the top and pull out the familiar wrapper. "You remember what I ordered?"

"Of course." He slides out the chair opposite mine. "But I got you an extra one. I didn't know how hungry you were."

I glance back into the bag and see three more tacos at the bottom. I laugh. "Kinda starving now that I smell it," I admit.

Ash leans across the table and snatches up the other two bags. I watch him lay out his food on the plate when my attention catches on his right hand working the wrapper off.

I gasp. "What did you do to your hand?" The skin on his knuckles is badly scuffed, like it had been bleeding.

"Eh, it's nothing," he replies, then chuckles. "You should've seen the other guy."

Watching his eyes drop to his plate, I feel a weight settle in my stomach. I assume he means Mason, and I have. I remember the cut above his eye.

So it was from an altercation with Ash and not some random guy he let his frustration out on.

"Just a minor disagreement between brothers," he adds, raising the taco to his mouth.

"*Minor?*" I'd hate to see the results of something serious. Then I wonder…

"What was the disagreement about?" I ask, waiting for his eyes to shift back to mine.

They don't. Chewing slowly, Ash keeps his stare deliberately on his food.

Guilt sears through me at his all-telling silence. "It was about me, wasn't it?" I concur.

Taco in one hand, Ash waves me off with the other. "Don't worry. We've had worse fights. He'll get over it."

Get over his beef with his brother or get over *me?*

Somehow I can't see Mason letting me go. He ignored my rejection before; who's to say he won't do so again? He thrives on the chase. I fear he'll never stop.

My appetite is gone after that, but I choke down the food he brought anyway. I don't want to be rude. He made such an effort.

I listen to Ash ramble on about work while watching him finish all eight of his tacos and the bottle of water. Replacing the cap on mine, which still has some left in it, I rise from my chair to clear the table.

I dump the trash and carry the plates to the sink to wash them. When I turn on the water, I hear the feet of Ash's chair skip along the floor.

He comes up beside me. "Has Mason stopped by?" he probes, taking the dish towel from the counter.

I feel his stare drilling a hole into me as I look down and run the soapy sponge over the plate. I sidestep the question. "He texted me, saying he wants to talk, but I blew him off."

My cheeks warm under Ash's scrutiny. I wonder if he noticed my diversion.

I hold my breath until his posture in my periphery relaxes. He shifts his weight and leans his hip against the edge of the counter, facing me. "If he *does* come by, promise me you won't let him in. I don't want you alone with him. He's not in his right mind."

"What do you mean?" I ask, handing him the clean plate to dry.

"He's had anger issues for years, and sometimes he can't even remember what he did. It's like he gets trapped in his head…" Ash's voice trails off. "I just don't want you caught up in one of his episodes." He gives the plate another run with the towel, then returns it to the cabinet above.

Submerged in water, my hands have stopped moving. My mind is replaying the scene from this morning, the confusion at my mentioning the message, and the way he looked at the mirror.

He didn't remember breaking into my apartment on Thursday.

A tremble runs through my grip on the second plate.

"Promise me, Em."

My eyes shift to Ash at the coaxing sound of my name. His right hand cups my face, fingers brushing along the curve of my cheek.

My focus lands on his mouth as his thumb traces my lips. "I could stay over if you want…" he drags out, his voice a heady breath, thick with arousal. "In case he drops by."

The seductive note coats me like honey. It's warm and sweet and makes my knees weak. I almost give in.

Mason's argument about Ash losing interest once a girl gives it up to him echoes in my ears; Ash himself admitted as much. Yet here he is, trying so hard, and I finally get why. As long as I care for them both, the conquest for me will never be accomplished. Ash has to win me over each time… make me choose him instead of his brother. *I'm* the catalyst. They feed on the rivalry as much as they feed *into* it, and I'm the only one who can stop it.

"No." I shake my head and pull away from his touch. "That's not necessary. I won't let him in. I promise," I add with a soft smile.

Ash's lips form a tight line. Either he doesn't believe me or he thinks Mason won't be deterred by a closed door.

"Alright," he sighs with a rough edge, letting his hand drop. I can't tell whether his tone is resignation or frustration at my shutting down his advances. "But I'm only a phone call away if you change your mind."

My smile crinkles. "Thanks." I hand him the other plate. I don't remember if I scrubbed it, but it looks clean when he takes it. "And thanks for dinner, too," I tag on.

"My pleasure." He tips his head in his signature casual air, and the tightness in my chest loosens when I detect no resentment.

I drain the water, and Ash finishes wiping the dish before sliding it back into the cabinet and closing the door.

He passes me the towel so I can dry off.

"I get it, you know?" He straightens and pivots my stance towards him, his height towering over mine.

I clench the rag in my grip. The hairs at my nape prickle when his hands slip underneath my shirt, tracing the waistband of my sweatpants. "You're a good person, Emily. Don't feel guilty. Mason's issues are not yours."

His touch inches higher, lazy fingertips brushing against the sensitive skin of my stomach. His head dips. "Don't let him ruin this," he says softly into my ear.

I press my palms to Ash's chest. "I should never have agreed to this. I was in over my head and didn't consider the consequences."

I step out of his embrace, tears pushing their way into my eyes. "I can't do this to him, Ash. I'm sorry."

The muscles along his face twitch. Through my blurring vision, I see his jaw clenching. His Adam's apple jerks.

Ash gives me a sullen nod.

With a weight pressing down on my chest, I watch him turn to leave. I track the fall of his boots down the hall. I hear the deadbolt on the door disengage, the sound of it opening and closing quietly, and then there's silence.

Fuck! My heart never felt so heavy.

I wipe my tears and trudge down the hallway toward my bedroom, turning the deadbolt over in passing. The urge to drop everything and run back home with my tail tucked between my legs is suffocating me. I proved everyone right. I won't survive here.

I grab the remote and turn on the TV as I scoot under the covers. The news channel is the first one that pops up.

Looking down, I bunch the blanket around me when the familiar voice of the anchorwoman from Channel 9 goes off, "This latest and most gruesome attack appears to have taken place in the early hours of Thursday."

My eyes shoot to the screen, my grip frozen on the remote.

"27-year-old Vincent Tucker was found stabbed to death in the parking lot of a popular pool hall downtown."

Oh God, no!

"A surveillance camera from the parking lot, which happens to be adjacent to the infamous *Black Lotus* gentleman's club, caught the attack. I must advise you, the footage is very graphic."

The news coverage cuts to the recorded feed, and I drop the remote to slap my hands over my mouth. Heart pounding in my ears, I stare at the fuzzy video of a guy in a black hood matching Mason's build, as he rips Vince backward by the hair and spins him around.

A knife flashes in his gloved grip. He plunges the blade into Vince's stomach repeatedly before slashing his throat in a final strike. Blood sprays out.

"At this time, it's unclear if the assailant knew Tucker personally," the anchorwoman supplies over the footage. "The victim was attacked unprovoked from behind as he dismounted his motorcycle."

With the pounding in my ears increasing, I keep watching as the raised hood slowly turns toward the camera like he knows exactly where it is. He knows someone is watching. He's going to show his face.

My eyes go wide. *Please, no!*

The killer looks right up into the camera, only instead of his face, an LED mask with blue stitching is revealed. *Mason's* mask! The one that's been haunting me since I moved here.

The newscast cuts back to the studio, showing the crew at their desks. "This recent attack puts Castle City's police department under even more pressure as the murders of 22-year-old Shelly Baker and 24-year-old Marisol Fuentes remain unsolved."

My hands start trembling, and a cold grip squeezes my throat. I see Mason's hands around Vince's neck… feel them around my own…

What if Mason strangled those girls and doesn't remember it?

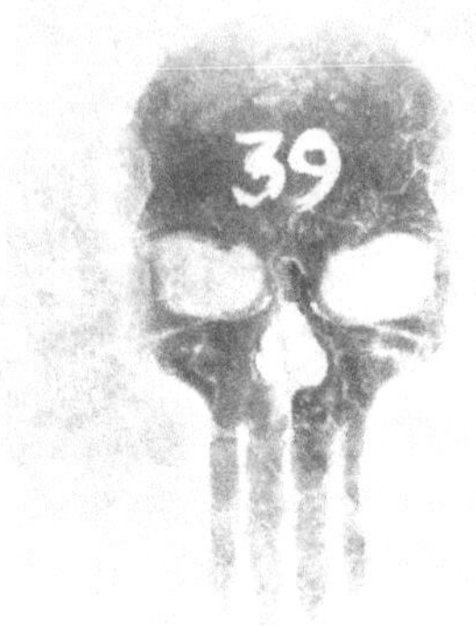

Em

My nerves have been on edge all day. I hardly slept, and work is rough as I replay the news footage over and over in my head. I can't believe it. All of Ash's warnings… Does he know that Vince is dead? Does he suspect Mason?

I didn't text Ash, and he hasn't reached out again. He accepted my final word.

"You alright, Emily?" Laura asks, fists digging into her waist when I come up to the counter to place an order. Her lightly grayed brown hair is pulled back into a loose bun as usual. "You've been looking out of sorts all night. You're not coming down with something, are you?"

I shake my head. "I'm fine," I assure her, a subtle curve to my lips for her concern.

I wipe a hand down my thigh, Laura's scrutinizing gaze still needling my back when I turn around. Her gut feeling is never wrong. She's too good at reading people.

I steel my spine and continue my shift, my eyes scanning the street through the large window sporadically where puddles are forming over the asphalt. The drizzle has been going for hours, and yet I chose to come to work on foot.

The weather is not the reason I can't stop checking the window, though. My skin prickles with dread. There's no black motorcycle parked across the diner, but I doubt a little rain will keep Mason at bay.

"Did you bring your car?"

"No," I sigh, putting my apron on the hook in the kitchen before facing the expression behind the motherly tone.

Laura nods toward a tall wicker basket near the door. "Take one of our umbrellas when you leave. The rain has picked up, and it's likely to get worse before it stops. Weatherman says we're expecting quite the storm," she supplies, hiking her thumb at Drew's TV in the back.

I thank her and do as she suggests, but it's of little use in this storm. I clutch the handle tighter and cower under the umbrella's shield. Wind whips around me, blowing my hair with wicked fury. I'm freezing.

Stripping my soaked clothes, I step into the shower, turning it as high as the water heater allows me. It's not hot by any means. It's just enough to make me more comfortable.

I dry off, brush my teeth, and change into my sleep clothes before returning to my room.

Thunder rolls in the distance as my wary gaze lingers on the window. I double-check the lock before slipping under the covers.

I'm jolted out of sleep by a loud crash that rocks my bed like a bomb has gone off outside. Lightning flashes through my room.

My heart punches up my throat as I move, my muscles jittery from the crude awakening. I reach for the lamp on my nightstand, but the room remains cloaked in darkness, other than flickers of more lightning through the curtains. The storm has knocked the power out.

I groan before rolling fully over onto my side to check the time on my phone. It's 4:42 in the morning. I've barely been asleep for an hour. The storm raging outside will likely keep me awake.

Dropping my phone back onto the nightstand, I swallow dryly. My throat is parched, and I forgot to grab some water from the fridge.

"*Fuuuck*," I growl into the dark room, then fling the covers aside, bracing for the chill to hit me.

My legs feel like jelly. Reluctantly, I trudge down the hall to the kitchen to lift a bottle from the fridge while lightning and thunder wreck the house simultaneously. At least I don't need a flashlight.

Cracking the plastic seal, I take several big gulps.

The mouth of the bottle stills against my lips. With the cold water on my tongue, my heartbeat suddenly picks up. The sound of a steady drip reaches my ears.

Instinctively, my eyes shoot to the faucet in the kitchen first, but the sound appears to come from somewhere down the hall. The bathroom, I figure.

Replacing the cap on the bottle, I creep down the hall and turn into the bathroom to check, only to find neither a leaky faucet nor shower head. The tile and sink are bone dry to my touch.

Drip, drip, it goes again behind me.

Lightning streaks through the hallway as I turn over my shoulder, and another round of thunder cracks so close the floorboard beneath my bare feet trembles.

My hackles raise. My breaths fall heavy.

On shaky steps I inch toward my bedroom door. The entire space reveals itself to me bit by bit until I can take in the full sight.

I barely feel the bottle slipping from my grip before the thud registers in my ears. Shoulders heaving, clothes soaking wet, Mason stands in front of the window, the air around him crackling with the same threatening energy as the storm outside. He's a towering mass of black, sucking the oxygen out of my lungs.

"Mason!" I gasp, my eyes locking with his in shock.

Slick, dark strands drape over his, adding to the menacing look of him. The rest of his face is hidden behind the half skull mask, but I can feel the cruel grin stretching underneath it as shivers chase down my spine. The cut above his eye still looks fresh. It glistens from the rain.

Drip. Drip.

He cocks his head. The dripping sound is coming from him.

I raise my palm in warning. "You need to leave," I tell him, willing my tone steady. "You can't keep coming back here."

Holding my gaze, he doesn't respond, and my fear doubles.

What if he's in a trance?

"Get out, Mason," I repeat more forcefully, using his name this time.

He still doesn't answer, but his head gives a deliberately slow shake while his dark stare pins me.

His gloved fingers flex.

Fuck!

I swing around to run, but a grip in my hair halts my escape when he crosses the distance to me in a split second. His left hand using the door frame for leverage, he rips me back into the bedroom.

I stumble while he stands firm, locking his arms around my middle and crushing me to his chest.

"Let me go!" I twist in his hold as my feet lose the ground underneath them. My fingernails claw at the bit of skin I catch between his gloves and the sleeves of his black sweatshirt.

The fact that he still doesn't speak to me only drives my fear higher. My racing pulse chokes my breath. The sandalwood and spice of his cologne strangle me like a noose.

He spins us around, using the momentum to throw me onto the bed. My body rebounds. I'm able to scramble on my knees to get to the lamp before he descends on me, but when I swing it at his head, he dodges my attempt and rips it out of my hands. It crashes into my mirror.

The sound of clattering shards fills the room at the same moment his right hand darts out, seizing the front of my throat and pushing me onto my back while his left hand cuffs my wrist. His knees come up in between my bent legs, his stance wide as he easily overpowers me.

A pit opens in my stomach. His tousled dark blond hair falls over his face, setting his irises into a shadow so deep there's no green left. The cut above his eye arches almost mockingly.

I've never been so afraid of him. I've seen him in this mask, but I don't recognize the look in his eyes. There's no trust. It's like I've never met this man before.

His weight drives my wrist into the mattress above my head when his masked face lowers to me, his nose almost brushing mine. "You like being choked, don't you, baby girl?" his voice rasps through the cloth.

His stare studies me. His gloved fingers flex around my throat, his thumb pressing down on my jugular vein.

"Stop. P-please, Mason," I stammer, tears streaming down my face. "You promised… you promised I'd be safe with you."

His lips press to the shell of my ear, his icy breath inciting more shivers. "I lied."

I want to scream at his betrayal, but my voice chokes on my tears. I know if I pass out, I'll never wake up again. I'll be the next girl in the news.

I feel my muscles start to relax as my body goes numb. My free hand shoves at him. My legs thrash. I fight Mason with everything I have.

As I flail in his hold, my right foot connects with the nightstand, knocking it over, and sending my phone skidding down the hallway on the wood flooring.

Fuck! I need to reach it. I need to call Ash.

Thunder roars outside, and in my periphery, the curtain billows in the wind from the still-open window. I see Mason's eyes flick toward it.

I take my shot, drawing my fist back and ramming the knuckles of my left hand into his Adam's apple.

The moment his hold on me slips, I kick off and run, swiping my phone off the floor before lunging into the bathroom and locking the door behind me.

Dropped into a crouch, I back up against the far wall. My fingers tremble as I open my contacts and click on Ash's name at the top. Listening for the dial tone, I wait for it to connect.

Then it rings…

…right outside the bathroom.

"Well shit!" Ash's voice calls out from the hallway.

There's a long beat when I don't understand.

"I was really hoping I could convince you I'm him, so you'd finally kick him, but I guess the cat's out of the bag now."

Ash?

In the next second, the bottom of his boot collides with the door in a deafening *BOOM!* The useless slab of wood flies inward, pieces from around the lock shooting toward where I cower. My arms come up to shield my head.

Three heavy strides rush me. Barging in, Ash snatches my phone from my grasp and flings it into the shower. I scream, watching it explode into pieces against the tile as I swat and kick at his hands trying to grab me again.

His grip locks around my ankle.

Another scream ruptures my throat when he yanks me down onto the ground to drag me out into the hallway. I kick with my free foot and flip onto my stomach, but my slick palms slide along the ground, finding no purchase.

Gripping my wrists, Ash flips me over and lays me out, my back hitting the ground. My head flings left and right, hair blocking my view as I fight him.

He straddles my hips before my knees can make contact with any part of him. My struggle is futile. He's so much stronger than me. His fingers only clamp tighter around my wrists.

"Fuck, Em." Pain flares in my forearms. Ash slams my hands down hard on either side of my head, a note of intrigue winding through his harsh breaths. "You really have some fight in you. This could've been fun."

His voice rings much clearer now. With his mask down, tucked under his chin, I recognize him but also not. He's like a different Ash I've never seen before, no longer hiding behind his jovial façade. The sharp lines of his face are hard in a way that has erased all the charm his features once held. *The cut on his eyebrow…* I assume he inflicted it on himself to match Mason's. All to fool me.

Even used his cologne.

He's the liar. *He's* the one I should've been afraid of.

"Such a shame that you had to figure it out." He shifts my arms, locking them in a one-handed grip above my head. His right hand wraps around the front of my throat once more, and his next comment seals my fate.

"Now I have to make sure you don't tell, but what's one more strangled girl?" he grates out, the words laced with a dark chuckle.

My bottom drops out. My voice attracts a quiver. "*You!*"

Ash is the one who killed the girls, and now he's going to kill me too.

His fingers tighten around my throat. His thumb strokes across my jugular in mocking of my ignorance. "You're so naïve, Em. You walked right into the lions' den and didn't even know it."

My sob hitches against the pressure of his palm. He's right. I was so blind to the danger I put myself in.

"Well, I hope that thrill you were looking for was worth your life." He releases my wrists, but it doesn't matter. I'm starting to feel light-headed. I can't lift my arms. They're too heavy to fight back.

Keeping the vise around my throat, his left hand traces the low cut of my shirt, teasing it down. "What do you think, baby girl? Should we let him watch one last time?"

His words carry as if underwater, dragging my conscience further and further away, and even though I can't move a muscle to save myself, I'm still fully aware of his body pressing down on me.

I feel him shift to pull out his phone.

Ash points the camera at me. I catch a glimpse of his grin before the flash comes on, blinding me.

His thumb twitches where it digs into my jugular vein. "Just a few more seconds, baby girl. Relax for me, yeah?"

This is it. My vision begins to fade at the edges as thunder rocks the floorboards again. The vibration chases tremors through my weak limbs.

Then two black gloves rip Ash off me by his shoulders.

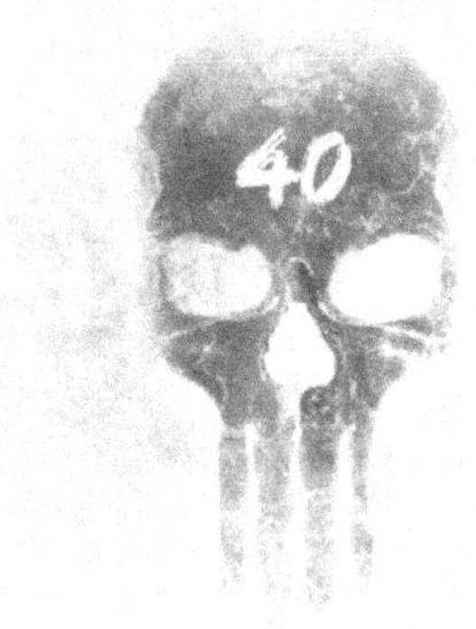

Mace

Fury ignites my blood.

I yank my twin off Emily, hauling him through the doorway and into the bedroom in the same move to get him as far away from her as possible. The remnants of the shattered mirror crunch underneath him as he crashes into her dresser across the room.

When I heard her scream, my body jumped into motion: I all but knocked my bike over, ripping my helmet off while taking a running start at her window. I couldn't get to her fast enough.

If I had been a second later…

Ash kicks to his feet, dusting himself off. "Well, well, well… brother," he says, leveling his glare. "Can't say I'm surprised you dropped by. I knew she was lying about seeing you."

He saunters toward me. Forefinger raised to my chest, he tips his head to the side and lifts his chin in a nod. "You thought I didn't know you were fucking her behind my back?"

I don't respond to his accusation. My face remains a blank mask, revealing none of the rage surging in my veins.

An equally calm expression stares back at me. "Walk away, Mason," Ash suggests.

"No!" My reply leaves my throat on a possessive growl. If he wants to get to Em, he'll have to go through me. "You won't touch so much as another hair on her head."

I feel her eyes rake over me from the hall to my right, but I don't take mine off Ash even for a split second. His right hand reaches toward the small of his back in a slow, deliberate manner, and I know he's going to draw a weapon.

His fingers clasp the knife loosely, letting me see the details of the grip before he flicks the switch to release the blade. He's brandishing a knife identical to the one I had, a twin to the one I got rid of after my blackout.

I saw the news on Vince. *My* knife. *My* mask. I couldn't believe my eyes, but the evidence had been right there on my clothes.

How can I not fucking remember?

I watched myself kill him in cold blood and still can't recall a single thing about that night, including the note I left on Em's mirror.

I hated the guy, but I didn't wish him dead. I'm not a murderer. What I did to Ely was justice. He was a predator. True evil. Vince was just a dick.

"Remember what happened the last time you tried taking me on," Ash warns. "You sure you wanna take that chance?"

I grind my teeth behind sealed lips. I have no intention of letting him lock me in a chokehold again.

He gets my answer when my fists come up. My feet shift into an attack stance, weight balanced and muscles primed.

"Fine." He raises the knife between us, the tip pointing toward me. "But no tapping out this time."

A roar bursts from me, and I charge him. Head low, I aim for his chest in a full-on tackle.

Ash's boots lose traction as I lift him. Wrapping his legs around my sides, he grabs a hold of my sweatshirt at the back before I slam him to the ground.

I feel the knife stab my left shoulder. Pain sears white-hot where it slices through the fabric to plunge into the muscle when I go down with him, but I don't let it stop me. My gloved fists descend on his skull in a blind fury.

Catching his wrist, I block the knife from taking another stab. I'm on my knees, Ash's ankles locked at my lower back as we roll through shards of glass, grappling each other.

I slam his hand to the floor, but his fingers remain locked around the blade's grip.

Clutching the front of his sweatshirt with my other hand, I lift him, then drop his back a second time.

Ash's ankles unlock at my back.

I flip him over, shoving his face into the floor. My left knee pins him down. With my grip still cuffing his wrist, I twist his arm behind his back and bend his elbow the wrong way.

"Drop it!" I shout when he howls in pain.

His grasp around the knife loosens. It hits the ground with a clatter, and I kick it out of his reach.

Ash uses my brief imbalance to free himself, spinning around and taking a swing at my temple. My skull rattles. My knees buckle.

He overpowers me. Tugging my arm forward, he locks me in a triangle choke with his legs. His thighs squeeze, but not enough to restrict the blood flow to my brain. He's toying with me like he was toying with Em.

"There's a question that's been burning on my mind forever," he says, his right hook crushing the reinforced knuckles of his glove into my cheekbone. "What's your kill count for DeMarco?"

The ringing in my ears picks up. "What?" *He's never ordered me to kill anyone.*

"Mine's 32."

I suck in a clipped breath.

"I don't even blink anymore," Ash boasts. "But there were a few extra ones I did on the side for free. Personal reasons, you know? Like Vince."

"*You* killed Vince?" My trapped hand fists his sweatshirt at the collar while I push against his leg with my other in an attempt to free myself. My boots get no traction.

"I really had you convinced you did it, hadn't I?" He snickers proudly. "I was just coming back to the club after silencing that rat Bates when I saw you with Vince."

I went to the Lotus? My muscles relax with the shock.

FUCK!

Jillian.

An image of my hands around the unconscious brunette's neck comes into focus.

FUCK! FUCK! FUCK!

"Man, I thought you were going to gut him right there," Ash continues, his legs giving me another squeeze. "I was so psyched to watch you hit him… but you didn't. You just walked away. What a bitch move. I couldn't believe it."

I *didn't* kill Vince! I want to feel relieved at that, but more images suddenly flood my mind.

"Well, I figured, if you weren't going to slice him up, then maybe I should," Ash rambles on blithely while my head is in a tailspin. "So I did. Shanked him real good. And then I went to see our girl here."

My attention snaps back when he nods toward Emily. "Left a little love note on her mirror while she was sleeping. I might have copped a feel too. She looked so peaceful. I wanted to hear whose name she would moan, yours or mine."

"And how did that go for you?" I quip in a knowing lilt.

Ash's high spirits drop. His jaw clenches, and the growl forming in his throat confirms my suspicion.

A spark of pride warms my chest. *That's my girl.*

"You don't fucking deserve her," he grates out.

"So you killed Vince, and you were going to frame me for it to get rid of me?"

"You made it too easy, brother. When I got home, you were sleeping. I switched our clothes. We've done it so many times, you didn't even notice. The gloves, too." He lifts his hand in the air in a taunting motion. "Can't even tell, can you?"

"Why, Ash?"

"You're weak, Mason. Ely saw it, and so does DeMarco. That's why he calls *me* when he needs someone to disappear for good."

To make a point, Ash stops fucking around. The triangle choke of his legs around my neck and arm lock tight.

"Don't forget." His voice drops into a low whisper. "You let me fuck her first… and all it cost me was a couple of donuts."

His words hit their mark. My rage rekindles with new fuel. I clench my left fist and ram the plastic covering my knuckles into his balls as hard as I can.

Ash howls again. His hold loosens.

The second I feel the release, I push up and scramble toward the knife I kicked away. It slid across the hardwood and came to a stop by the knocked-over nightstand.

Grabbing hold of my boot, Ash pulls my leg out from under me before I can reach it. I hit the ground. He dives for the blade and beats me to it, already twisting. I can't even draw a breath so fast. He reaches back and buries the knife in between my ribs.

I cry out in agony. It's lodged in deep—much deeper than the stab at my shoulder earlier caused by my tackle. Despite the adrenaline rush, this time I feel the pain everywhere. Fire ignites my muscles from head to toe, making me dread even the smallest movements, but I can't give up now. I can't let him get to her.

Ash jumps to his feet behind me. I hear the rustle of clothes. When I push up and swing around, I find him aiming the barrel of a gun at my chest.

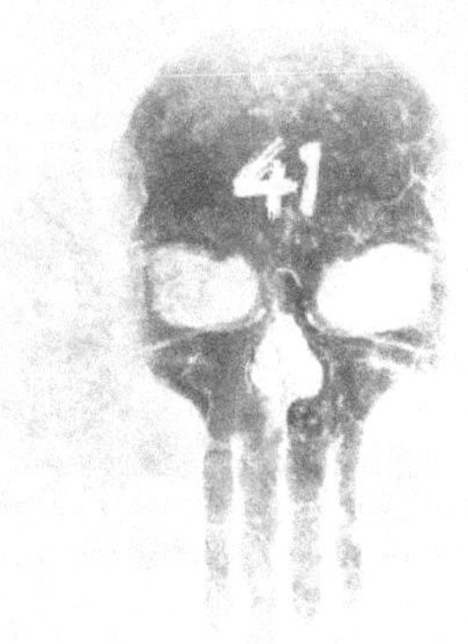

Em

His body angled toward me, Ash cocks his head. "You didn't think that was my only weapon, did you?" He glares down at Mason by his feet with the hilt of the knife protruding from his left side. "This is much more my style."

I slap my palms over my mouth to contain my sob as I cower in the hallway, my knees pulled into my chest.

Ash's fingers flex. "Last chance." He adjusts his grip around the gun. "Walk away. Don't make me fucking kill you."

"You already have my answer," Mason sneers, the muscles in his back and shoulders contracting visibly underneath his sweatshirt. His breathing appears labored.

"*She* is where you draw the line?" The gun shakes as Ash's anger takes over. "You choose *her* over your own blood? Your own *brother?*"

"You're no brother to me." Mason's right hand reaches across his body, and I flinch when he yanks out the knife in one sharp pull. "You made it clear how much blood means to you."

Bracing his injured side, he slowly pushes to his feet.

I can't imagine the physical pain he's containing on top of his brother's betrayal. Ash admitted to everything. He brought his deceit to light. He won't let me live knowing the truth. Mason is the only one standing in his way. He came back. Even after I hit him, after I told him I never wanted to see him again, he's defending me.

"I protected you," he growls, raising the bloody knife at Ash. "I should've let him kill us."

My eyes flick back and forth between them. I don't know who he's talking about. Who are Ely and DeMarco?

Mason gives air to another roar, then lunges at Ash again. He deflects the barrel of the gun toward the ceiling at the same time his brother blocks the knife.

A shot goes off, and I jump, covering my ears. My vision blurs from tears I can't hold in. I'm so scared for him, but I don't know what to do. If I get in between, I might make matters worse.

They push and pull. With bated breath, I watch Mason rear back, then his skull cracks against Ash's, sending him stumbling backward. Dazed, he drops his gun.

The knife also clatters to the ground in the process, but Mason doesn't give his twin a chance to recover either weapon. He spins on his foot. His leg swinging out, he throws a kick at Ash's head in a wide arch.

As Ash goes down, Mason straddles him. The last thing I see is his fist reeling back, Ash's hands at his throat, then they're blocked from view by my bed.

Along with their grunts, a relentless assault of kicks and punches carries to my ears before they reappear in my sight, but I've lost track. I don't know who's who.

The fight is a tangle of black limbs. Same hoodie. Same jeans and boots. Bloodied faces. I can't tell them apart.

Metal slides against wood. They tumble across the floor while scrambling for the scattered weapons, either one trying to stop the other from reaching them.

One gets a hold of the gun.

His twin kicks it out of his grip, diving for it himself. I see it skidding in my direction, then it all happens so fast. Stretched toward it flat on the floor, his fingers wrap around the grip. Behind him, his brother has found the knife that slid under my bed. The blade descends toward his back when he whips around and pulls the trigger, hitting his target dead center between the eyes.

—

His arm drops. His grip releases the weapon as it comes down, and when I hear it hitting the floor beside him, I know…

He's not the one who wants me dead.

Mason falls back, hands clasping his head as a sob hitches in his throat.

He killed his brother.

Despite the terrible things Ash has done, he was still his twin, his only family, and I feel his pain.

Ash's body collapsed where he stood when he raised the knife. I can't look. A pool of blood forms in my periphery as I kick off the floor and rush to Mason's side.

My fingers tremble at the sight of all the blood from the stab soaking his sweatshirt. He needs an ambulance.

"Mason!" I scoot under him to prop him up in my lap while putting pressure on his wound.

Through dark pink bangs, his eyes find mine. "Did he hurt you?"

"No." I shake my head to assure him. The bruises are minor. "You got here just in time. Stay with me, okay?"

I don't know how much blood he's lost. His skin looks pale, and his hand squeezing mine at his side has no strength left

I dig through his back pocket for his phone. "Fuck, come on," I curse as it slips through my bloody fingers until I finally tug it free.

I tap the screen. When the fingerprint prompt pops up, a burst of relief shoots out of me. I'm glad it doesn't require me to guess the PIN.

I rip off his right glove. Pressing his thumb to the screen to unlock it, I ignore the picture of me sleeping and dial 911.

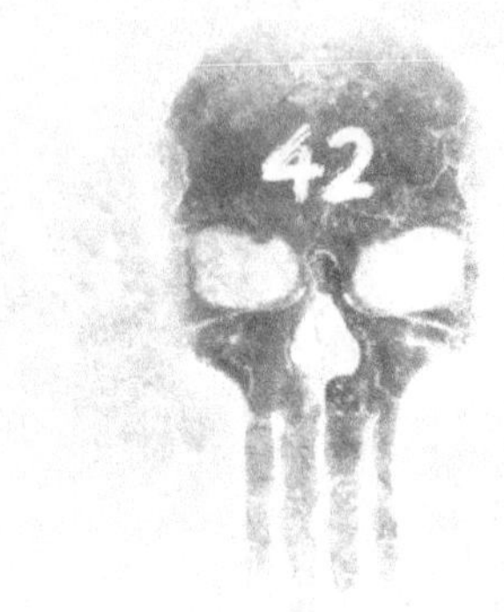

Mace

The noise of tools clanking rings in my ears. I step away from the truck I've been working on to grab a rag from the bench and wipe my hands.

Behind me, Rob and Jason are training the new hire while Isaac is out for the day.

An exasperated sigh bursts out of me. I hope to get back to painting soon. I prefer the sound of music blasting my eardrums.

My attention is drawn across the garage's workshop by a familiar female laugh that warms my heart.

I drop the rag and look through the glass at Em, leaning against the counter as she talks to the customer whose paint job I finished yesterday. She's still shadowing Tatum, but she quit her job at the diner and will take over sales full time next month.

A genuine smile curls the corner of my mouth. I haven't had a blackout in weeks, and I have a feeling they're gone for good.

She really does keep my demons at bay.

My eyes flick toward the TV mounted on the wall across from me. They're showing a follow-up on the strangler case.

My smile falls. My chest clenches.

Em told the cops everything about Ash, from him breaking into her apartment to his confession of killing Vince and strangling the girls before attempting to do the same to her. They were able to match his DNA to the samples found under the two victims' nails, and the case was officially closed without any further investigation into me…

…the only other guy with the same DNA.

If I have to guess, the police were happy to put an end to it to save face in front of the media after being criticized for their competence from the get-go.

I feel another twinge when the news channel pulls up the pictures of the females. I recognize their faces. I knew them both.

The cops never questioned Emily's statement…

My head snaps around. The door to the shop swings open, and she strolls in with the customer in tow.

The muscles in my body relax as my eyes rivet to my baby girl. *My beacon.* She never asked me why I happened to drop in that night. Maybe she doesn't want to know. The truth is, I have no answer for that. Her helmet was strapped to my bike, but I don't remember the ride to her place in the storm at all. My mind pulled out of the darkness the moment I heard her scream through the open window. Then I saw the Impala out front.

I hand the customer the keys to his bike, then show him out through the garage. When I come back, Em's arms are crossed in front of her chest, a hand clasping her throat as she stares up at the news report.

I know she's thinking about him. Thinking about how easily she could've ended up on that news report.

The channel's footage switches in my periphery as I stare at her. I catch the anchor's voice mentioning a familiar name. "The body of Alex Bates, a missing local man, was fished out of the lake this morning. Cause of death: a gunshot to the head," the female chimes without an inkling of empathy. "He is presumed to be a victim of the ongoing turf war between the leaders of Castle's underground syndicate. Bates was believed to have gone into hiding after agreeing to testify against Luca DeMarco, one of the ruthless leaders rumored to be running the city's illegal businesses. The FBI has been hunting him for years without gathering enough evidence to charge him."

My spine stiffens a little. I expect Emily to react to DeMarco's name after Ash's confession, but she doesn't. Her eyes swing around to me, and her lips twist as she changes the topic. "Are you still okay with going tomorrow?"

We're driving back to her hometown for her birthday. She wants me to meet her family.

"I'm looking forward to it," I assure her, although I haven't decided what to tell them about myself.

Ash's last comment rings on in my mind. Yes, I'd been willing to give her to my brother to reel her in, but I knew she'd be mine in the end.

"I bet you're wondering if I'll still let you choke me now," she says, the words chased by a light laugh.

I step into her. Winding my arms around her waist to pull her close, I drop my forehead on hers.

"I will, though." She stares up at me through her lashes, her hands warm on my chest. "I trust you, Mason. You know when to stop."

I press a kiss to her cheek and sink fully into our embrace. It took some practice, but I nailed it with her. Emily is the one who came back to me. She saved me in more ways than she knows.

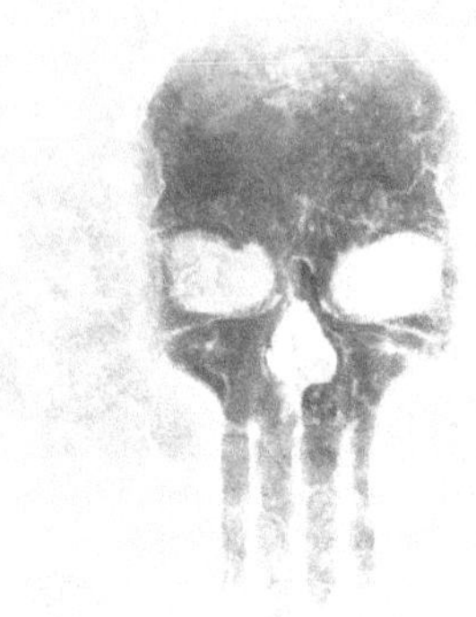

The night she chose me, consciously or not . . .

My fingers twitch in anticipation. I know I shouldn't be here. I *know* it's wrong, but that has never stopped me before.

I picked the lock and made my silent approach to find Emily sound asleep. She lies on her back, a hand resting beside her face on the pillow.

Leaning over her, I pull the covers aside to feast my eyes on the image of her in her pajamas. As usual, she's wearing skimpy shorts, black this time, with a pink camisole that stretches across her breasts, highlighting the weight I ache to cradle in my palm.

Before I even notice the outline of her nipples, blood rushes toward my groin, making my cock throb behind my fly at the sight of her.

My fingers slide underneath the hem of her shirt. Ever so slowly, I raise it higher, inch by maddening inch, until I lay her bare before me.

Fuck me, she's glorious. I bite my bottom lip, the ache in my thighs growing heavy.

Opening her legs with a light touch, I lower myself in between, my knees wide for balance as my weight settles on the mattress.

Emily doesn't stir. She's still completely oblivious to my presence.

The heat of her body reaches out toward me, bringing my lust for her to a boil as my sight drops to the sparse piece of cotton covering her pussy.

I want to touch her so badly. I want to feel her smooth skin beneath my fingertips, the slick glide of her flesh, her tight walls around my knuckles… I'll force the pleasure from her even if she tries to deny it.

Her nipples harden as though she can sense my stare. The tip of my cock tents my fly, pulsing viciously behind its confines. I've never ached for friction like this before. My skin pulls tight across my body. My muscles tremble.

I stifle a growl in the back of my throat. I can't believe I'm even contemplating this.

My eyes rivet to her face… to her relaxed features. She said she wanted to watch me, but she doesn't know about my past. She wouldn't understand why I can't get myself off. Not even for her. No matter how hard she makes me.

Fuck it! I undo my jeans and shove my hand into my briefs.

A shiver runs up my spine at the first touch, the silken skin shifting eagerly over the rigid length as it throbs against my palm.

My fingers curl on reflex. Fisting my restrained hard-on, I stroke it, lazily but firmly.

Goddamn, this feels good. The wet spot of cotton against my knuckles grows. My eyes fall to her exposed breasts again as I speed up. My palm swipes across my tip, grazing the barbell below, and I squeeze the head.

Heat floods my veins. Ripples shoot down my thighs and up my abs, contracting my muscles. Never has my own touch had this effect on me. I feel myself getting close. I think I might actually finish.

My fist pumps in a faster rhythm, fingers wrapping tighter around my pulsing shaft with the slickening motion from head to root—

"Mason."

Fuck! My spine arches, and I climax right at the moan of my name from her lips. A hot jet bursts from my tip, soaking my briefs.

My vision snaps to her face, expecting her glare, but she's still asleep, her eyes closed.

"Yeah, baby?" My voice is hoarse from the force of the orgasm as I release the grip on my cock and bend over her, hands on either side of her head.

Emily's fingers twist the front of my sweatshirt.

My brow creases. "Do you want this off?"

"Yes, Mason," she confirms with a soft whimper.

A smirk stretches my lips. I reach behind my head and straighten only long enough to shrug the hoodie off, letting it fall onto the bed beside me.

Em's hips roll impatiently on top of the mattress. Braced above her, I lick my lips. "Do you want my mouth on you, baby girl?"

"Yes," comes another immediate response, her breath juddering.

I sink down her front, my own warm breath feathering across her skin, the tip of my nose hovering. I inhale her scent. I devour her without touch.

When my fingertips curl at the waistband over her shorts, she lifts off the bed to let me slide them down.

I lower myself to her again. Splayed hands at the back of her thighs, spreading her wide, I give her one long, savory lick.

Her body shivers through a moan, and I look up to watch her face.

Pausing my piercing at her clit, I swirl in deliberately slow circles. I'm gentle, mindful with each stroke of the thin line between her sleepy haze and waking fully.

I'm on my knees for her, begging for each precious drop, desperate to draw her into me.

The way she moans my name when she comes undoes me. I want to sketch her like that, the tiny muscles in her face tense from the pleasure, her lips parted in a silent gasp. She's so fucking beautiful like that.

My cock swells with renewed vigor as I inch back up her body. I kiss the length of her flat belly, the valley between her breasts to the crease of her full mounds, before bringing my mouth down on one.

Positioned right at her entrance, I swirl my tongue around her nipple and prod her with light thrusts.

Emily's spine bows. She arches into me, eager to feel more, but I grant her only the tip before I retreat.

I release her nipple to watch her face. Her eyes don't flutter. She's still asleep.

I sink the head of my cock into her again, repeating the teasing play. Knees raised at my sides, Emily's hips rock to urge me on. Each time I ease into her, I feel her little muscles contract around me. She's going to come.

Her body stiffens. Then I feel the jolts. She trembles beneath me.

"Mason." Her lips part, her moan forming my name again, and fuck me, I want to plunge into her at the hoarse sound of it.

Pulling out, I chuckle. She's entirely conditioned to me. I claimed her body. It answers to me, whether she's conscious or not.

I dip my head toward her ear, letting my chest brush her sensitive nipples to rouse her.

Another dark laugh ruptures in my throat when she stirs at last.

"You're a heavy sleeper, aren't you, baby girl?" I drawl, my hips still nestled between her thighs without penetrating. I want her awake for this one. I want her to feel my next thrust in the deepest parts of her core.

I slide my cock across her slick pussy in warning. "Such a good girl…" My mouth lowers to hers as I close my eyes and pull my hips back. "You come for me even while you're asleep… calling out my name."

And then I push.

I seat the entire length inside her in a single thrust, relishing the feel of her as her heat welcomes me, and in that moment, I know: my scars may never heal completely, but somehow she quiets the self-destructive voices in my head. My soul is tethered to hers.

She's mine.

Beyond life.

Beyond death.

I'll never let her go.

She's my solace… and I'm entirely at her mercy.

Thank you for reading

Please consider leaving a review however long.
A review is always appreciated.

Other Works

Contemporary Romance:

OF APPLES AND TREES
FAIR TRADE (releasing 2026)

Paranormal Romance:

Bound by A Web Of Wyrd Trilogy
BLOOD BOUND — Book One
THE THREAD OF ALESSANDRO MARENA —
Prequel Novella and Book 1.5
SOUL BOUND — Book Two
OATH BOUND — Book Three

Check out my website for more details, and sign up for my
newsletter to receive all the latest details.
www.runikpress.com/renaterowlandbooks

Acknowledgments

As always, I would like to thank the amazing members of my Street Team, who keep me motivated with their continued support, as well as my Beta Readers Kelsey Stone, Nichole B, Mars Radkins, and Christin T.

Thank you to Disturbed Valkyrie Designs for this amazing cover art, which I fell in love with at first sight.

And I would also like to give a shoutout to the Dark Romance Team for all their support and the connection I have made through them.

Author Biography

Renate Rowland is an author of suspenseful romance. After being fortunate to have called three different continents her home, she has settled with her family in the US. She is an artist at heart, and although she expresses that in various ways, she held on to her stories until she felt it was time to give them air and let them breathe on their own. Finding much inspiration in music lyrics, she is driven by the desire to create something as powerful and moving as the artists she admires.

Follow me on social media:

Instagram & Threads: @renaterowland

Facebook: @renate.rowland.books